UNDENIABLE
RUSH

Also By S. C. Stephens

THOUGHTLESS SERIES

Thoughtless

Effortless (Book 2)

Reckless (Book 3)

Thoughtful (Thoughtless alternate POV)

Untamed (Book 4)

RUSH SERIES

Furious Rush

Dangerous Rush (Book 2)

Undeniable Rush (Book 3)

CONVERSION SERIES

Conversion

Bloodlines (Book 2)

'Til Death (Book 3)

The Next Generation (Book 4)

The Beast Within (Book 5)

Family is Forever (Book 6)

STANDALONE BOOKS

Collision Course

It's All Relative

UNDENIABLE RUSH

S.C. STEPHENS

This is a work of fiction. Names, characters, places, brands, media, and incidents are either the product of the author's imagination or are used fictitiously. The author acknowledges the trademarked status and trademark owners of various products referenced in this work of fiction, which have been used without permission. The publication/use of these trademarks is not authorized, associated with, or sponsored by the trademark owners.

Copyright © 2018 by S.C. Stephens
Cover design © Hang Le byhangle.com
Editing by Madison Seidler Editing Services //
www.madisonseidler.com
Formatting by JT Formatting

All rights reserved.
Without limiting the rights under copyright reserved above, no part of this publication may be reproduced, stored in or introduced into a retrieval system, or transmitted, in any form, or by any means (electronic, mechanical, photocopying, recording, or otherwise) without the prior written permission of the above copyright owner of this book.

First Edition: 2018
Library of Congress Cataloging-in-Publication Data
Undeniable Rush (Rush Series) – 1st ed
ISBN-13: 978-1724662200 | ISBN-10: 1724662201

ACKNOWLEDGEMENTS

A huge thank you to everyone who supported this series and asked for it to continue! I'm sad to let the characters go, but so happy for their journey.

A thousand thank yous to my agent, Kristyn Keene of ICM Partners, who was so supportive of this series, and such a huge help in making the books happen. Hugs to everyone at Forever/Grand Central Publishing, who has done such a great job promoting the original book, and a special thank you to Goldmann Verlag for picking up all three books for their German readers. I'm so excited to be able to share this series with my international fans!

Thank you to my two editors, Chelsea Kuhel and Madison Seidler, my formatter, Julie Titus of JT Formatting, my cover designer, Hang Le, and my web designer Lysa Lessieur of Pegasus Designs. I would be lost without your help! A very special thank you to Lori and Becky—this book would not exist without you! Thank you so much for fitting me into your busy schedule. I owe you, big time!

And to all the numerous blogs, readers, and authors who have supported me over the years—from the bottom of my heart, thank you so much! I wouldn't be able to continue in this business without your encouragement.

UNDENIABLE RUSH

CHAPTER 1

"Have you ever had too much to drink, then hopped on a roller coaster? And then during the ride you realized your stomach couldn't handle it, and you knew you were going to throw up, but you knew you couldn't throw up, so you willed yourself to hold it in until the ride was done?"

Turning my head, I looked over at Hayden sitting beside me in my truck. He was staring out the windshield at my father's two-story farmhouse, his usually tan cheeks pale. "No, can't say I've ever felt that way," I answered, smiling. "Are you nervous about dinner?"

He swallowed a lump in his throat, then twisted to look at me. "Yeah. I know I shouldn't be. I mean, I've confronted Jordan multiple times and while that kind of sucked, it never made me...nauseous."

Leaning over, I gave him a light kiss. "That's because you were *confronting* him...not coming over as a welcome guest. It's easier to face someone when you're not afraid of rejection."

As he pulled away from me, his mouth twisted into a scowl. "I'm not afraid of your dad not liking me." His expression softened. "And I wouldn't say I'm a 'welcome' guest. More like a tolerated one."

I knew he was right, but I had hope that one of these days Hayden would be as accepted here at my father's home as I was. Especially considering how far the two of them had come since I'd first started "seeing" Hayden. Dad almost smiled when he talked to him. *Almost*.

"Come on, it looks like we're the last ones here."

As I cracked open my door, Hayden ran his palms over his jeans. "Great…the entire family is here. Not awkward at all."

Raising an eyebrow at him, I said, "I've already met *your* entire family, it's only fair that you meet mine. And this isn't all of them—just my dad, my sisters, and their husbands."

He looked over at me with an amused grin on his face. "Thanks, that helps so much."

The look in his jade eyes, the curl of his full lips…he was dangerously attractive, and for a split-second, I considered climbing back into the truck, skipping dinner, and taking him back to my place. I knew he would say yes if I offered him an out like that. But no…just the fact that Dad had invited Hayden over tonight was monumental. I couldn't pass up the peace offering. And besides, Hayden and I were slowly easing back into our relationship. He hadn't even stepped foot inside my home since we'd restarted things, and the thought of inviting him over—of being alone, being intimate, being…bare—I couldn't deny the fact that it scared me a little.

Shaking my head, I told him, "You'll be fine."

Smiling at me, Hayden shook his head and stepped out of the truck. "Well, if I'm not, at least I'll still have you. I don't ever want to *not* have you again." The look on his face sent an icy chill racing along my skin. Our momentary breakup had been devastating, for both of us, and I knew, without a doubt, I'd rather advertise Benneti Motorsports on my ass again than lose Hayden. And feeling that way was terrifying.

"I don't ever want to not have you again either," I whispered.

Hayden stared at me a moment in the moonlight, then he stormed my way. Grabbing my face with both of his hands, he pulled me into him for a kiss bursting with pain and passion. My heart seized as his emotions rolled over me. I could feel how much he cared about me, like his love was a tangible object wrapping around us, warming us, protecting us. When Hayden put his heart out there, let himself connect with someone, he fought for them. Dedication and commitment were deeply ingrained in his soul. But those same traits had also been our downfall.

Lacing my arms around his neck, I deepened our connection. The undulating waves of passion and devotion started shifting into desire as our kiss became more heated. I could barely remember the last time Hayden and I had made love. I wasn't sure how much longer I could hold off on being with him, but at the same time, I wasn't sure if I was ready to move forward—my heart was still cluttered with uncertainty.

"Hayden," I murmured between the short breaks when our mouths separated. "I…"

I think I want to try… I think I want to take the next step. Take me home.

Before I could say any of that, a gruff voice intruded on our heart-swelling moment. "Mackenzie, stop that this instant and get your…"

I snapped my gaze to the front door, just in time to see my father take a deep breath. "Will you...please...come inside?" His voice was just as strained as his smile, and embarrassment heated my cheeks.

"Yeah, sorry. We were just..." I stopped trying to explain as I separated from Hayden and grabbed his hand to lead him inside.

Hayden cleared his throat, his expression uncertain as he approached Dad. "Hey, Jordan. It's nice to see you again," he said, running a hand through his scraggly blond hair.

Dad lifted an eyebrow. His steely gaze on Hayden was a mixture of resignation and indignation. "*Hey?*" Dad said slowly. While he hadn't actually berated Hayden for his word choice, his tone spoke volumes.

Hayden's hand tightened around mine, and I could see his posture straightening. Five seconds in, and Dad had already pissed him off. I instantly interceded. "Dad, you said you'd be nice."

Dad redirected his intimidating gaze to me. "I *am* being nice," he said, looking genuinely perplexed. I gave him a pointed look, and with a sigh, he returned his eyes to Hayden. Extending his hand, he politely intoned, "It's nice to see you as well, Hayden."

Hayden didn't take his hand right away, and I thought I might have to scold my boyfriend, as well as my father. They might have worked together to get Cox Racing up and running again—and in my name—but they weren't friends.

Just as I was about to elbow Hayden, he accepted my father's palm. The shake was almost too short to be considered polite, but at least they'd touched each other in a non-violent way; if we made it out of this dinner with no one getting socked, I'd consider it a success.

I stroked Hayden's hand with my thumb as we walked past Dad into the entryway. Anything to calm him down. As we stepped into the living room, I heard Hayden inhale a deep breath and slowly release it, and when he smiled, it looked completely natural.

"Oh good, you're here."

My oldest sister, Theresa, and her husband, Nick, rose from the couch to greet us. I instantly wrapped my arms around my sister, squeezing her tight. When we separated, I introduced Hayden to Nick. They shook hands—it was a much longer and more cordial shake than when Hayden and Dad shook hands.

"It's nice to finally meet you," Nick said. "I've heard...a lot." Nick's pale blue eyes flashed to my sister, and I instantly knew not everything he'd heard was good. Nick was a decent guy, though, and I was sure he would give Hayden a chance. But knowing that Nick had probably been preconditioned to not like or trust Hayden, sucked. If only Hayden and I had been given the chance to start out like a normal couple. Like my sisters and their husbands.

Hayden gave Nick an uneasy smile, and I knew he was also aware of what Nick had been told. "Well, don't believe everything you hear," he said.

Nick ran a hand through his dark hair as a nervous laugh escaped him. Then both men were looking anywhere but at each other.

With an inward sigh, I asked Theresa, "Where's Daphne?"

She pointed behind her. "Out back. Jeff wanted to try out the track."

That made me smile. Daphne's husband, Jeff, was sort of...straight-laced. I couldn't even picture him on a bike. Looking over at Hayden, I gave him a crooked grin. "Want to see the track?"

Hayden's expression instantly brightened. "You have a track here?"

He looked back at Dad, and Dad shrugged. "Just a simple practice track. Nothing like what you're used to."

My eyes widened as I stared at Dad. That was almost a compliment. Hayden smiled and gave Dad a small nod. Oh my God, was that...bonding that just happened? Feeling almost eager, I pulled Hayden to the backyard. Dad, Theresa and Nick followed.

A chuckle escaped me when we got to the track, and I saw Jeff sitting on an older Kawasaki 100cc dirt bike. I think it was mine from when I was six. He looked a little terrified, like he was straddling a rocket. Daphne was giving him pointers on how to ride. That made me laugh even harder. Daphne hadn't ridden a bike in ages, and back when she had ridden one...well, it was like watching someone on a golf cart.

Hayden's grin was enormous as he took in the scene. Dad rolled his eyes and sighed; I was pretty sure if I hadn't ended up a racer like him, he would have spent every day rolling his eyes and sighing.

Bouncing on his toes, Hayden turned to me; his grin was infectious. "Can I try it?"

I pointed at the track where Jeff was just now starting. "It's an oval. Why are you excited about this?"

Hayden pointed over to a bike next to Daphne. It was a little 50cc pocket bike, a bike that looked like it was made for a doll; it was no taller than Hayden's knees. "I've always wanted to ride one."

Dad cracked a smile. It had surprised me to no end when Dad had purchased the "toy" bike, but boys will be boys, even if they had hardened with age and discipline. And, of course, when I'd asked Dad about it, he'd had a perfectly reasonable excuse: he'd said it was good to mix up your training every once in a while, confuse the body. *Uh-huh.*

I shrugged at Hayden. "Go for it."

Looking like a kid on Christmas, he grabbed a nearby helmet and jumped on the tiny bike. A grown man on a bike that small was a ridiculous sight to see, and we were all laughing at him when he started it, but I knew from experience that it was exhilarating. Your entire perspective changed when you were that close to the ground—it felt like you were going 500 miles per hour.

Hayden took off, zooming after Jeff; he looked like a child chasing an adult. With Hayden's aggressive speed and profound skill, it didn't take him long to zoom around Jeff. Daphne frowned when her man was passed so quickly that he looked to be standing still, but then she started watching Hayden, and her expression turned appreciative. As I glanced around, I saw that everyone was watching Hayden with the same small smile on their faces. Even Dad looked impressed. Hayden was handling the small bike just like he would a full-sized one, ducking low in the corners, taking his time to pull out of them. Even on a toy, he was flawless.

His smile widening, Dad turned my way. "I think you made the right decision, hiring him onto your team."

Shock made my mouth pop open. As I regained my composure, I asked Dad, "And as a boyfriend? Did I make the right decision there?"

Dad's eyes flashed to the track, his lips pressing into a firm line. Jeff tossed his hands into the air in annoyance as he was lapped by Hayden. Again. Dad smiled. Returning his eyes to me, he shrugged. "It galls me to admit it, but I don't really know Hayden. It's too early for me to know for sure, but…so far, I like what I'm seeing."

He was appraising Hayden the same way he would a new rider, but, oh my God…just him confessing that was mind-boggling. I couldn't hold back my explosive grin. Dad's expression instantly shifted to a frown. "Having said that, the moment he hurts you…all bets are off."

Even that mild threat couldn't deflate my buoyant mood. Because it wasn't all that long ago that Hayden hurting me had been exactly what Dad had hoped for. He liked him. He still didn't *want* to like him, but he couldn't fool me anymore. My father *approved* of my boyfriend. Now if they could just stop getting on each other's nerves.

Once Hayden was finished, he headed back to us. Removing his helmet, he stepped off the bike. "Now, that was fun!" he exclaimed. I had to laugh at his expression. Doing something he was familiar with—something he was extremely good at—had made him more at ease. I doubted he still felt like he needed to throw up.

Without my help, Hayden walked over to Jeff and stuck out his hand. "Hayden Hayes. Nice race, man."

Jeff had been sulking at his obvious defeat, but hearing Hayden call it a "race," like he'd stood a chance against him, lifted his spirits. "Jeff. Thanks. You're not... half bad on that thing."

Hayden leaned toward him, his face mischievous. "You should see me on a real bike." Jeff smiled, his dark eyes amused, and Hayden lightly smacked his shoulder. "You should come to the track, race me on a big bike."

Daphne, Theresa, and my father all said, "No," at the same time.

Daphne shook her head and crossed her arms over her chest. "Don't you dare tempt him to do what you and Kenzie do, Hayden. You'll get him killed." Her face morphed into concern as she lovingly stroked Jeff's arm. Theresa's expression was the same; they both thought Jeff would die on one of our bikes.

Dad leaned toward me, and said in a low voice, "I'm more concerned about what he'd do to the *bike*. The boy has no talent for racing. None, whatsoever."

I stifled a snort, while Jeff gave Daphne a disheartened frown. Hayden leaned in close and whispered something in his ear. Jeff instantly brightened, and Daphne turned her irritation toward my boyfriend. "I said no, Hayden!"

He smiled at her, giving Jeff a conspiratorial look. "I know," he said, then he subtly bumped fists with Jeff.

I rolled my eyes. Here I'd been worried about my father being the one to murder my boyfriend, but if he took this any further, it would be my sister who put him six feet under. Striding over to Hayden, I grabbed his elbow and started pulling him toward the house. "How about we go inside and get started on dinner. Hayden has a lot to do tomorrow."

With a sigh, Hayden dropped his head. "God, I hate moving."

I gave him a wry smile as we walked back into the living room with everyone. "All of your stuff fits in one vehicle. How bad can it be?"

He grinned at me, then sighed. "It's the principle of the thing. I'm tired of bouncing around…"

Melancholy seeped into his voice, and I put a gentle hand on his arm in support. "You won't have to bounce around forever," I told him. It was as close to a promise of moving in together one day that I could give him. I couldn't proclaim our *happily ever after* when we were taking things easy.

Theresa, having overheard his comment about moving, told him, "You and Kenzie are moving in together? That's great!"

The happiness in Dad's eyes instantly faded, and he gave Hayden a look that clearly said, *Forget every nice thing I ever said about you.* Dad definitely wasn't ready for Hayden and me to shack up.

Hoping Dad remained nice, I told Theresa, "No, he's moving in with Nikki."

The entire room went quiet. Daphne looked between Hayden and me like she suddenly didn't understand what she was seeing. "He's moving in with…another woman… and you're cool with that?"

Hayden ran a hand through his hair, uncertainty on his face again. "It's not… She's not… I'm helping her out, she's helping me out…it's a friendship thing."

Daphne pursed her lips. "It always starts out that way."

Dad crossed his arms over his chest as he burned Hayden with his eyes. Glaring at everyone, I told the room, "Nikki's pregnant, and she's worried about money. Hayden is staying there to help her out *financially.*"

I stressed the word as I shot everyone nasty looks, daring anyone else to call my boyfriend a cheater. Unfortunately, they all knew I'd suspected the same thing not too long ago. They knew about the breakup, and they knew about the person who had triggered the whole thing. I firmed my face, showing them confidence in my relationship, and nothing else.

The room was thick with tension, and oddly, it was my father who broke it. "Nikki is pregnant? I didn't know she was seeing anyone."

I could tell from the way he said it that he wasn't comfortable talking about it but was just trying to change the subject. Relaxing my expression, I told him, "She's not. It was kind of…an accident."

"Who is the father?" Theresa asked, genuinely curious.

Cringing, I bit my lip. "Myles…"

My father's eyes narrowed into pinpricks. "Myles Kelley? He's the one who got her pregnant?"

Sighing, I immediately held up my hands. "Don't. I know that look on your face, and I know you want to 'have a talk' with him, but just…don't. Myles and Nikki are fine. They're working things out."

Dad indicated Hayden. "Then why is *he* moving in with her and not Myles? Why is Myles shirking his responsibilities?"

"He's not, but Myles and Nikki…they're…complicated," I said, knowing full well that wasn't going to be a good enough answer for my dad.

As I watched him slowly shake his head, I resisted the urge to smack myself in the face. I never should have brought up Nikki's situation around Dad, and I knew, without a doubt, Dad was going to have a conversation with Myles soon. And then Myles was going to have a conversation with me. Great.

* * *

After dinner, I drove Hayden back to my place, so he could pick up the car he was borrowing from Hookup before driving back to Hookup's place in San Diego. I was grateful this would be the last time he'd have to make the long, twice-daily trip. Once he was settled in with Nikki, his commute was going to be so much shorter.

"So, was that as bad as you feared it would be?" I asked him.

Face pensive, he took a moment before answering me. "Hmmm? Dinner? Oh, no…it was actually kind of fun."

I studied his face as we approached a stoplight. "Then why do you look like you're…reconsidering something?"

With a sigh, he looked my way. "I guess, because I am."

Even though I didn't want it to, my heart fluttered. Was this about us? "What do you mean?"

Hayden frowned, which didn't make me feel any better. "It's just…maybe your dad is right. Maybe I shouldn't be moving in with Nikki. Maybe Myles is the one who should be doing this, and I'm stepping on his toes or something."

Relief poured into me as I realized it had nothing to do with us. "Wait, you're *agreeing* with my dad now?" Hayden smiled and rolled his eyes, and I shook my head. "Myles is stuck in a lease, you know that. He can't move in with her right now."

He pursed his lips in thought. "I could switch places with him. The landlord would probably never know."

Shaking my head again, I told him, "Maybe...but Nikki isn't ready for that. She needs to ease into this parenting thing. Having Myles around all the time would just make it harder, I think."

"I thought they were best friends?" he asked, confused.

A long sigh escaped me as the light turned green. "Yeah...they are, but...there's tension now, you know?"

Hayden smirked at me. "Ah, yes...I am *very* familiar with tension."

I laughed, then asked, "Why are you really having second thoughts? It can't just be because you're worried about offending Myles."

Hayden didn't answer right away, and when I snuck a peek at him, his head was down in contemplation. Finally, he said, "I saw the way your sisters looked at me. I don't want you to ever look at me that way." Lifting his head, he stared my way. "Are you *sure* you're okay with this, Kenzie?"

I threw a carefree smile his way, letting him know just how untroubled about this I was. "I told you I was fine, and I meant it." Pursing my lips, I added, "And besides, I think I'd rather have you living with Nikki, then over at the bachelor pad, party house. You and Nikki together will give me far fewer ulcers."

Hayden laughed as he put a hand on my knee. "Good, because I don't want you worrying about me anymore. I'm not going anywhere."

"I know," I whispered, a tight grin on my lips. *Or at least, I hope I know.*

When we finally got to my house, it was difficult to say goodbye to Hayden. My head told me I was being silly, and I should take a chance and let him come inside. My heart was screaming at me to seal the windows and doors tight and prepare for the inevitable storm. I was torn, and because I was so torn, I knew it wasn't the right time—I needed to keep some space between us, just a little while longer.

Hayden didn't press me to come in, just gave me a series of soft kisses that left me breathless. I felt my resolve wavering as his mouth moved over mine. Maybe I *could* do this. Maybe if he just came into the living room. Maybe if we only sat on the couch and kissed. It didn't have to go further than that. I didn't have to strip off his shirt, feel every inch of his torso, place soft kisses down his abs...

I immediately pulled away from him and was shocked to find I was breathing heavier. Hayden's eyes were concerned, until he noticed how affected I was by him. "Kenzie," he murmured. "I know you wanted to take things slow...but if you're ready to go just a little faster...all you have to do is tell me."

I bit my lip as I studied his face. God, yes, a huge part of me did want to pick up the pace. But inviting him in, welcoming him into my heart, laying out my soul for him to take...just the thought made an apprehensive knot form in my stomach. As I contemplated progressing our relationship, the barrage of lies I'd endured from him recently whipped me across the face, stealing my desire. *I said I'd tell you the truth. I just never said when I'd tell you.*

Swallowing a hard lump in my throat, I shook my head at him. "I'm not..." My eyes stung as the ache of his betrayal poured through me, all over again. Would it ever completely leave me? God, I hoped so. "Not yet," I murmured.

Pain was on Hayden's face, but he nodded in understanding. "Okay, Kenzie." A moment of silent tension passed between us, and then he whispered, "I'm so sorry I hurt you."

My vision hazed with unshed tears, making it difficult to see him. "I know. I know you are..." I willed the moisture in my eyes back inside my body. There was no reason to fall apart, to indulge in unnecessary agony. We were back together, we were happy, we were moving forward again. I needed to let this go...before it destroyed us.

Slapping on as large of a smile as I could, I gave him a soft kiss on the cheek. "I'll see you tomorrow, Hayden. I'll be at your place bright and early...so don't stay up late." Mentioning staying up late made a well of pain crack open inside my chest. The distance between us had started because he'd been out late...with *her*.

Nothing happened, he did it for you. He chose you. He doesn't want her.

Begging my eyes to remain dry, I gave him one last kiss, then turned and started speed-walking to my front door. Best to get inside quickly, just in case. Hayden's voice stopped me as I was inserting the key. "I love you, Kenzie."

My back straightened, and every muscle went stiff. We'd played around with those words, but we'd avoided directly saying them. A mixture of emotions assaulted me as I turned to look back at Hayden—joy…and grief. "I love you, too," I whispered, a small, sad smile on my lips. Then I darted into the house, quickly closing the door behind me.

Exchanging those words should have lifted my spirit, should have made me feel light and airy, invincible. But that wasn't exactly how I felt. Part of me felt like I was walking through the clouds, blissfully buoyant. But another part of me, the scared, dark, hurt part, felt like a giant sinkhole had just opened up all around me, and any second now, I was going to stumble over the edge and fall into the abyss. All that was waiting for me on this path was pain. Inevitable pain.

No, that's not necessarily true. Not every relationship is doomed. As long as there is love, there is hope.

And I knew deep in my heart that he truly did love me. Fierce, unshakable love. Was that enough to fill this distance between us though? Once trust had been fractured, was it possible to regain unquestioning faith in the person who'd cracked it? Or would I always—from now until the end of my days—be haunted by doubt? Would these thorns inside my heart ceaselessly pierce me, forcing me to heal over and over again? Because that sounded exhausting.

Needing a little friendly support and advice, I pulled out my phone and called Nikki, my best friend, my confidant, my female other-half. I could hear Hayden's car pulling away as the phone rang; it intensified the confusion I was feeling. I wanted space from him, but I also wanted to pull him close. How both of those feelings were possible at the same time, I'd never understand.

"Hey, girlie," Nikki said, answering the line. "How did it go?"

Knowing she meant dinner at Dad's, I sighed. "It was...fine. Awkward at first, but then...fine."

"Then why do you sound like it didn't go well?" she asked.

Worn out from the emotional tug-of-war, I dropped to the couch. "Hayden told me he loved me," I said, melancholy in my voice.

"Normally I'd say congratulations...but I feel like that's the wrong thing to say right now. Why is that not a good thing? Are you changing your mind about him?" she asked.

Even though Nikki couldn't see me, I shook my head. "No, he's who I want, it just...sometimes it hurts to want him. Sometimes... I'm terrified. I don't want to get hurt again..."

A sympathetic noise met my ear. "I get it, Kenzie, I really do...but if you keep holding him back, then what's the point of being together? Eventually, you'll have to stop dipping your toes in the water and jump in."

Her swimming metaphor made me smile. "I know. It's just really...hard. I keep having these horrible thoughts. And the dreams...they're even worse than what I stress about during the day."

"Tell me about it," she said. "Last night I had a dream that the baby was actually an alien from space. It burst out of my va-jay-jay, then tried to kill me."

Before I could stop myself, I started laughing. Belly laughing. Nikki sniffed, like she was offended. "It's not funny, Kenzie. That could totally happen. It *is* Myles's baby, after all."

Wiping my eyes, I continued laughing for another full minute. When I was done, Nikki flatly intoned, "Feel better?"

And surprisingly enough, I did. Humor had an uncanny way of dissolving fear. "Yes, thank you...and please call me if you have any more nightmares like that."

Nikki finally laughed. "I will."

Feeling warm and at peace once more, I told her, "Thank you, Nikki, I needed that. And, just so you know, everything with the baby is going to be fine. You've got me, you've got Myles, you've got Hayden...you don't have to go through any of this alone."

She sniffed again, but it was laced with emotion this time. "Thank you, Kenzie. I'm kind of freaking out on a daily basis. I've got my first doctor's appointment next week...will you come with me?"

"Of course," I said, smiling into the phone. "Is Myles coming, too?" There was such a long pause, I could almost picture her gnawing on her lip. "Oh my God, Nikki. The second you hang up with me, call your baby-daddy and fill him in on what's going on. Okay?"

"Okay," she murmured, clearly unhappy.

"See you tomorrow," I said, disconnecting the phone before she could change her mind and weasel her way out of calling Myles. For some reason, Nikki wanted to pretend away the baby when it came to Myles. I supposed she had her own fears on the matter, and they probably went even deeper than mine.

Staring at my phone, I knew I needed to do something. I needed to push myself forward, even though I felt like retreating. Opening up my contacts, I scrolled to Hayden's assigned name—*Major Asshat*. Pressing the message icon, I sent him a brief text—one I hadn't sent in a really long time. *'I love you.'*

My heart pounded as I hit send, waiting for the confliction to return. But it didn't come. I still felt okay, and I took that small growth as a victory.

Hayden didn't respond to my text until he got home—good boy. *'I love you too. See you soon, sweetheart.'* As I read his message, I could easily picture the content grin on his face. It further eased my stress, and as I drifted off to sleep, I found peace in the fact that, at least for today, hope had conquered doubt.

CHAPTER 2

I left for Hayden and Hookup's place bright and early the next day, just as promised. Hookup lived in the heart of the city, in a neighborhood that looked a little sketchy. Everyone had chain-link fences in the front and back yard, and graffiti was plastered on just about everything. Hookup and Izzy had grown up near here, with Hayden joining them later. I tried to picture them running around as children, but I just couldn't see it.

When I got to the basic one-story house that belonged to Hookup, I couldn't help but notice that his place was the only house on the street with only one car in the driveway. I had to believe that was a rarity for Hookup's house, since Hayden had told me that before his recent change of heart, this house had been party central. Seeing how quiet it was now must be shocking to the neighbors.

Parking my truck behind Hookup's car, I got out and headed to the front door. I considered ringing the doorbell with a Christmas song, since that was how Hayden frequently greeted me, but I decided against it, since Hookup was probably still sleeping.

Instead of knocking, I texted Hayden and let him know I was at the door. He looked adorably tired and disheveled when he opened it to let me in. "Hey there, twenty-two," he said with a yawn. "I knew you said you'd be early, but I had no idea you'd be racing the sun to get here." He glanced up at the pale, morning light, then shook his head. "Sorry, babe, but I think you lost that race. I've got donuts as a consolation prize though."

He opened the door wide enough for me to come in, and I shot him a dirty look. "You know I can't eat that stuff while I'm training. In fact, you shouldn't be eating that stuff either. I need you in tip-top shape for the first race."

He raised an eyebrow at me as I passed by. "In March? I think I'll be fine." He lifted his shirt to show me a set of rock-hard abs that any male model would kill for. "See...all firm, no flab. When you see love handles, then you can take away my donuts."

The sight of his lean, flat stomach had me so distracted, all I could do was murmur, "Sure..."

Hayden laughed at the look on my face as he dropped his shirt, then he pulled me into him for a hug. "I'm glad you're here," he said, and there was something in his voice that seemed overly relieved, almost like he hadn't been sure I'd come.

Pulling back to look at him, I noted the concern in his eyes. "My boyfriend is moving in with my pregnant best friend...how could I possibly miss a moment of that?"

His emerald eyes lightened as he studied me, until finally, he laughed. "Yeah, if anything, this should be... interesting. Come on, join me for breakfast. We need food before we start."

Grabbing my hand, he led me toward the kitchen. My eyes drifted around as we walked. Hookup had been busy packing his stuff, and boxes were everywhere. He'd sold the place, so he could move into a house in a nicer neighborhood with Izzy and Antonia. Aside from purchasing all of the equipment I'd needed for Cox Racing, it was the most unselfish thing I'd ever seen him do.

When we got to the kitchen, I was shocked to see that Hookup was awake…and eating Hayden's donuts. Just because he'd changed, didn't mean he was an entirely different person. "Hey, man… Kenzie. Thanks for the grub," he said, lifting the apple fritter in his hand.

Hayden frowned. "I bought that for Kenzie…that's why there was a giant K on it."

"It's okay," I interceded. "My hips don't need it."

Hookup nodded, like he was agreeing with me. Yep. A part of him was still very much the same. Asshole. "See," he said, "I knew she wouldn't want it. Kind of sad that I know your girlfriend better than you do."

Hayden sighed, then shook his head. "Whatever, Tony. Did you save me some boxes?"

Taking another big bite, he nodded. "They're in the garage. Good luck, dude."

With that, he clapped Hayden on the back and walked out of the room. Hayden watched him go, then turned back to the donuts. His face compressed into a scowl. "Damnit, Tony, you ate the maple bar, too?" Hookup's laughter was the only response.

Face forlorn, Hayden looked over at me. "I can't wait to move."

Laughing, I picked up a jelly-filled donut and handed it to him. "Here, you better eat this quick before he comes back."

Hayden sighed, then devoured it in three bites. My eyes were huge as I watched him. "What?" he said. "You told me to eat it quick."

Shaking my head, I gave him a kiss on the cheek. "Keep that up, and those love handles won't be far behind."

Licking his fingers, he suggestively wriggled his eyebrows. "I'll just have to work them off then." His face immediately shifted. "When you're ready, of course."

Right...when I was ready. Ready to fully entrust my heart to him, ready to let go. Nikki's advice rang through my head, compounding my confusion. *If you keep holding him back, then what's the point of being together?* I knew she was right, but I wasn't there yet. Turning away from him, I quickly said, "We should get started. I'll go grab the boxes."

Hayden didn't say anything as I left the room, and I felt the silence between us, like a cold, wet blanket covering my skin, weighing me down. I hated this, and I felt like even though I was sure Hayden would wait as long as I asked, the countdown on our relationship had begun. I either let him in...or I let him go. Both options scared me, and even though Hayden wasn't pressuring me in any way, I felt like I was trapped inside an hourglass, struggling to remain calm as the sand began to bury me.

When I rejoined Hayden in his bedroom a few minutes later, he didn't seem fazed at all by me running away from him. In fact, he seemed downright cheery as I started opening the boxes; his joy made me feel better. We were fine...we'd get through this.

Grabbing some clothes off his bed, he told me, "It's going to be so nice to be close to you again, close to the track again. That commute was killing me. Plus, Tony was getting really tired of me borrowing his car every day. His newfound generous attitude only goes so far."

He laughed as he started tossing clothes into a box. "What *are* you going to drive now?" I asked.

Hayden paused with his lips pursed. "Honestly, I don't know. I'll have to find something soon though."

Chewing on my lip, I told him, "You could ride my street bike? I've got my truck, so technically, I don't need it."

Hayden shook his head before I even finished. "No, we're going slow, taking things easy. I don't want you to feel obligated to help me."

I crossed my arms over my chest. "So, I can't *ever* help my boyfriend?"

Tossing me a one-sided smile, he said, "You're helping me right now."

Lifting an eyebrow, I waited for a real answer to my question. With a sigh, he stopped working and faced me. "I don't want to take any sort of handout from you right now, Kenzie. I'm not blind. I know we're not 100 percent back to normal. And I don't want something to come between us while we're still so…fragile. No resentments, no hard feelings, no bitterness, no…anything. I don't want you to feel like I'm taking advantage of you or taking something from you." He cracked a small smile. "And besides…it's about time I stood on my own two feet. I want to do this by myself."

What he had to say about us not being 100 percent hurt to hear, but I knew he was right. And maybe he was also right about not adding any more complicated feelings to our relationship, although I didn't think I'd ever feel like he was taking advantage of me. "I understand wanting to make it on your own. That's one of the reasons why I purchased my own Ducatis, instead of letting my father buy them."

Hayden grinned. Shrugging my shoulders, I asked him, "Can I at least help you look for something?"

His grin was infectious. "Of course."

As I'd predicted, it didn't take long to gather everything of Hayden's and pack it into my truck. He just didn't have that much stuff. I wondered if Hayden's habit of living light would change as he continued fully embracing the roots he was putting down. Roots that still included me, thankfully.

After saying goodbye to Hookup, we got in my truck and made the trek back to Oceanside. Now that Hayden was sure I was okay with him moving in with my best friend, there was an excited energy about him. He bounced in his seat, drummed his fingers to the music as he hummed along to the radio, and he wouldn't stop grinning. He was excited for this transition, eager to turn a new page in his life. In *our* lives.

Even with my flip-flopping emotions, I was excited about this too. "I'm so glad this is happening today. I'm glad you're not going to be so far away now."

Hayden swung his dazzling smile my way. "I know. Even though Hookup is better company now than he used to be, it was lonely there. I missed you."

He reached over and put his hand on my knee, and my heart skipped a beat. "I missed you, too," I quietly told him. And in some ways, I still missed him. I missed us…what we were. Hopefully, what we could be again.

Sooner than I expected, we pulled up to Nikki's place. Her apartment was just a few blocks from my house. Luckily, it had two bedrooms, so Hayden would have his own space, at least until the baby got bigger.

I parked the truck beside Nikki's tiny smart car. She'd probably have to get something bigger soon. On the other side of Nikki's vehicle was a car that belonged to someone I hadn't expected to see today: Myles. Seeing him here made me grin. He was already trying to be a good father by supporting Nikki during this could-be-awkward change. Either that, or he was bored.

Hopping out of the truck, Hayden and I each grabbed a box, then made our way to Nikki's first floor apartment. When I got to the door, I could hear low and intense voices inside. It was kind of unusual, considering Myles was in there with her. Generally, all I heard was laughter when those two were together. "Nik," I yelled, banging on her door with my toe. "We're here."

The voices continued, but no one acknowledged me. "Nik?" I called again.

Finally, the voices drifted closer. As the door opened inward, I heard Myles saying, "I know, but that doesn't mean I have to like…" His voice trailed off as he stared at Hayden and me in the now-open doorway.

"Don't have to like what?" I asked.

Myles shot a brief glance at Hayden before tossing on a carefree smile. "Nothing. Glad you guys are here."

I looked over at Nikki in the doorway just in time to see her roll her eyes. "Come on in," she said, stepping back so we could enter.

Tension laced the room as I glanced between my two best friends, who had obviously been arguing about something. Or some*one*. "Is this a bad time?" I asked, repositioning the box in my hands.

Nikki shook her head, her long, dark ponytail bouncing around her shoulders. "Of course not. I'll show you to your new room, Hayden."

As she waved him inside, I noticed how unmistakable her pregnancy was now. Either she was finally wearing clothes that fit her, or her body had decided it was free to expand since we all knew about the baby now. I also noticed Myles's scowl when Hayden followed Nikki down the hallway.

I waited for the two of them to be out of earshot, then rounded on Myles. "What's going on?"

His face instantly corrected itself. "Nothing. This is awesome. Totally…awesome."

A frown curved my lips as I stared at him. "You said you were fine with Hayden. That you'd forgiven him."

He shook his head. "I have, and it's not him, per se." He pointed down the hallway, where I could hear Hayden and Nikki talking. "It's just, that's my kid growing in there, and that's my…" Pressing his lips together, he paused. "It's just weird having a guy living here, is all. Nikki's always been…single…for the most part. She's never had anything serious anyway."

"Well, Hayden's not here to move in on Nikki, if that's what you're worried about. If it will ease your mind, just think of him as a girl." I cringed the minute the words left my mouth.

Myles grinned at me. "I can't believe you just said that."

"And I can't believe you're jealous," I countered.

His expression instantly shifted into annoyance. "I'm not *jealous*. It's just…weird. I'm weirdous, and that's completely different."

I couldn't keep the smirk off my face. "Uh-huh."

"Kenzie?" Nikki shouted. "You get lost? It's not a very long hallway."

Still smiling, I told her, "On my way."

Myles rolled his eyes and stayed in the living room as I took my box down the hallway.

Hayden and I made two more trips to my truck, and that was all it took to unload all of Hayden's things. Once we were in his new—but small—bedroom, I looked around and frowned. "You don't have a bed. Or a dresser. You don't have much of…anything."

Hayden smiled as he sat on a box. "I guess that means we're done. Looks like I'll be living out of boxes for a while."

I frowned, not happy with that answer. "You can't sleep on boxes."

Standing, Hayden walked over to me and put his hands on my arms. "I'll sleep on the couch until I get a bed. I'll be fine."

Still unhappy about his situation, I shook my head. "Why don't you have anything? I mean, I know Keith supplied a lot of your stuff when you lived with him, but what about before then? Haven't you *ever* had stuff?"

Now Hayden frowned. "When Felicia and I…lived together, yes… I had stuff. But after she left, and it became very clear to me that she wasn't coming back… I kind of had a bonfire."

Even while a stab of pain went through me at hearing *her* name again, my mouth dropped open in surprise. "You burned all your stuff? All your furniture?"

Hayden nodded. "Hookup and Grunts helped me. It was kind of...cathartic...what I can remember of it anyway." A small laugh escaped him, and then he shrugged. "After that, I just didn't want to have anything I couldn't leave behind at a moment's notice. I wanted to be as mobile as possible. I felt that way for a long time, which is why I think I let Keith give me so much. It didn't feel permanent, because it wasn't mine. But now... I want permanence. I'm ready for it." Inhaling a deep breath, he smiled. "I'm ready for a bed. And, maybe, a dresser."

Smiling wide, I wrapped my arms around his neck. He lifted an eyebrow before encircling me in a hug. "Transportation comes first though. I'd rather get a kink in my neck than have to get a ride everywhere."

"Did I hear you say you needed transportation?" Nikki asked, appearing in the doorway with a plate of cookies. "Hungry?"

We both turned to look at her, and my mouth popped open again. Nikki didn't bake. She noticed my expression, and her cheeks flushed. Giving Hayden a pointed glance, she immediately said, "This isn't typical of living here. I don't supply food. Just wine...which I can't have anymore..." A soft sigh escaped her.

Hayden laughed, then took a cookie from her plate. I frowned as he popped it into his mouth. All he'd had today was fat and carbs. You sure couldn't tell he had bad eating habits from his body though. Damn high metabolism. "I don't expect anything from you, Nikki. I can take care of myself. Now what were you saying about transportation?"

Myles appeared behind her. Stepping into the doorway beside Nikki, he also grabbed cookies—three of them. Before the next season started, I was going to have to talk to my team about properly fueling their bodies. "I think she means me. I'm looking to sell my old street bike." He flashed a meaningful look at Nikki. "Priorities and all." Returning his eyes to Hayden, he said, "Anyway, are you looking to buy?"

Hayden grinned at me, then turned to face Myles. "Yeah. I'd love to take it out for a spin. Can we go now?"

He looked over at me for approval, and I smiled and nodded. "Sounds great." The more the four of us socialized together, the less awkward this would be for everyone.

Myles seemed unsure, but Nikki was thrilled about the idea. "Yeah, let's do it! We can stop by Kenzie's and pick up her bike, then we can all four go for a ride together. Assuming you're fine with Myles riding your bike, Kenzie?"

I was just about to tell her sure, when Myles shook his head. "No way. You can't ride a bike right now."

Nikki and I crossed our arms at the same time. "Why can't I?" Nikki asked, heat in her tone.

In answer, Myles pointed at her stomach. Nikki's expression heated even more. "Up until a few days ago, you didn't even know I was pregnant, and now you're telling me what I can and can't do?"

Myles tossed his hands into the air. "It's not my fault you didn't tell me the instant you knew. And actually, I'm still kind of ticked about that. So, yeah, I think that gives me an extra say in the matter. Like I get two votes and you get one."

Nikki's eyes widened. "What? That is the stupidest thing I've ever heard you say, Kelley...and I've heard you say some pretty stupid things."

Hayden shifted on his feet. "It's okay, we don't have to—"

Nikki pointed a finger at him. "No! We're going." Shifting her attention back to Myles, she said, "I have a doctor's appointment Wednesday. You're going to come with me, and we'll find out from a professional what I can and can't do. Until then, I get *all* the votes, got it?"

Myles sighed and rolled his eyes. "Fine," he snipped. Then he grabbed the rest of the cookies and stormed from the room.

Nikki closed her eyes, clearly counting to ten. When she reopened them, she gave me a tense smile. "He's driving me nuts. *Already*." Narrowing her eyes, she said, "If he doesn't knock it off, you might need another rider soon."

I offered her as supportive a smile as I could. "I'll talk to him, get him to relax. But maybe we should forgo the group ride until after your doctor's appointment. Just...to keep the peace?"

Nikki glared at me so hard, I felt the condemnation across my skin. "Fine," she sneered, in the exact same tone Myles had used. Then she left the room, and I heard her bedroom door across the hall slam shut.

Hayden sighed as he looked my way. "Like I said...it should be interesting living here."

Giving him a sympathetic smile, I said, "Why don't you and Myles go test out the bike. I'll stay here, try to calm Nikki down. It's so strange seeing them fight like this. They've always been so...compatible." Sadness washed over me as I realized how *all* of our relationships had shifted. Hayden and I were…different. Myles and Nikki were different. God, I hated change.

Hayden kissed my cheek. "They'll be fine. They just need time to…get used to how things are…now."

I knew from his tone and his face that he wasn't really talking about Myles and Nikki anymore. My mood brightened as I nodded. Yes. Time would fix this, and time would fix *us* too.

Hayden gave me a soft kiss full of meaning, full of promise, full of determination. When he pulled back, he cupped my cheeks, then kissed my forehead. I inhaled a deep, cleansing breath, filling myself with his strength, then I wished him good luck in his endeavor with Myles.

He rolled his eyes at me as he walked out the door. "We're gonna be riding bikes. We'll be fine." With a wink, he left me, so I could deal with my emotional best friend.

I inhaled another deep breath before I made the attempt. As I knocked on her door, I heard Myles and Hayden leaving the apartment. They were both laughing, so that was a good start. "Nikki? Are you…okay?"

I heard sniffling behind the closed wood. "Yep. I'm great."

With a sigh, I cracked open her door. "I know you're not. Want to talk about it?"

She quickly wiped her eyes dry, like she could hide her feelings from me. "Nothing to talk about, I'm peachy keen."

Sitting on the bed beside her, I put a hand on her knee. "I know you're not. Come on…you're always there for me, let me be there for you."

She sniffed again, then her deeply-tanned face swung my way. "It's just... Myles and I were always on the same page. Always. But now, it's almost like we're strangers. Or worse, it's like he doesn't see *me* anymore, just what I'm...carrying."

Biting my lip, I debated what to say to her. "Myles is just trying to figure things out, same as you. And I'm sure it's hard for him, since he's...not really a part of the process anymore. He's just worried, about both of you."

Nikki gave me a reluctant smile. "I know. I just... miss how we used to be."

Slinging my arm around her shoulder, I pulled her into me. "I know how hard it can be, when you miss the past. Just know the future is going to be okay. You guys are going to be okay. I know it."

Her grin turned warmer. "You really think so?"

No. But I hoped so. "Yeah... I do."

CHAPTER 3

It didn't take Hayden and me long to adjust to our new routine. Now that he lived so close to me, I would swing by his place every morning—usually waking him up—and we'd ride out to the track side by side, me on my bike, him on the bike he'd purchased from Myles.

I found myself climbing into bed every night looking forward to that early morning ride with Hayden. In a small, satisfying way it reminded me of the old days, when we'd snuck out to the track to do a little midnight racing. But unlike those stolen night rides, we tried to stay close to the speed limit on our morning rides. Or somewhat close.

Wednesday morning was different though. No, this morning Hayden was riding to the track alone, and I was going with Nikki to her very first doctor's appointment. I knew she was a nervous wreck, as she'd already texted me six times this week, asking if she really needed to see someone this early in the pregnancy. My response to her was always the same: yes. If it were left entirely up to Nikki, I think she would wait until her water broke to meet the doctor. Whatever she could do to convince herself this wasn't happening. Hopefully the appointment would firmly break through her wall of denial.

UNDENIABLE RUSH 35

Stepping up to her apartment door, I firmly rapped on the wood, then rang the doorbell. It would be just like Nikki to pretend she was sleeping and hadn't heard me. She couldn't ignore me with Hayden staying there, though, and I was positive I could wake him up if he was still sleeping. Or I could practice my more illicit skills and break in.

As I waited for some sort of response, I listened hard for some sound of life. Nothing. Were they both still sleeping? I was just about to ring the doorbell again, when I heard a deep, gruff voice mutter, "Coming," then heard the sounds of shuffling feet.

A bright smile took over my face when Hayden appeared in the doorway. He was so cute when he first woke up, his shaggy blonde hair all sexy and disheveled, wearing a ratty T-shirt and loose lounge pants, his hand to his mouth, covering a yawn. "Hi," I cheerily told him, not feeling the least bit tired. I'd already been up for a couple hours.

Giving me a sleepy grin, he murmured, "Hi," then stepped forward and wrapped his arms around me. His warmth and comfort instantly flooded my senses, and I closed my eyes, drinking him in as I returned his hug. This was my favorite part of the day.

"Good morning," he whispered in my ear, his breath tickling my skin.

A shiver went through me as I clenched him tight. "Morning."

Pulling back to look at me, Hayden frowned. "You're here for Nikki, aren't you?" He seemed so disheartened by that fact, like he already missed me.

Cupping his cheek, I nodded. Then I shook my head. "I'm here for both of you."

That made him smile, and leaning forward, he gave me a soft kiss. I reveled in the tender exchange, then reluctantly pulled away. "While I'd love to kiss you all morning, I'd better collect Nikki before she ducks out a window."

Hayden laughed, then stopped and nodded in agreement. Holding hands, we walked into the apartment. "Nik? You ready?" I asked. Silence answered me.

With a sigh, I looked up at Hayden. He shrugged. "I thought she was here, but maybe she already slipped out?"

Irritation pricked my skin, and, dropping his hand, I strode down the hallway to her bedroom. When I opened the door, the covers on her bed moved, like the person they were hiding was trying to burrow into the mattress. Rolling my eyes, I sauntered over to the bed and pulled off the comforter. Nikki was curled into a ball, trying to be as small and inconspicuous as her plump body would allow. Blinking her eyes, she peeked up at me. "Oh hey, Kenzie. I didn't know you were here."

I raised a pointed eyebrow at her, then relaxed my expression. "Ready to go?"

Still dressed in her pajamas, it was clear she wasn't ready to go anywhere. If she thought that would deter me, though, she was dead wrong—I'd drag her down there in her comfy fleece pants if needed. Nikki seemed to understand that as she looked up at me. With an annoyed groan, she uncurled her body. "Almost…"

Smiling, I stepped back so she could get up. "Is Myles meeting us here or there?" I asked as she grudgingly got out of bed.

"There," she murmured, trudging to her dresser.

I kind of wished he was coming here, another set of hands corralling her wouldn't be a bad thing. "Okay, well, I'll be in the living room waiting for you." She nodded, and I turned to leave. Pausing, I twisted around and told her, "Don't take too long, Nik. We really do need to go."

She gave me an exasperated look, but then nodded. Nikki liked being late, while I liked being early. But Nikki knew this was important. Otherwise she would have fought me more.

I could hear Hayden in his room when I left Nikki, so I headed that way. He was standing by a box of clothes, shirtless, buttoning his jeans. The defined lines of his abs stole my focus, and I couldn't help but stare at him. He glanced over when he felt my eyes burning holes into his body, and when our gazes locked, his lips slowly curved into a charming, crooked smile. "Are you sure you need to go so soon? If you've got time, I've got time." He held his arms open for a hug.

Resisting took every ounce of willpower I possessed. "I don't have time, sorry." And I wasn't sure if I was ready for a half-naked embrace. That would make me think and feel things I just wasn't ready for.

Not wanting to once again slip into doubt and confusion, I tossed on a carefree smile. Hayden grinned at seeing it, and my mood—thankfully—remained level. After he slipped on a fresh T-shirt, I walked over and innocently kissed his cheek. "I'll see you later at the track." I started to walk away, then paused and looked back at him. "I love you." It was a little easier to say this time, and my heart pleasantly fluttered in my chest, instead of pound like I was running a marathon.

Hayden's grin grew. Reaching out, he grabbed my hand and pulled me back to him. "I love you too," he said, then he crashed his lips down to mine. I lost myself to the feel of his mouth on mine. His hands ran up and down my spine, his tongue lightly flicked against me, igniting me, and the passion slowly began to burn away the fear and doubt that constantly lingered in the back of my brain. Maybe letting go wasn't such a bad thing after all...

"You tell me not to waste time getting ready, and here you are...practically getting it on with your boyfriend. Does this mean we're staying home?"

Hayden and I separated, and I spun around to see Nikki's amused smile. Even though there was a distinct smugness to her grin, there was happiness in her dark eyes. She wanted Hayden and I to get back to where we used to be...back when things were good.

Inhaling a deep breath, I tried to calm my surging heart. "No, we're still leaving," I firmly told her. She had places to be, and Hayden and I...couldn't go there yet.

Hayden looked satisfied when I looked back at him, like just the act of turning me on made him happy. I was glad to see the peace on his face, and I was feeling pretty content myself when I left the apartment with Nikki.

"You guys seem to be doing well," Nikki commented once we were in her tiny car. "Did you take my advice? Get back on that stallion?"

I pursed my lips at her comment, then sighed. "Yes... and no." She looked confused by that, so I clarified. "I'm trying not to push him away, trying not to let the fear win, but we're not having sex yet. Not even close." He still hadn't come inside my house yet. I should rectify that soon. Open a physical door, and a proverbial one.

Nikki furrowed her brows as she drove. "Well, I guess it's a step in the right direction. Just don't get stuck inside your head, Kenzie. Sometimes you need to feel things without thinking them through."

I pointed at her stomach. "Like you did with Myles?"

She shot me a glare before her eyes drifted back to the road. "Not funny. Don't compare my love life to yours."

"Is there a love life?" I asked, genuinely curious. The thought of them together didn't weird me out like it used to. They'd actually be pretty...perfect.

But Nikki snorted. "No, Kenzie, we're just friends. And barely that anymore." Her voice softened. "The only thing I am looking forward to today is the fact that maybe I can convince the doctor to make Myles relax...so I can have my friend back."

I had to bite my lip to stop myself from saying something. While this appointment might ease Myles's mind, it also might give him a lot more ammunition to use against her...and I had a feeling that was the way it was going to go. I really needed to have a conversation with him soon, before he permanently damaged their relationship.

When we got to the parking lot of Nikki's OB/GYN, Myles was already there, waiting in his car. He looked shocked when he saw Nikki pull up beside him. He'd probably assumed she'd be her usual late self.

Nikki let out a long, slow exhale as she shut off the car. "You all right?" I asked her.

She looked over at me with a strained expression. "Just feeling sick."

My eyes widened. "Morning sickness sick?" I started looking around for a bag, a bowl, something she could use.

Nikki let out a shaky laugh. "No, just nerves sick. I don't think I'll actually puke, knock on wood."

I put a supportive hand on her arm right as Myles opened her car door. "Oh good, you're early," he said, extending a hand to help Nikki out of the car.

She smiled up at him as she took his hand, relief and gratitude on her face. Then she frowned. "Of course, I'm early. Did you think I'd be late for this?"

Myles and I gave her the exact same disbelieving expression. Glancing between the both of us, she murmured, "Shut up," then let Myles pull her from the cramped vehicle.

I chuckled to myself as I got out and walked over to them. They both seemed so overwhelmed as they stood there, standing close to each other but not looking at each other. Myles kept running a hand back through his dark, piecey hair, and his equally dark eyes kept scanning the lot, like he was memorizing the escape routes. Nikki looked green. It was strange to see them so out-of-sorts, as both were usually so carefree and easygoing, always looking for a good time.

The day they'd met was crystal clear in my brain. Nikki had joined Cox Racing first, and we'd hit it off right away—even though I hadn't been an official rider yet, the track was my home, and I'd spent most of my time there. On Myles's first day, he'd ran into Nikki first.

Holding up his helmet and duffle bag, he'd asked her, "Do I give these to you?"

She'd glanced at me, and we'd shared a laugh. Then, showing Myles her grease-stained coveralls, she'd dryly told him, "Do I look like your personal assistant?"

A second later, he'd realized what her job was at the track, and like most men Nikki met...he'd been surprised. "Holy shit, you're a mechanic?"

Nikki's answer still made me laugh. "Yeah, weird, I know... I have tits, and yet, I know how to use tools." One day, I was getting that put on a T-shirt for her.

Instead of getting mad or irritated at her answer, instead of puffing up his chest like he had something to prove... Myles had started laughing—tears from his eyes, dying laughing. That was when I'd known the two of them would be friends for life.

Myles had invited her to go out with him after work, and they'd gone out almost every night after that. They were yin and yang, peas in a pod, kindred spirits...or at least, they used to be. Now, they were just stressed out parents-to-be.

Not sure if they'd be able to walk into the building without a little prodding, I said, "You guys ready?"

They both nodded, looking forlorn and uncomfortable, and the three of us began walking toward the front door. On the way, Myles looked back at Nikki's car. "You know, I was thinking, you should probably trade that thing in for a bigger car soon."

Nikki suddenly looked a lot less green as she stared at him. "What? No way."

Myles frowned. "It's practically a speed bump on wheels, Nik. What if someone hits you?"

Staring straight ahead, she inhaled a deep, calming breath. "It will be fine, Myles. I love that car, and I want to keep it."

Myles sighed as he pulled the front door and held it open. "Yeah, well I love…seeing you breathing. And that thing won't survive a crash."

There was an odd pause in his sentence, one that made me smile, but Nikki didn't seem to notice. She laughed as she walked through the door. "Says the man who rides 150 miles per hour on an open-air vehicle for a living."

His frown deepened after her comment, but even I had to admit she made a good point. What he did daily was far more dangerous than Nikki driving around in a microscopic smart car. I gave him an apologetic shrug as I walked into the building after her.

Myles sighed again as he followed us, and that was when Nikki decided to drop a bomb on him. Turning to face him, she quietly said, "Before I forget…my mom wants you to come over for family dinner on Sunday. It's not optional," she added, grimacing.

All the color left his face, and he glanced back at the front door like he was going to make a run for it. "Do they…know?" he asked, looking back at her.

Biting her lip, Nikki shook her head. "No."

"Fuck." Myles said that in a louder voice than Nikki had been using, and everyone waiting in the quiet lobby turned to look at him. His cheeks instantly filled with color as his eyes drifted to the ground. "Sorry," he murmured to the crowd.

A few of the women were still frowning as they went back to their magazines. If they only understood the situation, then they might be more sympathetic, less annoyed. Nikki's parents could be…intense. And on top of that, she had six—*very protective*—older brothers. I might never see my best racer again.

With one hand I rubbed Myles's arm in camaraderie. With the other, I clenched Nikki's elbow. Leaning in, I told her, "Don't let them murder him, okay?"

Nikki laughed...but it was nervous sounding.

The three of us looked for somewhere to sit in the lobby. Something must have been in the water in Oceanside, because pregnant women were everywhere, and most of them looked like they were about to explode at any moment. "Jesus," Nikki muttered. "Is that how big I'm going to get?" One of the mothers-to-be heard her and shot a nasty glare in our direction. The three of us weren't winning any popularity contests, that was for sure.

Myles had a strange look on his face as he looked around. "I don't think I'm supposed to be here," he whispered.

I understood why he felt that why. He was the only guy in the place. Smiling at him, I reassuringly told him, "It takes two to make a child, so you have just as much right to be here as they do."

Myles grinned in an unexpected way. He opened his mouth, but Nikki immediately interrupted. "No, that still doesn't give you two-to-one veto power."

His lips curved into a pout, and I let out a quiet laugh—a laugh that earned me glares too. Nikki pointed at some chairs across the room, then headed up to the receptionist. Once she was checked in, she joined Myles and me. Nikki spent the next fifteen minutes rocking in her chair and biting her nails, while Myles bounced his knees and drummed his thighs. Every single person in the lobby tossed an occasional annoyed glance our way. I tried to ease my friends' minds with pointless conversation, but they couldn't seem to stop being a bundle of nerves and anxiety.

Reaching over Myles, I patted Nikki's knee. "It's going to be okay," I said, glancing at both of them. "It's just a checkup."

Myles let out a long breath, stilling his legs. Nikki nodded and clenched my hand. "Thank you for being here. Both of you." Her eyes shifted to Myles. "I know I didn't really give you much of a choice…but thank you anyway."

Myles grinned, and seeing that boyish smile made Nikki visibly relax. "There's no place I'd rather be right now," he told her. Then his eyes darted around the room stuffed with pregnant women, and his grin shifted to a frown. "Well, no, actually, I can think of at least a thousand other places I'd rather be right now…" his eyes refocused on her, and his expression softened, "but there is nothing I'd rather be doing than supporting you. You're my best friend."

His voice was so soft, so sweet, so tender… I instantly knew I was a third wheel who didn't need to be here. This moment should belong to Myles and Nikki, and Myles and Nikki only. I was just debating how to tell my best friend I wasn't going in with her, when I heard someone loudly proclaim, "Nikki Ramirez?"

On the far side of the room, a nurse was holding open a door to the back rooms and scanning the crowd for her patient. Nikki shrank down in her seat, hiding, and I poked her in the side. "Go on, Nik."

She looked over at me with wide eyes. "Are you coming?"

Cringing, I looked between her and Myles. "Actually, I think the two of you should go in alone. This is your moment, and I don't want to intrude. But I'll be here when you get out."

Nikki opened her mouth to object, but Myles grabbed her hand. Their eyes locked, and Myles nodded at her. Nikki studied his expression for a few moments, then looked back at me, sighed, and said, "Okay…we'll see you in a few, Kenzie."

Waiting for Nikki and Myles to return from the doctor's office might have been the single most boring thing I'd ever done in my life. I couldn't even entertain myself with reading the magazines, since they were all pregnancy or parenting related. And I just couldn't think about that yet, not for myself anyway. But even still, as I mindlessly browsed the Internet on my phone, I wondered if that type of future was in the cards for Hayden and me.

Would he want kids? Would *I* want kids? Would we even be together long enough to contemplate having kids? Life was so unpredictable. That was practically the only thing anyone could count on.

But still…having a child with Hayden—his green eyes, my wavy brown hair—we'd make a beautiful baby, that was for sure. My heart suddenly constricted in pain. No, not pain…an ache. A deep, heart-wrenching ache that cut me to the core. And I knew in that moment that having a child was something I absolutely wanted. One day. And I absolutely wanted it…with Hayden. That warmed me and terrified me.

Just as I could feel an ulcer beginning to form in my stomach, the door Nikki and Myles had disappeared through swung open. Nikki strode through, her face reminding me of a turbulent sky about to unleash its fury. Worried, I stood up and started walking her way.

"Nik? Everything okay?" Even though she looked angry more than anything else, I started to fear that something was wrong with the baby. Could they tell that this early in the pregnancy?

Her eyes were hot when she met my gaze. I could feel the lethal penetration all the way to my bones. "I need a new doctor. Mine is an idiot."

Surprised by her answer, I looked behind her to the still-open door, where Myles was talking with an older man who I could only assume was her doctor. "Why?"

Nikki raised her hand to me. "Don't, I can't…" Not finishing her comment, she turned and headed for the front door. Myles spotted her leaving, hastily said goodbye to the doctor, and darted out the door after her.

Even more confused, and worried my ride was about to leave, I made my way outside. I got there right as Myles caught up to Nikki. "Come on, Nik," he told her, "just take a minute and think about it. That's all we're saying."

I had never seen Nikki this angry before. It was a little unnerving. "What's going on?" I asked. Maybe I should have gone in with them after all.

Myles sighed, and Nikki rolled her eyes. Not answering me, she addressed Myles. "I can't believe you bought that crap he was spewing."

Myles's lips compressed as he shook his head. "I know you want to act like having a baby won't change your life, but the truth is—it's *going* to change your life. It's not just *you* anymore. And the doctor was right—racetracks are messy, and dirty, and smelly, and loud. It's no place for a baby. You shouldn't be going to events."

My eyes widened as shock went through me. *Not go to events...?* The shock was quickly followed by icy truth. God...of course she shouldn't be going to events. Everything Myles had just said was absolutely true. Shit. She was my best mechanic—*my* mechanic. I couldn't even imagine someone else touching my bike. It was hers, and hers alone. What the hell were we going to do?

Nikki still didn't seem to want to accept her situation. Raising her chin, she stubbornly said, "I'll leave the baby with my mom. Problem solved. I'm not missing Cox Racing's first year back." She pointed a finger at me. "I'm not missing *Kenzie's* first year back."

I was warmed by her loyalty, but even I knew she wouldn't be able to leave her baby. Not in the beginning, not when it was only a few weeks old. Putting a smile on my face, even though I suddenly felt hollow inside, I tenderly put my hand on her shoulder. "Nik...you can't leave a newborn behind."

Rounding on me, her face a mixture of fury, resentment and fear, she snapped, "For a weekend? I think I can handle that."

I exchanged a look with Myles. He understood. He knew Nikki better than she knew herself, and while she wasn't excited about this pregnancy, wasn't embracing the changes in her life...her heart was pure gold. Once that baby was born, nothing else in the world was going to matter to her. Not even me.

With a sigh, Myles gently turned her to face him. "It's not just a weekend, Nikki, and you know that. How are you going to work at the track with a baby? The garage isn't safe for a child either. You should both be home. Together."

Nikki narrowed her eyes at him, but they were misty with tears now. "And how am I supposed to live, Myles? I *need* to work. I have bills to pay." Her voice hitched with emotion.

Myles swallowed, clearly hating her turmoil. Shaking his head, he softly said, "I don't know. I don't have all the answers. All I do know is that the baby shouldn't go to events, shouldn't spend all day at the track. And I have a feeling, when it's time, and you meet the little guy…or girl…you won't be able to leave him or her." His eyes intensified as they shifted to me. "We should have a plan ready, so when that day comes, Cox Racing isn't screwed."

The knot in my throat was almost impossible to push down. I was losing her. Maybe just temporarily…but maybe not. She could easily choose to never come back, to get a different job that was more in line with raising an infant…start a daycare or something. And with everything else in my life feeling so topsy-turvy, it was almost more than I could take. But I had to be strong, for her sake. Because she was barely holding on.

Nodding at Myles, I pulled Nikki in for a hug. "It's all going to be okay, Nik. I promise."

CHAPTER 4

When Nikki and I got back into her car, an unnatural silence filled the space with tension. I wanted to break it somehow, fill the sadness with laughter, but I just didn't know how. Myles drove away while we sat there, and Nikki watched him go with her keys clenched in her hand.

Wanting to redirect her thoughts—somehow—I tentatively asked a question. "So...did the doctor have *any* good news for you?" I half-cringed after asking, anticipating the question might make her upset again.

Nikki sighed, then a small smile brightened her expression. "Well...we were able to hear the heartbeat, and he gave us a picture of the baby."

Opening her purse, she grabbed a small photo from the bag and handed it to me. The grainy black and white image was unmistakable, and my eyes instantly watered. "Oh my God... There really is a little life growing in there," I murmured, a little mystified by it all.

Nikki laughed as she stared at the photo in my hands. "Yep...no denying it now. He said the baby is due in April..."

Glancing up at her, I quietly said, "We should go to the track and talk to John and my dad. The more time we have to find someone...the better."

Nikki lifted her tired eyes to mine. "Yeah...okay." Looking around the lot, she asked, "Do you want to go get your bike first?"

Feeling like she'd fall apart if I left her alone, I shook my head. "No, I'll get a ride with Hayden later. Let's just get going." Before she changed her mind.

Myles was already at the track when we got there, talking to Hayden in the garage. From the look on Hayden's face, it was clear Myles was telling him the bad news—we were losing Nikki. Temporarily. I had to remember that this wasn't a permanent problem. Nikki would come back to me. Come back to us.

A groan left Nikki's lips when she saw Myles and Hayden deep in conversation. "Everyone's going to know by the end of the day," she said.

"It's best that they do, Nik. You're not just my personal mechanic, you're the head mechanic for Cox Racing—the heart of the crew, the one who keeps everything running smoothly. We *all* need to get used to the idea that you're not going to be there." To stave off an emotional outburst, I quickly added, "For a little bit."

Nikki pursed her lips but didn't comment. I took that as a good sign.

When we stepped up to Myles and Hayden, Hayden gave Nikki a sympathetic smile. "Myles just told me the news... Sorry, Nik. I know you didn't want to miss anything this season."

She looked between all of us, irritation and sadness on her face. "It's just a precaution. I don't plan on missing anything."

The small smile remained plastered on Hayden's face, but his eyes broadcasted his disbelief. Having helped Izzy raise Antonia, he knew from experience how much a baby could change your priorities.

Giving Hayden a sly, *I agree with you* smile, I turned to Nikki. "I'll be in my office with John and my dad when you're ready, Nik."

Her eyes pleaded with me to reconsider, but eventually she nodded, then started trudging to the locker room to put away her stuff. Myles watched her leave for a minute, then turned to me. "I'm gonna make sure she's okay. This is really hard on her."

Seeing an opportunity, I briefly grabbed his arm to stop him. "The way you've been acting has also been hard on her."

Myles blinked, like he truly had no idea what I was talking about. "Me? All I've been is helpful."

"All you've been is overbearing. She doesn't need another father right now, she needs her best friend."

Myles tossed his hand into the air, annoyed. "She's living in denial, Kenzie. She doesn't want to do anything she's supposed to be doing."

"She's adjusting," I said, shaking my head. "And you need to give her time to adjust. You and I both know that she will do everything in her power to put that baby first…when she's ready." Softening my expression, I put a hand on his arm. "Just stop being a douche. That's all I'm asking."

Hayden laughed into his hand, and Myles finally cracked a smile. "Okay… I'll stop being a douche and try to relax more."

"Thank you." My grin was bright and cheery, and Myles shook his head at me before following after Nikki.

When Hayden and I were alone, he turned to me with concerned eyes. "You okay with this news? I know how much you rely on Nikki." He sighed. "After how amazing she was as my mechanic last year, I know I'm kind of freaking out."

Closing my eyes, I fought through a sudden bout of panic. What *was* I going to do? I shook my head as I looked at him. "Honestly, I think I'm still too in shock to really process it. I don't know why this didn't occur to me when she first told me."

Hayden gently grabbed my hands. "Maybe it did, and you just didn't want to think about it. But even though it sucks, it's still a good thing, you know?"

"Yeah…" Remembering my feelings at the doctor's office, I chewed on my lip, then asked, "Is that something you want…one day? Kids?"

Hayden's eyebrows rose, then his smile grew. "Well, it's no secret that I love kids…so…yeah, when the time is right, I'd love to have children." From the way his gaze softened with adoration, I knew he meant he'd love to have them with me.

Heat flushed my cheeks, and I felt a swell of love from deep inside me. It helped wash away the ache of his past betrayal with the promise of his future commitment. A part of me wanted to tell him right then and there that I was ready to move faster—a lot faster—but with how my moods tended to a spin on a dime recently, I knew I needed to be moderate with my decisions. I didn't want to hurt him—or myself—by being rash. But that didn't mean I couldn't still move forward…

Stroking my thumbs along his hands, I felt my nerves spike and my heartbeat quicken. "I, um, need a ride back to my bike after work."

Hayden looked confused as he studied my reaction. He probably didn't understand why this was making me nervous. He would soon. "Sure, of course."

Expecting that answer, I was already nodding. Avoiding his eyes, I quietly said, "And I was hoping, maybe after we got my bike…you and I could go get something to eat? And…take it back to my house?"

I flashed my gaze up to his eyes, so I could see his reaction, and was rewarded with a brilliant smile. "I would love that, Kenzie," he said, his voice soft with caring.

A thrill went up my spine. Even though we'd been together for a while now, somehow it felt like we were making a first date. But even still, my stomach was tight, and my muscles were rock hard, like I was waiting for an actual, physical blow to the gut. With a conscious effort, I forced my body to relax. Just like Nikki's pregnancy, Hayden and I, we were a good thing.

Grinning, I told him, "Good. Well, I should go find my dad, but I'll catch up with you later."

I reluctantly stepped away from him, and he reluctantly let me, holding hands until the last possible moment. But when our connection was finally severed, Hayden's tender voice stopped me in my tracks. "Hey, Kenzie?" Pausing, I looked back at him over my shoulder. He had his hands in his pockets, and his heart on his sleeve. "Do you…want kids? One day?"

A slight grimace marred his features, like he wasn't sure if he should be asking me that question or not. My heart thumped in my chest, but it was a good thud—an eager thud. Walking back over to him, I laced my arms around his neck. "Yes… I do." It felt oddly amazing to say those two words to him—I do—and I felt the pockets of resistant hurt inside me being slowly chipped away.

His lips came down to mine, and we sealed our desires for the future with a kiss, and somehow, I knew, this particular kiss would stay with me for the rest of my life.

* * *

Gathering John and my dad took more time than I thought it would, and Nikki was waiting in my office when I returned with them. Her lips lifted in a reluctant smile when we walked through the door, and I returned the sad sentiment. None of us really wanted to do this.

I hadn't told John or my dad why I wanted a meeting, so they were naturally confused when I shut the door on the four of us. "What's going on, Mackenzie?" Dad asked. Then his eyes strayed to my desk. It was nearly overflowing with paperwork. Bills I was trying to sort out, records on all my riders, forms for the various events, suggested travel itineraries, supply requests from the crew, quotes from painters and builders for my seemingly endless renovation of the Cox garages, and so much more. There was barely any free space on my desk anymore, and every day, more crap seemed to appear. The clutter grated against my need to be neat and tidy. Just walking in here lately was stressful.

"Do you need help with any of that?" he asked, indicating the mess. Walking over to the stacks, he started examining them.

Wanting to do as much as I could on my own, I shook my head. "No, there's a different matter we need to—"

He cut me off. Lifting a thick wad of papers, he said, "Mackenzie, these are for Daytona. You should get these forms in as soon as possible. Delaying isn't a good idea."

Gritting my teeth, I nodded. "I have plenty of time before the cut off."

Setting down the stack, he frowned. "You also have plenty of time to forget. If you need help getting all of this organized, that's what John and I are here for. Part of being a leader is delegating tasks, especially the difficult ones."

I could feel the hackles rising at his choice of words. Difficult? Like I was incapable of filling out paperwork correctly? Sure, the business side of things was still pretty new to me, but I wasn't an idiot. I could handle it. I could handle everything.

Ignoring my father, I turned to John, my crew chief and the true second in command here. Jordan Cox was merely a consultant. One I could listen to—or not listen to. The rising tension in the room didn't seem to faze John at all. He was quite used to my father and me butting heads. "John," I told him. "Nikki is pregnant, as I'm sure you know, and she'll be leaving us when the baby is born. Perhaps before…"

Nikki instantly shot to her feet. "No, I'm not leaving, I'm taking a temporary leave of absence…and even that might not happen."

Ignoring *her* now, I continued explaining. "We need to find someone to replace her." Nikki loudly cleared her throat, and I grudgingly amended my statement. "We need someone to *temporarily* replace her."

John ran his hand over his chin as he thought. John was just about the same age as my father, and they both had the stern, imposing demeanor down pat. I heard Nikki swallow as his eyes shifted to take her in. "I see," he said, his grey eyes narrowing. When his eyes returned to me, there was worry in them. "It's going to take some time to find the right person. True, we've got a few months, but I don't want to leave it to the last minute. Best to acclimate someone new to the team early."

"I agree," I said with a smile. "That's why I'm telling you now."

"This is ridiculous and pointless," Nikki mumbled, but she said it too low for John or my dad to hear. Deep down she knew it wasn't stupid. She'd do the same thing in my position.

John looked over at Jordan. "I'm going to go make some phone calls. I've got a couple of contacts over at MMTI. They might have some promising leads—recent graduates, or soon-to-be graduates."

My dad nodded at him, and John quickly left the room. It irritated me some that John always looked to my dad for confirmation, like Dad was still in charge. I should sit him down and explain to him how things worked now...once I had some spare time.

Nikki looked sad as she turned my way. "I guess that's it then, the clock is ticking."

Pursing my lips at her, I said, "Don't be overdramatic about this. Like I told John, it's a temporary replacement."

Her eyes narrowed as she studied me. "You only added that to appease me. 'Cause let's face it, this might be permanent. What if you find...someone great?"

"Then I'll have two great mechanics on the team." Thinking a moment, I added, "And Kevin."

Nikki laughed at my joke, then hugged me. "I better get back to work while I still have a job."

She started to leave, but my dad stopped her. "Nikki …a moment."

Her back was to my father, but I saw her close her eyes. I sympathized. Talking to my father, especially when he was disappointed, wasn't easy. Twisting around, Nikki seamlessly said, "Yes, Mr. Cox?"

I narrowed my eyes at Dad, warning him to be nice. Dad's eyes flicked from me to her, then he said, "I've been meaning to…congratulate you on the child you're having with… Myles." Myles's name came out with a definite growl to it. "While becoming a parent is a daunting prospect, I have no doubt you will be an excellent mother."

Nikki seemed shocked that he had anything positive to say on the matter. I was a little surprised too, and I had a feeling the same words wouldn't have been spoken if Myles were in the room. "Um…thank you."

Looking a little dazed, she glanced back at me, then headed out the open door. As she left, Dad muttered, "Now Myles…that's a completely different story."

I rolled my eyes at his comment. "Remember what I said—be nice to him. You don't need to berate him for his mistake. He's already well aware he messed up. And Nikki's aware of her mistakes, too, since she's just as much at fault as Myles."

Dad raised an eyebrow. "I'm assuming you and Hayden…won't be following down their reckless footsteps?" He grimaced after he said it, but his expression was nothing compared to mine. Was my father really asking me about my sex life? If I told him how slow Hayden and I were taking things, he'd probably be relieved. Not that I'd ever tell him.

"Uh, we're..." Closing my eyes, I held up my hand. "You don't need to worry about us."

When I opened my eyes, Dad was nodding, his expression thoughtful. I almost wanted to ask him what he was thinking about, and it had been a long time since I'd been curious. The bridge spanning the gap between us was thin-bare and rickety, like it could collapse at any moment.

Clearing his throat, Dad changed the feeling in the air by saying, "Your sisters...and I...enjoyed having dinner with you and Hayden. They'd like...*we* would like, to make it a more frequent thing." His eyes got a faraway look. "Time has a horrible way of sneaking up on you..."

Shaking his head, he returned his gaze to me. The usual steel in his blue eyes seemed softened, flexible—vulnerable. It was odd to see him that way. "Yeah...no, that sounds good. Let's do it." Glancing at the mountain of responsibility on my desk, I wondered if I'd be able to honor that agreement.

Dad looked over at my desk too, and I could almost see him biting his tongue. He gave me a tight smile instead, then turned to leave. He was almost through the door when his willpower dissolved.

With a sigh, he looked back at me. "I know you don't want to hear this, Mackenzie, especially from me, but you agreed to let me consult, so that is what I'm going to do. And for my first piece of advice...unless you want Cox Racing to go bankrupt in the next six months...again..." he paused to cringe, "...then I'd start working on lining up some sponsors. Some *big* sponsors. The few you have right now won't carry you far. Trust me."

I wanted to be angry with him for saying that, but I knew he was right. Icy dread crawled up my spine. It rose up my back and settled firmly around my shoulders. God...what if the business failed again, but this time it failed because of *me*? I didn't think I could handle that level of rejection.

Seeing that I understood the importance of what he'd just said, my dad nodded at me, then left the room. With a sigh of defeat, I collapsed into the chair behind my massive, intimidating desk. Staring at the piles, I debated what to work on first. Everything seemed a top priority. I had a feeling the bad dreams I'd been suffering from lately would now include never-ending stacks of paperwork.

I felt drained by the end of the day, and I hadn't even had a chance to work on the things that mattered for my career as a racer—maintaining my body, sharpening my riding skills. The season hadn't even begun yet, and I already felt behind. How could I possibly do all of this? But my father seemed like the only one who truly understood the business side of things and going to him with this... After everything he put me through last year, asking for his help now made me want to gouge out my eyeballs. No. I'd find a way on my own. I just needed to organize my time better.

A light knock on my door roused me from my troubling thoughts. Glancing at the clock, I saw that it was my typical time to leave. I felt so swamped, though, like I couldn't. Or shouldn't. Dad was right, I needed to get on this stuff.

"Come on in," I called out, feeling worn to the bone.

Hayden walked in, a bright, untroubled smile on his face. For a brief moment, I was jealous of his lightheartedness. "Ready to go?" he asked, not worried in the least about the mountain of things on my desk, things *he* didn't need to stress about.

Letting out a long sigh, I debated what to do. Putting it all aside for another day sounded amazing. But that was a short-term solution, one I'd been practicing for too long now. "I've got so much to do, Hayden. I don't think I can leave yet."

He bunched his brows as he finally noticed what I was drowning in. Then he shrugged and took a seat in the chair in the corner. "No problem, I'll wait."

Lifting my eyebrows, I shook my head. "It could be hours. I can't let you do that."

He shrugged again. "You kind of have to. I'm your ride."

Closing my eyes, I cursed myself for putting him in this position. Or giving him an excuse to stay. Either one made me feel incredibly guilty. Standing up, I made my way over to him. "I really can't let you do this," I said, placing my hand on his knee. "Nikki is probably still here. If you want, you can leave your bike for me, and get a ride home with her."

With a frown that clearly said he didn't like my perfectly reasonable solution, he told me, "But what about dinner at your place? I was…really looking forward to that."

My throat closed on me, and I had to swallow a few times to relax it. "I was, too, but I just feel so…behind. Another night, I promise."

With a sigh, Hayden stood up and clasped my hand. "Okay, but I'm holding you to that. Me, you, dinner, your place. Chinese or Thai, you decide."

Putting a hand on my stomach, I said, "Hayden, I really need to watch my—"

He put a finger to my lips, cutting me off. "You can eat that tofu, no-carb, no-taste diet every other day from then until the season starts. I just want one, real date with you, full of calories and fat. And chocolate. And beer."

Smiling under his finger, I rolled my eyes, then nodded. "Okay, fine."

He grinned at me, then looked at the mountain behind me. Returning his eyes to mine, he asked, "Is twenty-four hours really going to make a difference on that pile, Kenzie? The sooner we get this date out of the way, the sooner you can go back to bland, boring food?"

The humor in his eyes, the warmth on his face…it was all too much. And oddly, as I stared at him, my dad's words tumbled through my brain. *Time has a horrible way of sneaking up on you.* That could be applied to two different things in this situation—work and Hayden—but at the moment, Hayden felt more important. This was a big step for us, one I'd procrastinated on for too long already. Hayden was right. Work could wait just a few short hours. And I needed a break anyway.

"Okay, Hayden, you win…let's get out of here."

Hayden blinked, like he was shocked. "I can't believe that worked. I thought for sure you were going to call security and have my ass dragged off, so you could work in peace."

"We don't have security," I told him. "And you sold me with the chocolate."

Hayden laughed, then squeezed my fingers. "Good. I don't feel bad stooping to that level then." As I laughed at his comment, the humor fell from his face. "I don't want to stress you out, Kenzie. If you really need to stay...then stay. We can have our date night later. I'm not going anywhere."

Wrapping my arms around his waist, I let out a soft exhale as I searched his glum face. "I know I can stay. I know I *should* stay. But I also know... I want to make time for you, I want to be with you. All of this...it doesn't mean anything if I lose you in the process."

Hayden grinned, then leaned down and kissed me. "I'm really glad to hear you say that. I love you, Kenzie."

"I love you, too... Asshat."

Pulling back, he crooked a grin. "That's *Major* Asshat."

With a laugh, I pulled his lips back to mine. "Yes... yes, it is."

CHAPTER 5

The next couple of weeks were a whirlwind of stress and chaos. Every time I stepped into my office, my to-do list grew a bit longer, and my bank account shrank a little smaller. I'd managed to line up two more small sponsors, but Dad was right, it wasn't enough. I needed a big fish. A Fortune 500 company, a name everyone would recognize. Someone with deep pockets and money to burn. Unfortunately, most of those companies were already spoken for. And the ones who weren't, weren't talking to me.

"Damn it!" Hanging up the phone, I dropped my head onto the stacks of paper littering my desk. Yet another company had put me on permanent hold. The least they could do was outright tell me no, so I could get on with my day. But no, they just ignored me to death.

"This a bad time, Kenzie?"

I looked up to see my sisters in the doorway, staring at me with concerned eyes. Forcing a smile to my face, I shook my head. "No, it's fine. What are you two doing here?"

Theresa shrugged as she walked closer. "You've been so busy lately, we thought we'd surprise you, take you out to lunch."

Daphne grinned as she surged forward. "I have to tell you all about my plans to get pregnant in the next three months."

"I think you just did," I said with a tired smile. Shaking my head, I looked between the both of them. "I'm sorry, guys, I just can't today. Maybe later."

Frowning, Theresa crossed her arms over her chest. "That's what you always say lately, Kenzie. We're starting to worry about you."

Disgruntlement over my last failed phone call made me snap. "You weren't worried about me when I didn't have a job. When no one in the family would talk to me. You seemed right as rain then." I knew the minute I said it, that I shouldn't have. They'd already apologized, and I'd already forgiven them. Continually throwing it in their faces wasn't fair.

Both Daphne and Theresa shifted their gazes to the floor, their pale blue eyes full of guilt and regret. "I'm sorry," I said, standing up and walking over to them. "I'm just...stressed. Dad made all of this look so easy, and it's anything but."

Theresa lifted a blonde eyebrow at me. "Easy? You do remember his marriage falling apart, right?"

With a dry laugh, Daphne added, "And how we barely saw him...unless we came here. Sound familiar?" she added.

I smirked at her comment. "I know, I get it. I won't be like that, I *want* balance...but this first year, while I'm learning the ropes, I might be kind of ghost-like, okay?"

They both looked at each other, then back to me. "Okay, Kenzie," Theresa said. "We'll give you some time to adjust, but after that, we'll kidnap you if we have to."

Smiling, I told her, "You won't have to, but thank you."

"Okay, well, if you change your mind, call us." Theresa's eyes scanned my desk. "And if you need help with any of this, just ask. I'm more than happy to lend you a hand."

"Me too," Daphne chimed in. "Although, I don't know how helpful I'd be. I never really paid attention to what Dad did behind the scenes here…"

That was certainly true. Dad had often commented on Daphne's lack of interest. Daph tended to focus on Daph. Still, I appreciated the gesture, from both of them. "Thank you, guys, but I'm fine. I've got this under control." Or I would have it under control. Soon.

My sisters sighed, nodded, then turned to leave. Regret pulled at my heart as I watched them go, and for a moment, I wanted to tell them I'd changed my mind. Lunch was only an hour, and I needed to eat anyway. But then I remembered how distant they'd been to me, back when I'd really needed them, and my heart started to reharden. I might have forgiven my sisters, but I'd never forget. So, I let them go. And felt even worse when I sat down again.

A heartbeat later, Nikki walked into my office. "Hey, Kenzie, I'm leaving for the day."

Her statement surprised me, and when I glanced up at the clock on the wall, I saw that hours had flown by instead of minutes. "Oh my God, is it really that time already?"

Nikki's brow bunched in concern. "Yeah…you've been up here all day. You didn't even take your bike out. Everything…okay?"

Not wanting to get into it with her, I nodded. "Yeah, it's fine. Just catching up on stuff."

She looked like she didn't believe me, but instead of calling me on it, she said, "Okay, well, we're all here for you, if you decide you need some help."

Again, I appreciated the gesture, but the problem was, none of them knew how to do this part of the job any more than I did. We were all just...winging it. "Thanks, Nik, I appreciate that." She put a hand on her stomach, and I instantly remembered that we hadn't really talked about her telling her family the news. "So, what did your parents say when you told them about the baby? Did Myles...lose anything?"

Nikki snorted, then cringed. "It was awful, Kenzie. Mom was pissed, Dad was disappointed, and my brothers..." She let out a long sigh. "All six of them managed to make it down the aisle before impregnating their wives, so I'm basically the black sheep of the family now. Especially after I told everyone that Myles and I weren't getting married." She lifted an eyebrow. "Mom chewed my ass for thirty minutes about that, until Dad let it slip that they barely made it on time with Carlos." She rolled her eyes. "I still can't believe they lied about their wedding date. Unbelievable."

My eyes widened at the news. "Wow...that's...surprising."

She laughed, then nodded. "Yeah, it pretty much redirected the conversation for the rest of the evening. I thanked my dad later."

A small laugh escaped me, and feeling more lighthearted, I decided to broach a question I'd had. "So... I know you don't want to marry Myles, but what about... dating him? I think you guys would be cute together."

The look she gave me was completely void of emotion. "Please tell me you're not hopping on the *Date Myles* train, because I really can't take one more person telling me what to do."

I held up my hands. "I'm not. Just throwing it out there, in case you hadn't considered it."

With a sigh, she shook her head. "We're not like that, Kenzie, and we never will be."

Never say never. Wisely, I didn't say that out loud.

Nikki looked sad for a moment, then she smiled. "Myles has eased up on bossing me around, though, which I really appreciate. Did you have anything to do with that?" she asked, tilting her head.

Doing my best to contain my smile, I shrugged. "I might have threatened him with bodily harm. I'm glad he listened. I really need him to ride this year."

Nikki laughed, then walked over to hug me in my chair. "Well, thank you. *I* was about to do him bodily harm."

Her eyes sparkled with mischief when she pulled away. "Hayden told me about your date night. I know he had a good time, but what about you...any issues?"

A huge smile brightened my face and lightened my heart. "No...it was good, fun. I mean, we didn't sleep together or anything, and he didn't spend the night, so maybe it wasn't a huge step forward, but it was a really good night."

Nikki smirked at me. "Really, that's all dating is. Creating a series of really good nights."

"Says the girl whose longest relationship was three months long, and that was because he was away for two of those months?"

Keeping the smirk on her face, she flipped me off. "Just because I don't follow my own advice, doesn't mean my advice isn't sound. I'm a fountain of knowledge. You're lucky to know me."

I belly laughed at that. Yes, I definitely was lucky to know her. She'd gotten me through some really dark times, and she always had a way of making me feel better. I hoped I could return the favor now, when her life was so uncertain. "I am lucky. Love you, Nik. See you later."

She gave me a wave goodbye, then shuffled out the door. I was just about to return to my paperwork, when Hayden stepped inside the room. If I didn't love the people who were interrupting me so much, I would start locking the door.

Hayden was all smiles, until he noticed the look on my face. "I'm on my own tonight, aren't I?"

With a sigh, I nodded. "Yeah, I really need to put a dent in this pile." I stuck my finger out, pointing at him. "And no talking me out of it tonight. I gave you your date night."

His grin returned. "Yes, you did, and what a night it was... Thai and *Total Recall*...that's pretty much perfection."

I laughed at his comment, then stood up to give him a hug—I could at least take a couple minutes off to share a moment with my boyfriend. Lacing my arms around his neck, I murmured, "I'm sorry I've been so busy lately. And I'm sorry our date night wasn't a sleepover. Or a hot-sweaty-sex-over. I'm sure you would have preferred that…" We hadn't gotten anywhere near sex yet, and sometimes I worried how long he'd put up with a PG-13 relationship. I'd just been so busy…and I didn't want to rush taking that final step, breaking down that final wall. When we did go there again, I wanted things to be perfect.

Wrapping his arms around my waist, Hayden gave me a carefree smile. "I had a great date night, Kenzie, and I can't wait until you have time for another one. But I don't want you to stress about sex. It's not an issue for me. Hot, sweaty sex isn't why I'm with you." Surprised at his candid answer, I lifted an eyebrow. He laughed at my expression. "I'm with you…because I love you. Because I'm a better man by your side. Because I can't imagine life without you. And none of those things have an expiration date, so if you need more time, if you're too busy right now…that's okay. I can wait."

My heart tugged, listening to him put my fears to rest. "How are you so amazing?"

Hayden grinned as he leaned back to look at me. "I'm pretty sure I just answered that. You, Kenzie. I'm so amazing, because of *you*." Leaning forward, he gave me a light kiss.

I savored the connection, then cursed my fragmented heart and overwhelming schedule. Because after that speech, I really wanted to have sex with him again.

Hayden pulled away after a few sweet kisses. After kissing my cheek, he released me. "I'll let you get to work. See you tomorrow afternoon?"

My mind totally blank, all I could do was stare at him. He sighed, then cringed. "You forgot about going to Izzy's, didn't you? You can still go, right? Because Izzy is pretty much dying to show you her new place. Antonia too…"

From the look on his face, I knew he didn't want to guilt me into going, he just wanted me to realize that he wasn't the only one who wanted to see me. God, I had so much to do, but it was Izzy and Antonia, so I really couldn't cancel. Feeling like my brain was about to burst, I nodded. Smile tight, I told him, "I'll meet you at your place."

* * *

The following afternoon, I hopped on my bike and made my way over to Hayden and Nikki's apartment. Traveling to Nikki's place always reminded me of the fact that she was leaving soon. I kept telling her it was a temporary change, but a part of me was worried it would become a permanent decision once she fell in love with her newborn baby. I couldn't imagine Nikki leaving Cox Racing for good—I didn't want to. And while we'd been searching, we still hadn't found a suitable mechanic to replace her. Time was running out—one more thing for me to stress about.

I was in sort of a melancholy mood when I knocked on Hayden's door. I hadn't slept well last night—my head had spun with all the things I should be doing instead of sleeping and socializing. The anxiety eased when Hayden opened the door and smiled at me. His smile always had been my undoing.

"Hey, come on in. I'm almost ready, then we can head out."

Nikki stood in the living room, glaring at Hayden. Were they not getting along as roommates? I'd really thought they would—they were both pretty easy going. But from the look on Nikki's face, he'd left the toilet seat up one too many times.

"Everything okay?" I asked.

Hayden turned, and instead of answering me, he raised a finger to her. "Pout all you want, I'm not getting involved, Nikki."

Nikki ignored me, too, directing her comment to him. "All I'm asking for is an opinion. Surely you have one of those?"

Hayden rolled his eyes, then shook his head. Nikki's glare intensified. A little irritated now, I spat out, "Will someone fill me in please? What are you guys talking about?"

Nikki turned to me, her face softening. "Myles wants the baby to have his last name instead of mine," she softly said. "He said he wants to be more than a name on a birth certificate."

A warm smile crossed my lips. "That's very…sweet."

Nikki briefly closed her eyes. "I know, but… I'm not sure that's what I want to do. I mean, we're not together like that, and we're not going to get married. I'd *always* have a different name than my child. That's weird to me."

I bit my lip, reconsidering. She made a good point, with no chance of them getting together, she'd have to continuously explain why her child had a different last name than her. It would disconnect her from the baby. But on the flip side…it would give Myles a more profound connection than he'd typically have. "Damn…that's a tough one, Nik."

She tossed her hands in the air. "I know, that's why I need advice."

She looked between Hayden and me. Hayden lifted his hands in the air. "I'm not touching this one. Myles is finally talking to me. Willingly. I'm not messing that up by getting in the middle."

Nikki grunted, then looked over at me, hope in her eyes. While Hayden disappeared to get his things, I walked over to her. "You've got time...you don't have to decide anything right now," I tentatively told her.

With a frown, she plopped onto the couch. "Yeah, I know..."

I sat beside her, silently sharing in her misery, until Hayden came out of his recently-furnished bedroom. Smile on his face, he pulled me to my feet. "Come on, let's go check out Tony's house in the burbs. Because I'm never going to believe it until I see it."

I laughed in agreement, then said goodbye to Nikki and followed him out the door.

Twenty minutes later, we approached a cute, split-level house on a dead-end street. Izzy and Hookup's new home had a huge fenced-in backyard complete with a swing set and a trampoline. The neighborhood was so quiet that when Hayden and I shut off our bikes, all I heard was a lawnmower somewhere in the distance. It was peaceful and subdued—about as different from Hookup's old place as you could get.

Izzy's car was in the driveway, along with Hookup's. When I peeked inside Hookup's car as we walked past, I couldn't help but spot the crayons, toys, and Happy Meal boxes, clear evidence that he'd been hanging out with his niece. That was also a far cry from the old Hookup. I was extremely grateful to see that he'd changed. But the most mindboggling thing in his car was the uniform tucked in the backseat. Hookup had somehow convinced Glenn to hire him on as a cook at Oysters, and from what I'd heard...he was good at it. Even still, I'd never get over the fact that Hookup had an honest-to-God, legit, W2-providing job. It almost seemed against the laws of nature.

Hayden and I held hands as we walked up the flower-lined walkway to the front door. When Hayden rang the doorbell, a small, spritely face greeted us. Hayden's favorite little girl—Antonia. "Uncle Hayden! Aunt Kenzie! Come see my room!" She grabbed Hayden's hand and pulled him inside. They disappeared downstairs so fast, it was almost like they'd teleported.

"Izzy? We're here," I shouted into the rest of the house.

Izzy appeared seconds later, at the top of a short set of stairs. "Kenzie, hey. Glad you could make it!" she exclaimed, hurrying down the dozen steps to give me a hug. "You've been so busy lately. Where's Hayden?"

"He got dragged away," I said, indicating downstairs with my thumb.

Izzy smiled as she listened to her daughter showing off her space. Turning back to me, she said, "You've got to see the kitchen. It's at least twice the size of my old one." The joy in the home was so contagious, I couldn't stop grinning, and I was instantly glad I hadn't gone into work today.

Grabbing my hand, Izzy pulled me up the steps to the kitchen, dining, and living area. A slider in the kitchen showed me the large backyard; Antonia's dog, Sundae, was back there, barking at a squirrel. "This is amazing,

Izzy. Just what the two of you need. And Hookup, too, I guess."

Izzy nodded. "Yeah, and I haven't even shown you the most amazing part yet. Follow me."

Curious, I followed as she walked down a hallway that led to the upstairs bathroom and bedrooms. Izzy stopped at the last door and pointed inside. "This is my room, the master. Tony's is across the hall."

Not following why this was "amazing", I shook my head. "I don't…"

Izzy nodded her chin and walked over to Hookup's room. "Tony took the smallest room. He could have claimed the master, or taken the massive room downstairs, but he didn't. He insisted we take them, then set himself up in this tiny place. I feel kind of bad about it, but I also understand. He's trying to atone." She smiled, and there was both pride and empathy in the expression.

As I glanced into Hookup's miniature bedroom, I marveled at the rapid turnaround his life had taken. I couldn't help but wonder if Hayden had helped spark the change when he'd cut him out of his life. Even if it was only a temporary removal, it had to have affected him. I know my own temporary removal from my loved ones had been devastating.

Looking back at Izzy, I gave her a beaming smile. "I'm so happy for you. For all of you."

Izzy put her hand on my arm. "For all of *us*, Kenzie. We are where we're supposed to be, and you and Hayden are where you're supposed to be. Everything is finally falling into place."

I kept the smile on my face, but it was a struggle. My life felt like a swiftly flowing river recently, and I was doing all I could to not be pulled under. And Hayden... I'd barely had time for him. But we would make it through this. So long as neither one of us gave up...we'd be fine.

"Come on, Uncle Hayden. You've got to see the doghouse Uncle Tony made for Sundae. It's amazing!"

I looked down the hallway to see Hayden being pulled toward the slider. It was hard to tell who was beaming brighter—Antonia or Hayden. He glanced down the hallway as he walked past, then winked when he saw me. My heart skipped a beat, and warmth exploded over my chest, filling me with hope and love.

Hearing Izzy's soft laughter, I looked over at her. "Want to go see it? Tony actually did a pretty good job." With a laugh, I nodded, and we followed Hayden and Antonia outside.

Hayden was being coated in sloppy puppy kisses when we got there. He was laughing, and Antonia was grinning so hard I was sure her cheeks would be sore tomorrow. "Isn't she cute, Aunt Kenzie?" she asked.

Smiling at the frail child, I wrapped my arms around her shoulders. "Yeah, she's pretty adorable. Just like you."

Antonia giggled while Hayden stood up. He swiveled his head when he noticed Hookup walking around the corner of the yard. He was holding a pair of pruning shears, of all things. "Hey guys, good timing. I just finished trimming all the bushes. This place could be in one of those fancy home magazines now."

Hayden shook his head as he stared at his friend. "Who are you, and what have you done with Tony?"

Hookup smirked at Hayden, then flipped him off. Laughing, Hayden pointed at the sturdy wooden doggie hut. "Not bad, man. I didn't know you even knew how to use a hammer." He frowned. "In the right way."

Hookup gave Hayden a grin that hinted at all the nefarious ways he'd probably used the seemingly innocent tool. Brushing the past off with a wave of his hand, he told him, "It was easy, nothing to it. I'm gonna finish the deck next. Make a kickass outdoor kitchen. You guys will be practically living here, we're gonna have so many barbeques."

"Barbeques, decks, tools…" Hayden slid his eyes to Izzy. "I think you broke him."

Izzy slapped his arm. "Be nice."

As I laughed at the trio, I happened to notice movement from the corner of my eye. Twisting my head, I looked over to the gate in the fence that was slowly opening. A tall, leggy brunette stepped through the opening and my heart sank. Felicia. I hadn't seen much of her since Hayden and Nikki had moved over to my side of the track. In all honesty, I'd kind of forgotten she was still at the track. Of course, I had a lot to do there now—running Cox Racing was enough work for about three people.

Seeing her now was a shock to the system—she was one of the major reasons why Hayden and I had broken up, and for the longest time, I'd been positive they'd slept together. She'd definitely wanted that outcome and had tried her best to make it happen. Even though I'd made my peace with her, I'd never be able to forget what had happened. Not completely.

As I stood there, staring at the gate, I felt Hayden's hand wrap around mine. I squeezed it back, hard. "We can go," he said in my ear.

God, that was tempting. But I hated the idea of fleeing every time she came around. And, unfortunately, there would be times when she would come around. Hayden may have cut ties with her, but Izzy and Hookup hadn't. They'd accepted her back with open arms, and unless I did the same, our group would be forever divided.

"No, it's fine. We can stay."

Hayden looked like he was just about to ask me if I was sure, when something caught his eye, making him frown. Dread and curiosity made me turn to look too. Then surprise hit me. Felicia wasn't alone. Rodney, one of Keith Benneti's riders, was walking in behind her. And after closing the gate, he reached out and grabbed her hand. Were they dating? And if they were...would Hayden be okay with that?

My eyes instantly returned to Hayden's face, searching for some clue to his emotional state of mind. His expression was blank now though. If he was feeling anything, I couldn't tell what. And rather than reassure me, not seeing a reaction filled me with dread.

"Hayden, Kenzie! How's it going?" Rodney said, his expression bright and carefree.

Hayden's face effortlessly morphed into a relaxed smile. "Hey, man. I didn't expect to see you here." *With her.* The unspoken words hung in the air as Hayden's eyes drifted to Felicia. Was he mad? Sad? Relieved?

Felicia pulled Rodney into her side as she lifted her free hand and curled her fingers in a wave. "I'm sorry if we're intruding. I didn't expect...everyone to be here." She briefly met Hayden's gaze, then mine, then snapped her eyes back to Izzy. Tension swelled in the air. It was so thick, I could almost see it hovering between our two groups.

Izzy's eyes darted from Hayden and me to Felicia and Rodney. She looked at a loss over what to do—apologize to us or invite them over. Knowing I was the only one who could diffuse the situation made a tremor of irritation run up my spine. How had I somehow become the peacekeeper? But moving on and moving forward were two incredibly different things, and I had to make a choice right now which way our group was going to go. Damn it.

With a concentrated effort, I made myself smile. "Hello, Felicia. It's…good to see you."

Hayden looked at me with surprise on his face. Izzy and Felicia looked equally stunned. Okay, maybe that had been a little too much good will. It was too late to take it back, though, not without stepping on some toes.

Felicia's shocked face slowly shifted into a smile as she finished walking over to us. "Thank you, Kenzie. It's…good to see you, too." I expected her to steal a glance at Hayden after saying that, but surprising the hell out of me, she didn't. Her warm gaze was still on my face, and it was clear she'd meant what she'd said. "Ready for Daytona?" she asked, excitement flashing in her eyes.

"Yeah, I'm…almost ready," I answered, wishing I had a more solid reply. And wishing I had more time to train. I kind of missed the old days, when all I had to worry about was my track times. Not that I would confess that to Felicia.

Felicia giggled and looked over at Rodney with affection and interest clear in her eyes. "I can't wait to get back out there." She sighed, and the sound was laced with regret. "I don't ever want to miss another race."

Hayden shifted his feet, and his hand clenched mine tighter. I could tell he was uncomfortable, but I wasn't 100 percent sure why he felt that way. "It's been nice catching up," he said, looking at everyone in turn, "but Kenzie and I have a...thing we need to get to."

Confusion coursed through me as I looked up at him. Our only plan today had been to hang out with Izzy and Hookup. I'd told him I was fine staying. Clearly, he didn't feel the same. And that worried me.

Hayden gave me a pleading expression as I searched his eyes. He was practically screaming, *Let's just go.* Irritation and fear bristled throughout me. He wanted me to trust him, but how could I, when his ex still affected him like this? "Yeah, that's right... I almost forgot about that...thing."

Pulling my eyes from Hayden, I looked over at Izzy. "I'm sorry, Iz. We'll stay longer next time." Antonia immediately started whining, but Hayden scooped her up, promising we'd be back soon.

Izzy's eyes were concerned as she studied me. "Okay." She flicked a glance at Felicia, then mouthed, *Sorry.* I nodded, since it was all I could do.

Once Hayden had perked Antonia's spirits, he said goodbye to Izzy and Hookup. Grabbing my hand, he slapped Rodney on the shoulder. "See you at the track, man."

Rodney looked confused, but he nodded. "Yeah, see ya."

Hayden started to walk away, then sighed and looked over at Felicia. "Bye," was his short response.

Brows furrowed, Felicia nodded. "Bye, Hayden. Kenzie."

I waved a goodbye, then let Hayden lead me to the gate. As soon as the wood closed behind us, my fear and confusion got the best of me. "What was that?" I snipped.

Hayden's face compressed into a mixture of confusion and anger. It was a look I hadn't seen on him in a while. "What was what?"

Yanking my hand away, I stopped and stared at him. "You're running. Why?"

Hayden scowled, then sighed. He briefly looked over my shoulder before returning his eyes to mine. "I'm not running," he said. "It was just time to go."

"Bullshit." My hands balled into fists, and my heart started pounding. "Is this because she's with Rodney now? Are you...jealous?"

He immediately shook his head. "No, of course not. I wanted them together. When it was obvious he was interested in her, I told him to go for it."

My anger faded at hearing that revelation. "Oh...then why...?"

Hayden grabbed my fingers and interlaced our hands. "I know what I did to us. And I know what you're trying to do by...accepting her. And it's not fair to you. You've already sacrificed so much for our relationship. I won't ask you...no, I won't *let* you sacrifice more. You don't have to hang out with her. Ever."

I bit my lip, moved and unsure, all at the same time. "I don't want to be the reason your friends are split."

Hayden smiled, then tucked a strand of hair behind my ear. "You're not. Felicia is the one who split us. Izzy and Hookup, they don't expect us to all be like we were before. And if that means that we miss out on a few barbeques, then I'm fine with that. What I'm not fine with is you putting up with something that hurts you, because you think it's what I want. It's not. All I want is your happiness. *Yours*. Above everyone else's. Do you understand?"

I did, and it made tears spring to my eyes. He wasn't uncomfortable being around her, or jealous because she'd moved on. He was worried…about me. In the end, his feelings always swung back around to me. I knew I should excuse myself and go back to work—get some much-needed crap done—but instead, I wrapped my arms around his neck and whispered the words that were surging through my heart. "Spend the night with me."

Hayden tilted his head as he regarded me. "Are you sure, Kenzie?"

Biting my lip, I nodded. "Yes. I'd like… I'd like you to come over. And stay. I want to wake up with you."

Hayden smiled, then placed a soft kiss on my lips. "All right, sweetheart. Whatever you want…or don't want…is yours."

God, I loved this man.

CHAPTER 6

Hayden and I spent the next several hours enjoying each other's company in my home. It was still a little strange having him in my living room, and the thought of him being in my bedroom later made my palms sweaty. I was cracking open a piece of my heart, letting him inside fully and completely, and that was terrifying. The thought of getting hurt again chilled me to the bone. He was so sweet, though, so warm, loving, tender and patient. Even if it scared me, I wanted this to happen.

Unfortunately, I also had work on my mind, so I found myself being frequently distracted. As much as I wanted to be 100 percent in the moment, I was closer to 75 percent. Sometimes 50.

"Kenzie? Did you hear me?" Blinking out of my trance, I looked over at Hayden. He was standing in front of me, holding a couple of movies in his hands. Tilting his head, he said, "I asked which one you wanted to watch."

I gave him a sheepish smile. "Sorry… I was thinking about something else."

With a sigh, he sat beside me. "Work…or Felicia." He cringed after he said it.

Oddly, she hadn't been on my mind at all. I shook my head. "Work. And...having you stay here tonight. It's been a while... I'm kind of nervous."

With a soft smile on his face, he brushed his fingers over my cheek. "Don't be nervous about that. Like I said, I'm not expecting sex. In fact, I'm taking sex off the table. Banning it."

My amused grin was uncontainable. "You're banning sex?"

He nodded, his face firm. "Yep. All I'm going to do tonight is wrap my arms around you as we fall asleep. And no matter how much you beg and plead, you're not getting in my pants. Sorry."

With a laugh, I shook my head, then picked out a movie. "Let's watch that one."

Hayden kissed my cheek, then got up to start the movie. And as he sat back down next to me, I felt a sense of calm wash over me. Having him take that worry off my plate was surprisingly cathartic. And for the rest of the night, I allowed my mind to completely shut off, and I just enjoyed the simplicity of his fingers tangled in mine.

My newfound peace faded at precisely 4:23 in the morning, when I woke up with a jolt. Hayden was sleeping peacefully beside me in my dark room. Lying on his side with his back to me, his breath was slow and steady, untroubled. I blinked back tears as I tried to calm my shaky breaths. Considering how wonderful my evening had been, my dream had been particularly cruel.

The dream had started out mimicking reality. Hayden and I had walked to my room hand-in-hand. We talked about the movie while getting ready for bed, then we'd crawled under the covers, curled into each other's arms, and fallen asleep—utter bliss. But then my dream had deviated from actual events. I'd woken up mere seconds later in my dream, and Hayden had been gone; his side of the bed had been ice cold, like he'd never even been there.

Panic had rushed through my veins as I'd searched the house looking for him. All his clothes were gone, along with his bike. Desperate, I'd hopped on my bike, and in a way that was only possible in dreams, I'd easily tracked him down. I'd found him at a street race, celebrating a victory with his lips on Felicia's. As I watched, their kiss intensified. Then they started ripping off their clothes, right there on the side of the street. Hayden cupped her ass, massaged her breasts, and moment by moment more skin was exposed. I couldn't look away.

That alone would have made it a top-notch nightmare, but no, my subconscious hadn't been satisfied to leave it at that. While I watched Hayden and Felicia passionately attack each other, my father tapped me on the shoulder. With sad, aged eyes, he'd handed me a slip of paper. "The bank foreclosed, Mackenzie. You weren't good enough. You lost the track. And it would seem, you lost Hayden too. I'm so sorry, but you've got nothing now. Just like me."

That had been when I'd woken up. My heart still thudded in my chest as I tried to separate what was real, and what wasn't. Hayden was here, in my bedroom. He wasn't night-racing with Felicia, he wasn't making out with her, wasn't having sex with her. The bank couldn't foreclose on the property—thanks to Hayden, I owned it free and clear. I hadn't failed anything yet. But sadly…that didn't mean I couldn't fail later. If I didn't get a steady stream of cash coming, I wouldn't be able to keep Cox

Racing going. I'd be the proud owner of an empty building. And Hayden might feel compelled to race again. And Felicia might follow him again. And this time, Hayden might not be able to resist her, especially if all we were doing was cuddling...

No. It was just a bad dream. Not a premonition. I wasn't going to fail...Hayden and I weren't going to fail.

Shucking off the covers, I got out of bed. There was no way I could go back to sleep after that mind-fuck. Hayden stirred as I stood up. He rolled onto his back but didn't wake up. The moonlight streaming through the window highlighted his face—his full lips, his rugged jawline, the gritty layer of stubble, the tantalizing scar through his right eyebrow. Fearless, aggressive, dangerous...loyal, compassionate, loving. He was truly a marvel of a man, and I was a very lucky girl. But my dream was making me question—all over again—just how long I'd remain lucky.

I wished I could grab my board and go surfing, but it was too cold. I needed to let off some steam, though, so I decided to go for a run instead. Careful to not wake Hayden, I changed into my workout clothes and slipped out the door.

Being outside in the cool, crisp air helped press the remnants of my dream to the very back of my mind. It felt so good to get my heart thumping, to get my arms and legs moving. I'd been spending way too much time behind a desk recently, and not nearly enough time in the gym. A fact that became readily apparent to me when I was only a mile into my run, and already huffing and puffing. Damn it. I couldn't let my body slip, couldn't let the day-to-day intricacies of the business slip, couldn't let my relationship with Hayden and my friends slip. But there wasn't enough of me to go around. Something had to give, and wondering just what that would be, scared the living crap out of me.

When I got back home, I felt both rejuvenated and depleted. I needed to do more, I needed to be better. Somehow.

Hayden was up when I walked through the door. "Where have you been?" he asked. "I was worried sick."

God, I was such an ass. In my need to get out of the house, I'd kind of made a part of my nightmare come true—but for him. "Sorry, I had a bad dream. I couldn't get back to sleep, so I decided to go for a run. And then I learned just how out of shape I am." Sure, I'd made it through the entire thing, but I used to be able to do it a heck of a lot faster.

Hayden's expression softened as he walked over to me. "You had a bad dream? Want to tell me about it?"

Biting my lip, I shook my head. "No." I didn't even think I could get the words out.

For a moment, he looked like he was going to press me, but then he changed his mind. Smiling, he wrapped his arms around my waist. "Except for the last 30 minutes or so, spending the night with you was incredible. I slept better than I have in a long time." His smile shifted to a frown. "I'm sorry it wasn't quite so peaceful for you."

Lacing my arms around his neck, I shook my head. "It was a great night, and I'm glad it happened."

Hayden cocked an eyebrow. "Will it be happening again? Soon?"

I stifled a sigh. "It will happen again, but... I'm not sure when. I've got a feeling I've got some late nights at the track in my future."

Hayden's smile slipped some, then he grinned. "Maybe I'll pack up my new bed and put it in your office. We'll just live at the track until things settle down."

A part of me thought that was a great idea, but I knew having him there twenty-four-seven would be entirely too distracting. Especially once he was done "working" for the day. "Thank you, but no." Leaning up, I gave him a kiss. "I need to take a shower and get going, but thank you for the wonderful evening."

"You're kicking me out before breakfast?" he asked, his face a mixture of playfulness and seriousness.

"Unfortunately, yes. As always, I have so much to do…"

Hayden didn't object any more, but I could feel his disappointment crawling across my skin. God, I hated letting people down. Especially him.

* * *

I'd like to say things settled down over the next few weeks, but no, they really didn't. It seemed like there were a thousand little fires that I needed to put out, sometimes hourly. The last batch of tires I ordered were completely wrong when they came in. They weren't even motorcycles tires, which really made me reconsider staying with my vendor. The contractor I'd hired to repaint the outside of the buildings—so Cox Racing looked successful instead of dilapidated—kept finding new things to charge me for, like the window he'd inadvertently shattered with his ladder.

Keith was still on a rampage about our two teams being on the track at the same time. My phone rang at least three times a day, and I had to waste time listening to Keith complain that so-and-so was messing with so-and-so's times. Like my guys were purposely slowing down his riders or something. Every time I told him my guys had every right to be out there whenever they wanted, and he'd just have to get used to it. His response was, "Then you'll have to get used to me calling you." I dreaded every time the phone rang.

One of the treadmills in the gym wasn't working, and neither was one of the toilets in the locker room. The vendor who we purchased nuts, bolts, and sparkplugs from suddenly went out of business, and I desperately needed to shop around and find someone else. I needed to update everyone's bikes and leathers with the new sponsor logos we'd acquired, but I was putting it off, since I hoped to nab some more before the season started. And on top of all that, every five minutes, someone walked into my office wanting to talk to me about…something.

"Kenzie, you're not going to believe what happened yesterday."

Glancing up at Nikki in my doorway, I said, "People stopped stealing Kevin's lunch? Because I'm really tired of hearing him complain about it every day."

Nikki snorted, like that trivial—but distracting—annoyance was funny. "No, Myles and I went to the baby store." Her face took on a dreamy expression. "You should have seen him, Kenzie. He knew exactly what to buy, exactly what not to buy, and then he paid for everything with the money Hayden gave him for his bike. It was pretty… incredible."

Dropping into a chair in front of my desk, she let out a long sigh. "It also reminded me just how unprepared for all of this I am. I have no idea what I'm doing."

Join the club. Brushing aside that thought, I gave her an encouraging smile. "Well, it sounds like Myles does, so...don't worry about it. He'll take care of everything."

She gave me a dry expression. "That's your advice? Let the man take care of everything?"

With a sigh, I ran my hands back through my hair. It was greasy, which reminded me... I hadn't showered in a couple of days. Gross. "No, I'm just saying...don't stress. It will be fine. You'll figure it out."

Studying my face, she seemed to understand that I wasn't really talking about her. "You okay, Kenzie? You seem...anxious or something. And you haven't touched your bike in days. Are you going to take her out soon?"

Closing my eyes, I let out a long exhale. "I want to, Nik. Trust me, that's all I think about when I'm up here, but I just...don't have time." As if to punctuate my point, my phone started ringing. Knowing it was most likely Keith, I let it ring. He could vent to my voicemail.

Nikki's brows bunched in concern. "I almost hate to ask, but...how is the search for my replacement going? My *temporary* replacement."

I felt the strength leeching from my muscles as I thought about *that* problem. Thankfully, John was spearheading the search, but I was making inquiries too. When I could. "Nothing yet, but...we'll find someone." *We have to.*

Nikki's face was apologetic. "I'm so sorry for adding to the chaos, Kenzie. You know I didn't meant to."

Giving her a smile, I nodded. "I know." My smile grew as I thought about what she'd originally told me. "Baby shopping, huh? Is Myles…okay about the whole last name thing then?"

She swished her hand. "Oh yeah, I took him to Oysters and we worked it out. Of course, we worked it out by me getting him completely plastered, so he'd agree to anything I said, but he's fine with it now. He even thinks it's his idea." She laughed. "Sometimes not being able to drink has its advantages."

I laughed at her answer, then sighed. "I wish I could have seen that." I wished I could run Cox Racing *and* have a life.

"Yeah," Nikki said, her voice wistful. Then she glanced around the room before saying, "We almost kissed at the baby store."

My eyes widened. "Really? How…what happened?"

She scrunched her face in an expression of confusion. "I honestly don't know. I was thanking him for buying everything, because I'd kind of been freaking out about how to pay for it, and then suddenly, our eyes locked…and he leaned forward, I leaned forward…" She stared right through me, lost in the memory. "My heart was racing, and I thought I was going to die if he didn't touch me…" Shaking her head, she snapped herself out of it. "Then a car honked at us to get out of their way and the moment was over." Scrunching her face in annoyance, she put a hand on her stomach. "I don't know what sparked it… honestly, I think it was all the hormones this little mutant is pumping into me."

Her denial made me smirk. "Right. No *actual* feelings there, just a hormonal imbalance."

Her eyes narrowed as she studied my expression. "Quit trying to play matchmaker, Kenzie. You suck at it. Both you and Hayden suck at it."

"Hayden talks to you about Myles?" I asked, surprised.

She rolled her eyes. "No, Hayden tells me I should stop denying my feelings and take a chance on love...blah, blah, blah." She stuck her finger in her mouth. "You've turned him into such a sap. I can't believe he was ever a rebel."

I grinned at her comment, then chewed on my lip. "How is he?"

Confusion marred her features again. "What do you mean? You see him as much as I do, don't you?"

"Not really. Not as much as we'd both like." Pausing, I shook my head. "I was just wondering if he'd said anything about the fact that we haven't...done the deed yet."

Nikki pursed her lips. "We're not really best buds who talk about our sex lives, Kenzie. But...he does take really long showers..." A long sigh escaped me, and Nikki quickly added, "He doesn't seem unhappy, if that's what you're worried about. He just seems...in love. All smiley and crap. It's kind of annoying actually. Maybe you *could* get in a fight with him? Make him a little more...broody. Then maybe he'll stop trying to set me up with Myles."

A much-needed laugh escaped me, and I let the guilt go. "I'll see what I can do," I told her.

Even though she was keeping me from things I needed to do, I missed Nikki when she left. In the span of just a few minutes, she'd eased my worries, made me laugh, and made me feel like I wasn't pushing a huge boulder up a steep hill. I wasn't entirely sure I'd reciprocated the feeling and eased *her* stress, but honestly...she was fooling herself if she truly thought that near-kiss with Myles was caused by the baby. Ridiculous and stubborn. I could relate—Hayden and I had started much the same way.

No one else bothered me for the rest of the afternoon, and time surged forward in leaps and bounds. Before I knew it, the windows were showing me that it was pitch black outside. Surprise and disappointment flooded me. While Nikki and Myles didn't always remember to say goodbye, Hayden never failed. Until tonight. Loneliness hit me so hard, I almost debated staying at work until morning. Maybe I could actually get caught up if I didn't sleep.

Annoyed that work was my life now, I pushed away from my desk. Hadn't I vowed to maintain balance when I'd first reopened the business? As I'd quickly learned, that was easier said than done. I had a grudging, newfound respect for my dad.

Feeling like I could sleep for a thousand years, I turned off my light, and trudged my way down to the garage. All the lights were on when I got there, and I cursed my careless employees. "Damn it, guys. Power doesn't grow on trees."

I was about to flick the lights off when a voice answered me. "Sorry about that."

Spinning around, I saw I wasn't alone. Hayden was still here. In his leathers. Holding my bike. "Hayden, you scared me. What are you doing?"

His grin was a mile wide as he pushed my bike over to me. "You've been so busy, you haven't had time to practice. I seem to recall the two of us fitting in racing at very inappropriate hours, and you seem to be done with work for the day, so…what do you say? Race me or chase me?"

Tears stung my eyes as I stared at him in utter disbelief. "You stayed down here, all alone, waiting for me to finish?"

He shrugged, like it was no big deal. "I didn't have anything else going on."

Running over to him, I tossed my arms around his neck. "Yes! God, yes, I'd love to race you."

With a laugh, he put one arm around me. "If I would have known you'd be this excited about it, I would have suggested it a while ago. Actually, I feel kind of guilty for not thinking of it sooner." Pulling back, he gave me an apologetic grimace.

Shaking my head, I brushed off his apology. "I'm just glad you thought of it now. I'm gonna change, then we can head out there." I kind of felt like we were at an event, about to compete for real. Damn, it had been way too long.

I changed into my leathers in record time. I'd been a little worried they'd be tight, but I hadn't been eating as much as I should, and they were actually a little loose. I made a mental note to pack bigger lunches. I was so excited to get on my bike, I ran back to Hayden. He was grinning when I skidded to a stop in front of him. "I've haven't seen you smile that hard in a long time. Ready for this, twenty-two?"

I practically ripped my bike out of his hands in answer. Hayden laughed as he grabbed his, then we made our way out to the track. Adrenaline started pumping through my veins as I anticipated the thrill we were about to experience. There was nothing in the world like this sport. Expect maybe being in love with Hayden.

Surprisingly, when we made it out to the track, we could hear the sounds of bikes racing. We weren't the only ones here. Hayden and I looked at each other through our helmets, and Hayden shrugged. He didn't know who was out there, so he hadn't planned on this being a multi-person event.

Two bikes suddenly came around a corner, almost neck and neck. I frowned as I recognized the motorcycles...and the team colors. Rodney and Felicia. What the hell were they doing here this late at night? Annoyed, I started my bike and chased after the pair; I heard Hayden start his bike a heartbeat behind me.

Even though I was chasing a couple of people I didn't entirely care for, the thrill of being back on my bike, back in the thick of things, made a huge grin break out on my face. The brightly-lit concrete surged underneath my wheels, and the vibration of the road traveled all the way up my arms, activating every cell in my body. My core tensed, and my legs instinctively gripped the bike. It felt like coming home.

I caught up to Rodney and Felicia in no time, then I ducked low...and prepared to pass them. It took a moment for my window to open up, but once it did, I punched it. They both glanced my way when I shot through the middle of them—they hadn't even known I was following. They both slowed down, but I didn't slow with them. I was too ingrained in the moment, too excited to be racing someone —*anyone*. I didn't want to stop now. Keeping low on the bike, I maintained my speed. They'd either decide to chase me, or they'd pull off the track; I kind of hoped they decided to pursue me. I needed a win.

After a few moments of focusing on the road ahead of me, I risked a glance back. All three of them were there—Hayden, Rodney, and Felicia—and they were all gunning for me. Laughing, I refocused on track, on maintaining my lead, my high. I raised my hand to signal three more—that's how long they had to catch me.

When we started the third and final lap, my muscles were shaking with fatigue, but I was still in the lead. I occasionally saw tires in my peripheries, but I never let them scoot around me. This track was mine. I was breathing heavy when the last lap was over, and I seriously needed water before my muscles started cramping, but I didn't care—I'd won!

I thrust both hands into the air as my bike slowed. Hayden pulled beside me, then lifted his visor. Grinning, he shook his head at me; he loved the way I cherished my victories.

As my bike slowed to a stop, I looked behind me to see Rodney and Felicia sheepishly keeping their distance. Raising my visor, I made my way over to them. "What are you guys doing here this late?" I asked, annoyance no longer boiling through my veins. "Does Keith know you're here?"

Rodney took off his helmet, then scratched his head with his gloved hand. "Uh, no, actually, he doesn't. And if you don't mind, we'd really appreciate it if you didn't tell him. He has a thing about when his riders can and can't use the track."

That made me laugh. "Tell me about it. Even still, you guys shouldn't be here this late. It's not safe. And technically…we're closed."

Hayden gave me a look, but I ignored him. We might have snuck in ourselves as riders, but as an owner, I couldn't exactly tell them: *Sure, use the track twenty-four-seven, I don't care.* I was partly responsible for their safety now, and the safety of the track. That thought made some of the stress of my responsibilities settle around my shoulders again. Damn it.

Felicia nodded at my words after taking off her helmet. "It won't happen again, Kenzie, we're sorry." Her face broke into a wide smile. "But you have to admit, that was fun!"

I wanted to deny it, but I couldn't. "Yeah, it was pretty fun. Especially when I kicked your asses."

Rodney and Felicia both laughed, then Rodney said, "I'll get you next time. Same time tomorrow?" Felicia rolled her eyes while Rodney's hopeful gaze flashed between Hayden and me.

Hayden shook his head. "No, she's right, you guys shouldn't be here this late."

Rodney looked dejected, but he shrugged. "Okay, let's go drinking instead. I think it would be fun if we all hung out." Felicia flashed him a look that clearly said, *Shut up, idiot!* I almost wanted to laugh at her flustered expression. But then I remembered my nightmare.

I opened my mouth to say something, but Hayden beat me to it. "Uh, actually... I don't think that's a good idea." He pointed at Felicia. "We used to date, as I'm sure you know."

Rodney looked at Felicia and shrugged. "Yeah, I know, but that was ages ago. You're with Kenzie now," he said, indicating me.

Hayden cringed. "Yeah, but it's weird, man."

Rodney blinked. "How is it weird? You're not into Felicia anymore, she's not into you. You and I are friends. Felicia and Kenzie have so much in common they'll be besties in no time. Hanging out together, it just...makes sense."

Felicia dropped her head in her hand, like she was mortified Rodney didn't get it. Hayden opened his mouth to give Rodney another rejection, but I beat him to it. "Sounds great, Rodney."

Hayden snapped his gaze to me, bewilderment on his face. I only smiled at him in answer. Beside his family—Hookup, Izzy, and Antonia—Hayden didn't have a whole lot of friends. Practically none at the track. But somehow he'd bonded with Rodney last season, and I didn't want to break that friendship by denying him access to it because of Felicia. And besides, Rodney was right about practically everything he'd just said. Everything except Felicia and I being besties. That was something I didn't *ever* see happening.

Felicia was looking at me with wide eyes too, but Rodney was ecstatic. "Excellent! It's a date!"

Inwardly, I sighed. Crap. I'd nearly forgotten that I had absolutely zero time for a social life. But I didn't really have a way to back out of it now, and I couldn't cancel and let Hayden go on his own. Hayden, Rodney, and Felicia on a date together...that was just unsettling. Jesus, what did I just agree to?

CHAPTER 7

Hayden and I started meeting up most nights to go riding. It cut into my sleep schedule, but it was so exhilarating to be out on the track again, I didn't care. It also gave me a legitimate reason to avoid going on a double date with Rodney and Felicia. Not that Hayden was pushing me to make that happen. He assumed I'd only said yes to that to be nice. And maybe that was true, partly, but I'd also wanted him to have a real relationship with his friend. I just wished Felicia wasn't part of the Rodney package. Maybe if I kept delaying, they'd break up, and I wouldn't have to worry about it. Then I'd just have to worry about Felicia being single, and stalking Hayden from across the track. Lord help her if she started texting him again.

"That was great, Kenzie. Your times are right where they need to be."

Taking off my helmet, I smiled over at Hayden. "I know. I'm beating you pretty consistently now."

Hayden frowned as he glanced over at the track. "Yeah, I'm going to have to stop taking it easy on you."

Laughing, I pulled off a glove and threw it at him. He smirked at me, then tilted his head. "I hate to bring this up, but Rodney cornered me the other day. He wants to meet up soon, go out together."

Inhaling a deep breath, I held it a second before letting it go. "Christmas is in a couple of days, then New Years is after that. And I already promised Nikki we'd go out with her and Myles. Maybe sometime after that…if I've got a free night once the holidays are over."

Hayden gave me a look that clearly said he knew I was purposely avoiding going out with them. "While I appreciate you agreeing to this, Kenzie, it isn't necessary. You don't have to go on a double date with my ex."

"I'm not," I countered. "I'm going on a double date with your friend. Who happens to be dating your ex. Totally different."

He laughed, then shook his head. "You're pretty amazing, you know that, right?"

Exhaustion suddenly swept over me. "If I were amazing, I'd have landed the Lowes sponsorship." My eyes narrowed into pinpricks. "I can't believe they went with Keith. He's got so many sponsors, there's no way he can give them the exposure I could have. They'll be lucky to get a spot on his fender. But me…hell, I would have given them the entire fucking bike." Closing my eyes, I counted to ten. It would be fine. I'd find someone else.

I opened my eyes when I felt Hayden's bare hand on my cheek. "I'm so sorry, Kenzie. If I knew anything about that kind of shit, you know I'd help you."

Smiling under his caress, I nodded. "I know you would. I just wish… I wish I had the schmoozing gene. But clearly, I don't." A tired sigh escaped me. "I really thought having the reigning champion on my team would make it easy to get sponsors. I just… I had no idea how thick the politics were, and with my father punching Keith, then the team going under, then me being blacklisted for a year, and the rumors that Keith spread about you, and my lead mechanic leaving the team for the season...well, nobody wants to take a chance on me right now. And if they all wait too long, then it might just be too late for Cox Racing."

Tears filled my eyes as I contemplated losing it all. Again. Hayden's thumb stroked my cheek, his expression a mixture of worry and sympathy. In a way, Hayden had a lot more to lose than I did. If Cox Racing failed, I could probably get hired somewhere else, since my dad was no longer pulling strings to keep me benched. But Hayden... Keith had spread rumors that he was a street-racer and a thief. He'd made him un-hirable. Hayden was truly blacklisted, and if Cox Racing went under, he was screwed.

"I won't let you down," I whispered.

Hayden shook his head. "Don't worry about me. Either way, I'll be fine." He smiled. "I've got you, and I don't have a problem being your umbrella boy."

A tension-relieving laugh escaped me, and I gave him an appreciative kiss. But while I was grateful for Hayden turning the potentially bad situation into a joke, I knew the truth. I knew Hayden's soul, and he *needed* to race, same as me. If he lost that—permanently lost that—he'd never be the same person. He'd be a shell, just like I was last year. I wouldn't let him go through that, not without putting up a damn good fight.

* * *

It was hard to leave work behind for the holidays, but I knew my father would be all up in my business—interfering with *everything*—if I didn't show up for

Christmas dinner. Even still, I was inundated with the feeling that I was forgetting something. Like worrying about having left the stove on or the door unlocked, I just felt... preoccupied...as we parked in my father's driveway. I managed to push the feeling away by reminding myself that today wasn't optional. I *needed* to be here.

Hayden had dressed up for the occasion, and he looked like a freaking model in his gray slacks and white button-up shirt. He was even wearing a matching gray tie and really nice dress shoes. I was shocked he even owned those last two things. Hayden was typically more casual with his clothes.

"Did you buy those just for today?" I asked, teasing him.

"Of course," he said, straightening his tie as we climbed out of my truck. "Wouldn't want your dad to think I'm always a slob."

Rolling my eyes at him, I looked down at my outfit, a simple black dress. I kind of looked like I was dressed for a funeral. In fact, I think I *did* wear this to a funeral once. It wasn't exactly screaming holiday cheer. Maybe I should have gone shopping too, gotten something with sparkles. Nikki would have; she always looked like a million bucks when she dressed up.

"You look amazing," Hayden said, grabbing my hand as he seemingly read my mind.

"Almost as good as you," I said, clenching his fingers tight. Hayden laughed as we walked to my father's door hand-in-hand. Opening Dad's door, I pulled us inside. "Dad? We're here."

Dad came out of the kitchen, wiping his hands on a towel. "Right on time, good," he said. His eyes drifted over Hayden's outfit, and I swear he cracked a smile of approval. "Theresa is on her way, and Daphne is running late. Some problem with Jeff." He frowned, like he hoped their drama didn't follow them over here.

Setting my bag down near the door, I asked him, "Can I help with anything?" I'd asked Dad a few days ago if I should bring anything, but he'd told me I had more important things to do than bake. I'd agreed with him, but now that I was here empty-handed, I felt bad.

Dad shook his head. "Nope, it's all under control. Just sit down and relax. I'm sure you haven't had much of a chance to do that lately." Dad indicated the living room, and my eyes nearly bugged out of my skull. He was really trying.

"Okay...thanks."

Theresa and her husband got there just a few minutes after us, and we greeted her and Nick with hugs and well wishes. Daphne didn't arrive for another half hour, and when she got there, she was fuming. Striding into the living room, she pointed a finger squarely at Hayden. "You! This is all your fault."

Hayden looked around himself, like he was sure someone was hiding behind him. "Me?" he asked, pointing at his chest.

"Yes, you," Daphne said, putting her hands on her hips.

"Uh, Daph, what did Hayden do?" I asked. And *when* had he done it?

Her fiery eyes turned to me. "He convinced Jeff to get a motorcycle. He practically started the timer on his life!"

Jeff walked into the room behind her, rolling his eyes. "You're overacting, Daphne."

Spinning on her heel, she snipped, "No, I'm not. You've left our baby fatherless. I hope you're happy."

"You're pregnant?" Theresa and I said at almost the same time.

Daphne swished her hand. "Not yet, but still...if he does manage to knock me up before he croaks, then I'm clearly raising the baby alone. Because he's on the fast-track to Organ Donor Ville."

Hayden raised his hand. "Can we go back to how this is *my* fault? I'm confused..."

Daphne drilled into him with her eyes. "You got him all excited about motorcycles, made him think he was a racer, like you. And don't tell me you haven't exchanged texts about meeting up at the track, because I know you have."

Hayden crossed his arms over his chest. "We've talked about it, sure, but we haven't actually done it." He swished his finger around the room. "But considering the fact that he married into a racing family, I'd say I'm not *entirely* to blame."

Daphne pursed her lips but didn't argue. Jeff put a hand on her shoulder. "It will be all right, honey. I'm very careful."

She jerked her head around so fast, Jeff backed up a step. "You knew I was against it, and you did it anyway. That's the opposite of careful. You really do have a death wish."

Jeff sighed and looked away. The room swam with tension. And that was when my father walked in. "Daphne, Jeff, good timing, I just finished setting everything on the table."

"I'm not hungry," Daphne told him. "But I will take some wine." She immediately turned and left the room.

"What's her problem?" Dad asked. Then he looked sorry he'd asked.

Sensing the mood in the air, Hayden smiled and said, "Dinner smells amazing, Jordan. And I'm starving. It's been ages since I've had a good homecooked meal."

I knew Hayden frequently met up with Izzy for dinner, and she was an amazing cook, so what he'd just said wasn't entirely true, but I appreciated his attempt to change the subject. Unfortunately, by doing so, he made himself a target.

"Nikki doesn't feed you?" my dad asked. His frown grew as his eyes danced between Hayden and me.

Theresa cleared her throat, uncomfortable, and poor Nick looked like he wanted to be anywhere but here. Hayden opened his mouth to answer Dad, but Daphne walked back into the room, glass of wine in hand. "I can't believe you're still living with another woman, Hayden. And how are you okay with that, Kenzie? I'd put a stop to it if I were you."

I knew Daphne was just lashing out because she was mad at her husband, but I was about ten seconds away from going off on her. After *everything* she'd put me through, she didn't get to question my life. Now or ever.

Maybe sensing that World War III was about to break out, Hayden stepped forward and interceded. "Daphne, how about I teach Jeff how to ride a bike properly?" He lifted his hands and his eyebrows. "The best way to keep him safe is to give him as much information as possible, right?"

Daphne firmed her lips, but she looked like she was considering it. "Not on the track. Not as fast as you and Kenzie go."

Hayden shook his head. "Of course not. We'll find a nice, empty parking lot. And I'll get him some leathers, the best stuff available. It's like armor, so he'll be almost impenetrable."

I knew that wasn't true, as leathers couldn't stop you from being squished or decapitated, but Daphne seemed swayed. "Well, maybe..." Jeff bounced a little in his excitement, and Daphne turned to face him. "I'm still angry. You should have talked to me."

He instantly stopped moving. "I know. I'm sorry."

Daphne sighed, but the tension in the air melted away. Looking back at Hayden, she said, "Thank you. And I'm sorry I was snarky about you living with another girl. I'm sure it's fine. I mean, she *is* pregnant after all. It's not like you're going to dump Kenzie for an instant family...right?"

Anger zipped up my spine again. *Jesus, Daphne.* I opened my mouth, but Hayden held his hand up, subtly asking me to let him handle it. Addressing the room, he said, "Kenzie is my world. I could be living in the Playboy mansion with three dozen loose women and it wouldn't matter. *She* has my heart...and my body," he added with a smirk.

I wanted to drop my head into my hands, but oddly, Daphne seemed impressed by his declaration. "Well, okay then."

"Okay then?" I asked. "You're not going to make a stink about this anymore?"

She shrugged. "Nah. If he would turn down whores for you, then I feel pretty confident he'll turn down your best friend."

I had to close my eyes. There were so many things wrong with that statement. I heard someone snigger, then my dad grumbled, "For the love of God, can we go eat?"

Everyone seemed to agree, because we all moved into the dining room at the same time. When I got there, I was...confused. All of my favorite foods were on display, and most of them weren't traditional Christmas food—my mom's world-famous lasagna, bacon-wrapped scallops, cinnamon rolls, gummy bears, and a tofu stir-fry. Nobody but me liked tofu. "What is all this?" I asked, looking around the room.

Daphne and Theresa smiled, while Dad looked sheepish. "Well, after...what happened...last Christmas, when we..."

"When you screwed me over?" I supplied.

Dad cringed but nodded. "We just wanted to make sure we made up for it this year."

My eyes watered as I looked around the room. "Thank you. Last year, without you guys...really sucked."

And just like that, I felt something heal between my family and me...even between Daphne and me. And it felt wonderful.

* * *

After dinner, Hayden and I said our goodbyes, then made our way to our second stop for the night—Izzy's house for drinks and dessert. Not that I could eat any more food. Or could handle any more sweets. I'd massively overindulged on gummy bears. So much for getting back on track. Damn my thoughtful, overcompensating family.

Antonia greeted us at the door when we got there. She was dressed up, too, in a bright red dress with white fluff at the neckline and sleeves. Her hair was coming in nicely now, and she had it pulled back with a red hairband that matched her dress. She was the epitome of Christmas.

"Uncle Hayden! Aunt Kenzie! Like my dress? Uncle Tony bought it for me."

She did a little twirl and Hayden laughed. "It's beautiful, Bookworm. Almost as beautiful as you." He winked at her and she giggled.

"Come on in, Mom made rosettes. They're amazing!"

She turned and ran up the stairs to the kitchen. I grabbed my stomach and groaned. "I can't, Hayden... I just can't."

Hayden grinned at me, then shook his head. "Lightweight."

I gently socked him in the stomach, then we followed Antonia upstairs. I froze when we got to the kitchen. Izzy was there, dolling out fried dough covered in powdered sugar. Hookup was there, too, leaning against the counter, drinking a beer. And Rodney and Felicia were there...picking through a tray of cheese and crackers. It hadn't occurred to me that they'd be here tonight, but of course they would be. It was Christmas, and Hookup and Izzy were Felicia's family, same as they were Hayden's.

Rodney spotted us before Felicia. "Hayden! Kenzie! Glad you could finally make it." He grabbed a bottle of beer from the counter and handed it to Hayden. "Catch up," he told him. "We've been here a while."

Hayden took the bottle, but he seemed tentative about taking it. Looking at me, he said, "Do you want something?" That was what his mouth said, but his eyes were clearly telling me *Say the word and we're gone.*

I smiled and answered his asked and unasked question. "No, I'm good, thank you."

Hayden gave me a minute to change my mind, then opened his beer. "Thanks, man," he told Rodney.

Felicia had been intent on the cheese tray, waiting to see how everything turned out. When it seemed we weren't fleeing, she looked up at us. "Hi," she said, addressing us both.

Feeling odd and out of place, I raised my hand. "Hey..." Would being around her ever not feel weird?

Tension started building in the room, and I hated that for the second time today, things were awkward. I looked around the kitchen, debating what we could possibly talk about. Hayden started digging through the cheeses. Felicia cleared her throat and sipped on her wine, while Hookup chugged his beer. Izzy just kept offering people rosettes. Rodney was the only one who looked unaffected. Rodney and Antonia.

"Why does everyone look so glum?" Antonia asked. "Is it because we haven't done presents yet? I've already opened mine, but you could do yours?" She innocently pointed at Rodney and Felica, and Hayden and me, and the weird feeling in the room tripled. Hayden, feeling impatient, had already given Antonia and Izzy their presents, and the two of us had exchanged between ourselves this morning. It hadn't occurred to me to get Rodney and Felicia gifts...and I really hoped it hadn't occurred to Hayden either. Maybe Rodney...but not Felicia. That crossed a line.

Letting out an awkward chuckle, Izzy said, "No, sweetie, adults don't really do that."

"Oh," she said, a confused expression on her face. "Then what's the matter?"

"Nothing, Bookworm," Hayden said. "Maybe we should all play a game. Your choice."

Antonia brightened as she thought. "Let's play Spoons!"

Hayden cringed, but nodded. "Sounds great, I'll get some cards."

As he left, I whispered to Izzy, "What's Spoons?"

Felicia, hearing me, answered instead. "You set a group of spoons on the table, one less than the number of people playing. Then the lead person starts going through the deck. When someone gets four of a kind, they grab a spoon. Then everyone else is free to grab a spoon. The person who doesn't get one is out. It's kind of...organized chaos."

Antonia clapped her hands. "It's so much fun! Uncle Hayden nearly broke the table last time."

Izzy sighed and shook her head. "He better not break this one, it's brand new."

Antonia...and Rodney...looked really eager to play. I wasn't so sure, but I didn't want to be the wet blanket of the party, so I sucked it up and took a spot next to Hayden. The game was exceedingly simple, but I was shocked at how quickly the anticipation built up. I found myself watching the spoons more than I was watching my cards, and when Hookup slyly reached out and grabbed one—doing his best to go unnoticed—I practically leapt on the table to get mine. I even accidently elbowed Hayden in the ribs. Maybe that was why he was a split-second too late in grabbing the last spoon.

"Oh my God," he said, looking at me. "You knocked me out."

"I did not... Rodney grabbed the last one." Rodney then proceeded to wave the spoon back and forth, taunting Hayden. Antonia laughed, and I did my best to not join in with her.

Hayden gave me a look of mock indignation, then he glanced at Antonia. "You better win this, small fry. I'm counting on you."

Antonia nodded, then gave him a thumbs-up. Unfortunately, she got knocked out the next round. Then Izzy. Then Tony. Then Rodney. When it was just down to Felicia and me, all of the previous tension in the room had completely vanished—everyone was whistling and cheering, and I had no idea which one of us they were cheering for. And I didn't care. I had to shake my head in amusement. "A year ago, I never would have pictured this moment happening," I told her.

She laughed in response. "Me either. Ready?"

"Let's do it," I answered.

Hayden rubbed my back while Felicia started going through the deck. She had a slight advantage, since she saw the cards first, but there was also a small advantage to me, since I knew which cards she was passing on. With only one spoon left on the table, the adrenaline in the air skyrocketed. Antonia was jumping up and down, causing Sundae to periodically bark at her.

After only a few minutes into the round, I had three sevens in my hand—I just needed one more. There were multiple decks in the pile Felicia was pawing through, so I knew my odds were good. So long as Felicia didn't get her four of a kind first.

And then it happened—a fourth seven. My hand shot out, reaching for the spoon, but Felicia either got her last card at the same time, or was reacting to my movement. Whatever the reason, we both jumped for the spoon at the same time. Neither of us were able to grasp it though, and somehow, we sent it spinning across the table, onto the floor. Antonia snorted with laughter. Felicia and I stared at each other for a split second, then our competitive natures took over, and we both dove for the spoon.

As I collided with the floor, I heard Izzy saying, "Careful, careful!" And Tony saying, "Twenty on Cox!"

If I'd had time to say anything, I would have taken him up on that bet, because my fingers curled around the spoon just a split-second before hers. Victory! Felicia was laughing as I yanked the spoon away and held it tight to my body. Rodney and Hayden were laughing too. Then I started laughing. I was going to be sore as hell tomorrow for that harsh landing, but it was so worth it.

Felicia helped me to my feet, and I again marveled at the fact that I wasn't trying to murder her. I wasn't even angry at her. Not really.

Shaking his head, Hayden wrapped his arms around me in a hug. Over his shoulder, I saw Rodney clutching Felicia in a similar manner. And they both looked just as happy as Hayden and me.

"Anyone break a bone?" Izzy asked, grinning.

I started shaking my head, but then I noticed the spoon…it was completely bent in half. "Sorry, Iz…there *was* one casualty."

Antonia started laughing even harder as she grabbed the spoon from me. "Didn't I tell you this game was fun, Aunt Kenzie?" She looked back at her mom. "Can we play again?"

Izzy sighed, but nodded. As Hookup grabbed the cards and started shuffling them, Rodney looked over at Hayden. "See, I told you they'd get along great. Let's plan that double date. What are you guys doing New Year's Eve?"

Hayden looked at me. "Uh…we're hanging out with Nikki and Myles."

"Perfect!" Rodney said. "The more the merrier."

Oh God. They were going to crash our double date. Shit.

CHAPTER 8

These back to back holidays were going to be the death of me. Not only was I eating too much, but I was hardly getting anything done. And it seemed like everyone I needed to talk to was either gone on vacation or their entire business was closed. Who closed up shop just because of a couple of holidays? A lot of people, apparently. It was so frustrating, watching the tiny fires around me turn into much bigger blazes, and not being able to do anything about it. The whole thing made me want to pull my hair out.

But it was almost over. Once this year finally kicked over to the next one, things would return to normal…with me holding everything together with a very thin thread. God, I hoped I got some good news soon.

My phone chimed with a message, and I reluctantly looked at it. *'You're still coming tonight, right? Because I think you need this even more than I do.'* That was from Nikki. She'd hounded me all week about this party. I generally preferred to stay home for New Year's, but it had been forever since we'd all gone out together, and she was looking forward to it so much… I felt obligated to go.

'Just finishing up work. I'll be there.'

Her response was instant. *'It's New Year's Eve. Why the hell are you at work?'*

Because I was hoping I could get some shit done today, but apparently, I can't. Knowing it sounded bitchy, I didn't text that to her. Instead, I ignored her message, tucked my phone into my bag and prepared to head home. To change. For a party I wasn't excited about.

I was still getting ready when Hayden knocked on my door. Setting down my curling iron, I hurried to the door to let him in. He looked fabulous in a pair of black jeans and a Cox Racing T-shirt. I smirked at his shirt and he grinned wider. "What? It seemed like the perfect night to advertise."

Shaking my head, I let him inside. "It's a hell of lot better than that obnoxious Benneti jacket. You burned that thing, right?"

Closing the door behind him, he nodded. "You bet your sweet ass I did."

Laughing, I walked back to my bathroom to finish curling my hair. Hayden watched me with curious eyes. "Can I ask a stupid question?" he said.

"Of course," I answered with a smile.

"Why are you curling your hair? It's already curly?"

"It's wavy and chaotic." Closing my eyes, I sighed. "I just want something to be in order…"

He obviously knew I wasn't talking about my hair anymore and gave me a sympathetic smile. "Well, you look beautiful. More than beautiful. Stunning…breathtaking…"

I gave him a dry look. "I'm wearing the exact same thing I wore for Christmas." There just hadn't been any time to shop for something new and cute.

Hayden's smile widened. "I know. I like that dress. You should wear it every day."

I rolled my eyes, but I was beaming the entire time I finished getting ready. Once I was as presentable as I was going to be, we got into my truck and headed to Oysters. The nautical-themed bar was making a big to-do out of tonight. Hookup had told Hayden that they'd brought in a DJ and a fog machine. Myles was giddy, because his signature drink was on special tonight. Glenn had taken Nikki's off the menu, out of respect for her condition. He promised he would bring it back once the baby was born... and then name another drink for the baby.

The parking lot was packed when we got there, and I had to admit, I was surprised. I'd kind of thought the place was going to be a ghost town. Hayden pointed to a truck a few spaces over. "Rodney's here." Which meant Felicia was too. Well, Christmas had ended up entertaining, maybe this would too. Positive thinking was going to get me through tonight.

Merely smiling at Hayden's observation, I shut my truck off and climbed out. Hayden was by my side a moment later, hand extended for me. I grabbed his fingers, and we made our way toward the door. The music was booming loud, even from outside, and I could see the swirl of "fog" as people opened the door. It was going to be insane inside, I just knew it. Glenn should stick to seafood.

When Hayden pulled the door open for us, the deep bass from the music combined with the cacophony of hundreds of voices talking at once hit me in the face like the heat blast from an oven. I even took a step back as my body adjusted. Hayden grinned at me as he pulled me inside.

Myles was the first person we spotted—once we could see through the haze of the fog. Like he'd been watching the door, he instantly approached us, two bright blue/green drinks in hand. "Hey, guys! Have a Myles." He thrust the drinks out to us, an eager grin on his boyish face. He loved this.

"Where's Nikki?" I asked over the music.

Myles tilted his head toward the back. "Bathroom. I swear she has to pee every five minutes. Weird, since she's not drinking. We've got a table though." He started walking, then glanced at us over his shoulder. "The whole gang's here."

I smiled when I saw Eli, Ralph, and Kevin crowded around a circular table, sipping on blue-green drinks. "Hey, guys," I said, tossing my hand up in a wave.

They each gave us a greeting, none of them looking at Hayden twice; they'd fully acclimated to an ex-Benneti being on the team. And being my boyfriend. Just as I was thinking the Benneti rivalry was well and truly gone, all four of my employees scowled. Wondering why they were all acting like guard dogs protecting their territory, I glanced behind me. Then I understood. Rodney was heading our way, Felicia in tow.

"What are they doing?" Myles asked, eyes narrowed.

Hayden looked apologetic. "They're, uh, here for us," he said, indicating me.

Myles's eyes widened. "For you?" His gaze swung to me, his dark eyes full of disbelief. While Nikki had been my main confidant during the whole Felica-Hayden-fiasco, Myles had known about it, and he knew I wasn't fond of her.

I gave him a tight smile. "Rodney and Hayden are friends, so we invited them out." Kind of.

Myles scoffed, then frowned at Hayden. I had a feeling their newfound, friendly relationship had just taken a hit.

Nikki returned to the table just in time to see everybody staring at the approaching couple. "Holy shit! Are they coming over here?"

My smile grew even tighter. "Hey, Nik. It's fine. It's all...fine."

She seemed to buy that just as much as Myles, but there was nothing they could do—Rodney and Felicia were upon us. "Hey, guys!" Rodney said. "What the hell are you drinking? It's blue."

"It's The Myles, named after me," Myles said, his voice flat.

Rodney raised an eyebrow, then laughed. "Well, it looks like a chick drink, dude. If I were going to have a drink named after me, it would be Scotch. On the rocks."

Eli cracked a smile. "Rodney's Rocks?"

"Exactly," Rodney said, snapping his fingers.

Eli sniggered, but Felicia practically purred as she placed her hand on Rodney's chest. "I'd order a Rodney's Rocks."

"Or a Hayden's Rocks," Nikki said under the music. Thankfully, I was the only one who heard her. I shot her a look, and she cringed in apology.

Hayden and Rodney started in on a conversation, with Felicia standing next to both of them. They were kind of apart from the group, in their own little trio, a realization that didn't exactly sit well with me. But neither did butting into their circle. That felt a little too obvious.

Myles shook his head as he watched the dynamics. "You okay with this, Kenzie? Like, for real okay with this?" He still seemed mystified.

I wanted to say no. I wanted to say yes. Instead, I shrugged. "I'm okay with Hayden hanging out with his friend."

Myles smirked. "Nice job sidestepping the issue."

Stepping closer to him, I flicked a glance at Nikki. "I'm not the only one sidestepping issues."

His brows drew together, confused. Rolling my eyes, I said, "Nikki told me you two almost kissed at the baby store."

He blankly stared at me for a solid ten seconds, then shrugged. "It was nothing. We got caught up in a moment. It happens."

"It happens?" I said with a laugh. "Have you and I ever got caught up in a moment?" He suddenly looked disgusted, and I smacked his arm. "Exactly. I don't think you got caught up in anything, Myles. I think you finally let your guard down. Both of you."

Myles rolled his eyes, but then his gaze drifted to Nikki, and he looked...thoughtful. I was just about to tell him to go ask her to dance, when I felt my purse vibrating. Worried it was some sort of emergency with the business, I pulled my phone out of my tiny bag and checked the screen. New message from John? He never texted me.

Unlocking the phone, I checked the text. My jaw dropped after reading it. "What's wrong?" Myles asked.

Shaking my head, I looked up at him. "Nothing. He found someone."

Myles looked lost, until I reached over and tapped Nikki on the shoulder, interrupting her conversation with

Ralph. She looked back at me, and I raised my phone. "John found a mechanic. He'll be there Monday."

All the color faded from Nikki's cheeks. It happened so quickly, I worried she was about to pass out. "Nik? You okay?"

She nodded and forced a smile to her face. "Yeah, I'm great. This is...great." Her eyes, thick with moisture, shifted to Myles. "I have to go to the bathroom." She spun and left without another word.

"Damn it, I didn't mean to upset her. I know she's freaking out, but this is good news. Really good news." And I'd been desperately needing some good news. I already felt a weight being lifted from my shoulders. But it was quickly replaced with guilt. "I should go talk to her."

I started to move away, but Myles stopped me. "Hold up, Kenzie. I think I should be the one to talk to her." I wanted to argue, but the look in his eyes—the compassion, the warmth—I nodded, and let him go rescue his damsel.

Once he was gone, I twisted to find my boyfriend. He was laughing with Rodney and Felicia. They looked so damn perfect together, like a trio of best friends. It made a surge of jealousy rush through me, but I forcefully shoved it aside. Best friends were a lot different than lovers. And I could...maybe, somehow, be okay with them all being friends. So long as Rodney was the glue holding them together, and Felicia was just an unavoidable consequence.

Shaking aside my darker thoughts, I walked over to Hayden. Still laughing with Rodney, he put his arm around me, then leaned over and kissed my head. "Hey, babe." Then he seemed to realize their threesome had shifted away from the main group, and he suddenly looked very uncomfortable, like he hadn't meant for that to happen.

Not wanting him to worry about offending me, I smiled. "Guess what I just found out about?" He shrugged, and I said, "John found a replacement mechanic for Nikki. He's starting Monday."

Hayden smiled, but it was brief. He looked around for Nikki. "How is she doing?"

My smile faltered. "She's... Myles is with her."

Hayden nodded, his face full of compassion. Rodney smacked him on the arm, interrupting our conversation. "Hayes, grab your woman, we're dancing."

I bristled at the term *woman*, then saw that Felicia looked annoyed too. "Woman?" she said, ice in her voice.

Rodney's entire demeanor changed. "Goddess of a girlfriend?" he suggested. Then he added, "I didn't want to say that in case you got jealous."

Felicia's eyes widened, then snapped to Hayden. He shifted on his feet, uncomfortable. My chest tightened with familiar anxiety—was she still wanting my boyfriend? "Jealous?" Felicia said, almost too quiet to hear.

Rodney nodded, oblivious to the discomfort in the air. "Yeah, you know, me calling someone else a goddess." His arms wrapped around her waist. "I wouldn't want you to think I was hitting on her, 'cause I'm not. You're the only goddess in my eyes."

Felicia laughed, and her eyes sparkled with affection. The ache in my heart lifted, and the tension in the air dissolved. Not wanting to not think or feel anything for a while, I pulled Hayden over to the makeshift dance floor Glenn had put in the middle of the bar. It was crowded with people, but we found a space along the edge. Rodney and Felicia positioned themselves right next to us. I wasn't thrilled with that, but I let it go as I lost myself to the music.

Hayden and I danced together so closely, our legs were intertwined—more grinding than dancing. As our bodies moved in complete sync, Hayden's passionate green eyes locked onto mine, and I felt my body responding, opening. I wasn't sure if it was the intimate way we were moving, or the fact that Felicia seemed genuinely invested in Rodney, or the relief that John had found someone he deemed worthy to replace Nikki, taking a huge burden off of my mind, but I found myself *wanting* Hayden. It had been ages since we'd last made love, since I'd felt that powerful, intimate, soul-bearing connection. I had wanted to take our second-chance slowly, fearful of him breaking my heart again, but as we stood close together, just a few feet away from his ex-lover, I didn't feel scared or worried. I just felt…cherished.

Wanting to subtly let him know I was ready for him—ready for more—I leaned up and placed my lips against his. His mouth was warm and receptive, caressing me with each tender movement. Yes…we were ready. *I* was ready. But before we left, before we gave ourselves to each other, I wanted to take advantage of this moment, and savor dancing with him. Savor this foreplay with him.

Time surged by, and before I knew it, the entire bar was doing a countdown for midnight. Smile on my face, I pulled away from Hayden and looked around the room filled with my friends and coworkers. Hookup was working tonight, and he'd come out of the kitchen and was loudly counting down with his coworkers. Rodney and Felicia had moved more toward the center of the dancefloor—they were already kissing. Eli, Ralph, and Kevin were still at the table, holding up mugs of beer in anticipation, and Myles and Nikki were on the dance floor right beside Hayden and me. I'd been so entranced with Hayden, I hadn't even realized they'd joined us. They were staring at each other, seemingly lost to everyone and everything around them. And then...when the crowd reached the number one, they leaned forward, and shared a kiss that was *anything* but platonic. Hormonal imbalance my ass.

I was so shocked they were kissing, I couldn't help but stare—missing my own midnight moment. Hayden had to physically move my head, so he could kiss me. I started to tell him what had happened, but his lips were on me before I could. My heart surged as our mouths moved together, and every last wall crumbled to the ground. I could have kissed him forever, but I didn't want to do it here anymore. I wanted to be alone with him. I wanted to be home with him.

Shifting my mouth up to his ear, I breathily told him, "Take me home." Then I pulled back, so he could see the heat in my eyes, so he would know just what I'd really meant. *Take me*.

Hayden's tongue flicked out to moisten his lower lip, then he turned and started pulling us toward the exit. I thought to say goodbye to Myles and Nikki, but they were still kissing. Oh my God...would this night finally break them of their "just friends" resistance to dating? I hoped so, for their sakes.

Hayden got us out the front door in record time. The cool air and the diminished noise was a welcome treat. So was the look of desire on Hayden's face as he rushed us to the truck. Not ten minutes later we were stumbling through my front door, mouths and hands all over each other. Hayden managed to kick the front door closed with his foot, then lock it without looking. We made our way to the bedroom, bumping into tables and walls along the way. By the time we got to my room, I'd torn Hayden's Cox Racing T-shirt off and kicked away my high heels.

Hayden closed my bedroom door, then held up his hand to stop me from ravishing him. "Are you sure about this, Kenzie. I don't want to rush you." His eyes were hot with desire, but I knew if I changed my mind right now, he'd smile and say, *Okay*. And that was exactly why I didn't want to stop. He was incredible, and he was mine. I was positive of that.

"I'm sure," I told him. "I love you. And I know you love me…you show me every day. You love me so much, sometimes I have no idea what I did to deserve you. I want to share this with you, I want to take this last step with you." Tossing my arms around his neck, I softly told him, "I want to make love to you. Will you make love to me, Hayden?"

A stuttered exhale left his lips, then his mouth lowered to mine in a definite *yes*. His hands reached down to pick me up, and I wrapped my legs around his waist as he walked us to the bed. He gently laid us down, his lips never leaving mine. His body, hard and needy, pressed against me, and I gasped with the rush of pure pleasure. "Oh God…"

Hayden's mouth drifted to my neck. "I love you so much, Kenzie. I've missed you so much…"

Closing my eyes, I reveled in the feel of his body pressing against every inch of me. His words reached deep into my heart, filling me with confidence, with certainty.

"I love you too, Hayden. So much." *And I've missed this too.*

We methodically took our time undressing. I had a feeling Hayden was purposely taking his time, waiting to see if I changed my mind. I wasn't going to. I wanted this too much, wanted him too much. When his tongue ran up my core, making me cry out, and I clutched his head to me in absolute need—that was when he finally believed I was 100 percent on board.

He sucked and teased me right to the brink of release, then he stopped and repositioned himself, so he could plunge inside me. When our bodies were fully connected, he paused. Both of us were breathing hard, our hearts racing. Cupping my cheek, Hayden stared at me with love and adoration on his face. He leaned down to gently kiss me, then he began to move. My heart swelled with love, while my body swelled with need. This was the man I was going to be with for forever—of that, I had no doubts. Not anymore. Not after all of the challenges we'd faced—and conquered.

Our bodies moved together with more urgency, more need, and the desire inside me rose higher and higher, slowly but steadily reaching an apex. I gripped Hayden tighter as I felt the edge of euphoria approaching, and I felt him do the same. The rush of release hit me a second later, and I cried out as I cherished the feeling, the connection, the sense of utter belonging. God, I'd missed this…

Hayden hit his climax a moment later, and I held him to me, loving how good it felt to give him this moment, this gift. The high began to fade shortly after, but not the bliss behind it. For once, I felt genuinely at peace.

Breath still fast, heart still surging, Hayden lifted himself to look at me. "You're my everything, Kenzie. I hope you know that."

Cupping his cheek, I smiled. "I do." And I truly did... fully and completely. I had Hayden's heart, and he had mine too. And nothing was going to tear us apart again. Whatever challenges were coming our way, we'd face them *together*.

CHAPTER 9

I spent most of the weekend in bed with Hayden, reconnecting with him over and over. It was bliss. Absolute, total bliss, and I felt recharged afterward, ready to take on the daunting task of running Cox Racing. Monday morning came around, and I headed to the track with determination in my heart. But the minute I stepped into my office, brimming with responsibility, I felt the familiar heaviness and anxiety settle over me, and regret started intruding on my euphoria. Maybe I should have come in at least *one* of those days and done…something.

Inhaling a deep breath, I sat down and got to work. At the very least, I should be able to get ahold of people today.

I was on hold with our tire supplier, still trying to figure out why they kept sending me the wrong part, when Nikki suddenly burst into my office. Like someone was chasing her, she slammed my office door and put her back against it.

Her sudden appearance startled me, and my heart started thudding against my chest. "Jesus, Nik. Are you trying to give me a heart attack?"

Leaning her head against the glass, she shook her head. "Sorry, I just wanted to talk to you before I ran into…" She paused to swallow, then spat out, "We slept together. Again."

I immediately hung up the phone. "You…what?"

Looking like she was about to have a psychotic break, she ambled over to my desk, and plopped down into a chair. "I have no idea how it happened," she murmured.

Lifting an eyebrow, I pointedly looked at her stomach. Frowning, she told me, "I know how it happened, I just don't understand…how it happened. I mean, we're just friends…"

I flicked a glance at my phone, and all the things I should be doing with it. "Well, Nik, maybe it's time you accept the fact that you're…not just friends. Maybe you haven't been just friends for a while."

Her expression was blank for a moment, then her eyes filled with moisture. "We have to be just friends," she told me, her voice completely serious.

"Why? What's so wrong with being more than friends? It will only add to your relationship, make it deeper, stronger."

She swallowed again, then nodded. "Yeah, but when it ends, and let's face it, most relationships end, I don't just lose a super-cool boyfriend. I lose my best friend. My *best* friend, Kenzie. That's not something I want to bet on."

As I watched a tear roll down her cheek, I wondered what I could possibly say to make her feel better. The problem was… I completely understood what she was talking about. When Hayden and I had split, that had been the part of our separation that was almost too much to bear. Losing his friendship.

"For what it's worth, Nik, I don't think you guys would split up. I think you'd make it." How could they not? They were practically the same person. But then again, sometimes being too similar wasn't a good thing, not in a relationship anyway.

Nikki gave me a halfhearted smile as she wiped away her tear, then her expression brightened. "You and Hayden disappeared without a trace from the party. And he didn't come home all weekend. How did your night go?"

I couldn't contain my grin, and I knew my cheeks were flushing with color. "It was...good."

"Binge-watched Netflix good, or my toes curled, and I saw stars good?"

My grin grew. "The second one." That night—and my entire weekend for that matter—flashed through my brain, making me sigh. "It was amazing, Nikki. Just so... amazing. I'm glad we waited. And I'm glad I took your advice and let him in. He's...worth the risk."

I raised an eyebrow, subtly suggesting that maybe Myles was worth it too. She looked away from me, her face both annoyed and thoughtful. Then she inhaled a deep breath and looked back at me. "I'm happy for you, Kenzie. You and Hayden, you both deserve happiness."

"So do you, Nik," I told her.

Her face got a forlorn expression. "I can't stop thinking about him, Kenzie. Like literally, that night is always on my mind all the time. I've had some really crazy dreams about it too." She gave me a small smile. "It's probably a good thing Hayden hasn't been around." Her smile slipped as she shook her head. "It was even better than the first time."

Curious, I asked her, "Have you...talked to Myles since it happened?" Her eyes instantly dropped to her lap.

"Oh my God, Nik, you two are horrible. Didn't you learn anything the first time?"

She looked up at me, her dark eyes annoyed. "Yes, we used protection this time."

I just about died laughing, and Nikki cracked a smile. Then sighed. "It's just weird talking to him about it. I'm afraid he's gonna…"

She stopped talking and looked away. "Afraid he'll what?" I asked.

Looking back at me, she shrugged. "Honestly, I'm afraid he'll blow me off, *and* I'm afraid he'll say we should go for it. It's a lose-lose for me, so I just…pretend he doesn't exist."

"But…if you're pretending he doesn't exist, then haven't you already lost your best friend?"

She stared at me a moment, then shook her head. "Wow…sex made you deep."

Smirking at her comment, I flipped her off. Nikki laughed, then her expression sobered. "So, you and Hayden…now that you're back together in *every* way…is he gonna move in with you?"

The look on her face tore me in two—it was panic laced with guilt. The entire reason Hayden had moved in with her was to help her pay for her rent. While him moving in with me would be great for our relationship, it would completely screw over Nikki. But, thankfully, Hayden and I weren't there yet. We'd ramped things up, but we were still on a slow-moving course. "Not yet, Nik. We're not ready for that step. And we might not be for a while."

She visibly relaxed. "Thank God. I mean, I'm totally a Hayden-Kenzie fan, but he's been such a big help." She frowned. "Financially. As a roommate, he's kind of a slob. Did you know he drinks milk right out of the carton?" She made a disgusted face. "Who does that?"

I laughed at her expression, then nodded. "Yeah, I know…it's gross. I'm trying to break him of it."

Just as Nikki told me good luck, my office door was knocked on. Nikki instantly tensed. Rolling my eyes at her, I said, "Come on in."

It wasn't Myles who walked in though. It wasn't anyone I knew. The stranger in front of me was tall, with pitch-black hair, piercing blue eyes, and a thick patch of nearly-black stubble that shockingly emphasized his manliness. He had a commanding presence, and a sensual kind of good looks that made women fantasize about spending all day and night in bed with him. Most women, not me. My eyes were firmly fixed on a blonde-haired, green-eyed god of a man. Nikki was certainly captivated though.

Jumping to her feet, she extended her hand. "Nikki Ramirez. What can I help you with tall, dark, and gorgeous?"

I gave her a *Please be professional* look, but she wasn't paying any attention to me. The stranger smiled at his shoes in an adorable way. Then he took her hand and gave her a charming smile. "Dex Covington. I'm looking for Mackenzie Cox?"

His pale eyes drifted to me, and I startled in recognition. "You're the new mechanic."

Nikki instantly dropped his hand. Dex seemed surprised by that, but his smile quickly returned. Stepping to the edge of the desk, he extended his hand to me. "You must be Mackenzie."

Standing, I clasped his hand. "Yes...hi, welcome...to the team."

Dex shook my hand, smiling brightly. "It's a pleasure to be here." Nikki huffed behind him, and I indicated her way with my hand. "Nikki here is the mechanic you're replacing." Nikki's eyes narrowed, and I instantly amended my statement. "*Temporarily* replacing, while she's out with her baby."

Dex nodded at her, then his eyes flashed to her stomach before returning to her face. "Congratulations. Babies are amazing, you're going to love your little one."

Nikki put a hand on her stomach, and I quietly heard her murmur, "I hope so."

Dex seemed unsure what to do with that, so stepping around my desk, I pointed to the door. "Would you like to take a look around? Meet the rest of the team?"

Dex smiled at me, his face appreciative. "I would love that, thank you." I almost missed it, but his eyes slipped down my body as I walked past him. Hmmm. I supposed I could ignore being checked out once, but if it became a habit, I'd have to have a conversation with him about appropriate workplace behavior.

Nikki followed us out of my office, probably to make sure Dex didn't touch any of her tools. Since we were upstairs, I showed Dex everything of interest. The break room, the storage room, John's office, and the gym. Dex seemed impressed by the assortment of cardio and weight-lifting machines in the gym and let out a low whistle as he looked around. "This is pretty spectacular," he said. "I suppose it has to be since the athletes need to be in tip-top shape."

I nodded, then subconsciously patted my stomach. I needed to get in there more often. "We try. Some of us do better than others."

Nikki smiled at my statement. "Don't even, Kenzie. Your arms and legs are rocks. Even if you've cut back a little, you're still in amazing shape. Me, however…"

She sighed as she rubbed her stomach. A chuckle escaped me at the forlorn look on her face. Dex turned to me, surprised. "You're a rider? John only mentioned that you were the owner."

Now I was the one sighing. "Probably because I don't get to the track nearly as often as I should." Shaking my head, I told him, "My bike will actually be your main priority. Well, my bike and Hayden's."

Dex smiled, and the look of interest on his face was unmistakable. "Beautiful, ambitious and talented. A deadly combination."

His comment made me frown. Guess I *was* going to have to have that talk with him. I opened my mouth to start, but unfortunately, someone else had heard him say that. "What's going on here?"

I looked over my shoulder to see Hayden, dressed in his workout clothes, heading our way. "Hey, Hayden. This is Dex…our new mechanic. I'm just showing him around. Dex, this is Hayden Hayes."

Hayden walked right up to my side and put his arm around my shoulders. It was so obvious, he might as well have spray-painted *She's mine* on my forehead. Dex extended a hand to him, but Hayden didn't take it. Dex dropped his hand, a knowing smile on his face. Pointing at the two of us, he said, "I take it you two are a couple."

Hayden nodded. "Most definitely."

With a sigh, I ducked to escape Hayden's embrace. "Yes, but while Hayden and I are a couple...and Myles and Nikki are—"

"Are friends," Nikki quickly interrupted.

"Are *something*...there's still a certain decorum I expect from my employees while they are on the premises."

Dex pursed his lips. "You don't want me to call you beautiful anymore, do you?"

I couldn't help but smile. "I'd appreciate it if you didn't."

"So would I," Hayden muttered.

Dex held up his hands. "Sorry, natural flirt. I can't help it." I raised an eyebrow at him, and he added, "But I *will* try. I swear. I understand I'm not at school anymore. This is a job. A professional job. I got it."

His earnestness made me smile, and then his eyes flicked over my face. "I just never expected my new boss to be so..." Clearing his throat, he shook his head. "Total professional here. No worries."

Shaking my head at him, I nodded toward the stairs. "Come on, let's go check out the fun stuff—the bikes."

I started leading Dex over to the stairs. Nikki followed. And so did Hayden. I wanted to roll my eyes and tell them both to get back to work, but I kind of understood. Change was hard.

Myles was coming up the stairs. He paused, taking us all in. Nikki ducked behind me, like she'd be invisible if I were partly hiding her. "What's, uh...going on?" he asked. His eyes kept drifting to Nikki, and an odd tension built up.

"This is Dex, he's our new mechanic. I'm just showing him around." I glanced back at my shadows. "Why

Nikki and Hayden are following us, I'm not entirely sure." Hayden frowned at me, and Nikki poked me in the back. *Sorry, guys, but you're both overreacting.*

Myles's expression didn't change. "Oh…" Tilting his head, he tried to get Nikki's attention. "Hey, Nik, can I talk to you…alone?"

From behind me, I heard, "Sorry, Myles, can't. I'm following Kenzie, because Dex needs to learn my job, and who better to teach him than me?"

She leaned out a little, so she could glare at me. Dex took in the exchange with a confused expression on his face. Then he snapped his fingers and pointed at Myles. "It's your baby!"

We all shifted to look at him, and he cringed. "Sorry, I also tend to blurt out the obvious, even when it's an unnecessary, unwanted observation." Miming a zipper, he zipped his lips closed.

Turning my head, I looked back at Nikki. "I'm just showing him around today. You can show him the ropes tomorrow. Go talk to Myles. Your *friend*."

Nikki was evaporating me in her mind, but this was for her own good. Nikki and Myles had avoided each other for way too long the first time, and Myles seemed willing, even eager to have a conversation about it. The least Nikki could do was listen to what he had to say.

Nikki tried to win the argument by having a staring contest with me, but that wasn't going to be enough this time. With a huff, she finally gave up and said, "Fine." Then she started walking back up the stairs. Or more accurately, stomping up the stairs.

Myles gave me a grateful smile, then threaded through us to follow her. Dex watched them leave with an amused smile on his face. "Never a dull moment around here, huh?" he commented.

Looking back at him, I shook my head. "It's not usually like this. We're pretty mellow around here."

Hayden suddenly grabbed my hand, pulling me toward him, and Dex's grin grew. "Uh-huh," he said, his bright eyes sparkling with delight.

"Come on," I said, indicating downstairs.

Once we were in the shop, I introduced Dex to Eli, Ralph, and Kevin. While he was questioning Kevin about the thrills of working the pit during an event, I turned to Hayden. "You can let go of my hand now," I discretely told him. "Dex knows I'm off the market. You've done your job."

Hayden glared over at Dex. "I don't know about this, Kenzie. There's something about him that rubs me the wrong way."

Reaching up, I grabbed his cheek. "The only problem here is that another man is testing the waters with me, and it's making you uncomfortable. But Hayden, he can test all he wants, it doesn't change how I feel about you, how I feel about us."

Hayden sighed, his expression worried. "Are you sure, Kenzie? I can't help but think that…"

"That what?" I asked, searching his face.

"That he's…new. No pain, no history. He's never hurt you." His gaze drifted to the floor and I sighed.

"That's completely true." Hayden's eyes snapped up to mine, and there was heat in them. Hot, steamy, he's-not-getting-you-without-a-fight heat. Seeing it made my heart surge, made me want to call it a day and take him home. Smiling, I drew my finger over his lips. "But what you're forgetting is the fact that I don't want new. I want you. Scars and all..."

I briefly traced the scar in his eyebrow, then leaned forward and kissed him. We were interrupted by an amused Dex, clearing his throat. "I'd love to see your bikes now...if you're not busy."

Hayden scratched his head, then gave me a pained look. "I'm gonna go upstairs...get started on my workout. See you...later."

He was clearly reluctant to leave me with another man. I understood that. But just like I had to trust him, he had to trust me. And by walking away, he *was* trusting me. I was very proud of him.

After showing Dex everything there was at Cox Racing, including the track outside, that he would never really have a reason to use, I sent him to John to fill out paperwork. Then I trudged back to my office to try to get something done today.

Myles was waiting for me when I got there, and I almost cried. *I have so much to do.* "Hey, Myles," I made myself say. "How did it go with Nikki?"

He ran his hands back through his thick hair. "I'm assuming she told you what happened New Year's Eve?"

Wrinkling my nose, I nodded. "Yeah, she told me you guys...yeah, she, uh, mentioned it."

He fell into the chair in front of my desk. A chair that was beginning to feel like a therapist's couch. "She didn't want to get into it. She just kept saying it was no big deal, and we had nothing to talk about. *Nothing.*" He shook his head, disbelieving, while I moved to my chair and sat down. "I just don't understand her," he said, looking dejected.

A really weird feeling washed over me. I knew exactly why Nikki wanted to sweep it under the rug, and I *could* tell Myles, make him partly understand her. And in so doing, I'd betray my best friend's confidence. I was the monkey in the middle, and it sucked.

"Myles, I can't..." Folding my hands on my lap, I told him, "I want to help you, I want to help both of you, but it's really not my place. I'm her friend, I'm your friend, and... I'm your boss, both of you."

Myles nodded, then looked down. He seemed so lost, I truly wished I could ease his pain. "Can I ask you a question?" I said.

He peeked up at me with a wry smile. "Isn't that going against what you just said?"

With a sigh, I shrugged. "Yeah, but can I ask anyway?" He looked down again, then nodded. "Do you like her?" I asked.

He closed his eyes before looking up at me. "Of course, I like her. We're best friends."

I pursed my lips at his avoidance. "You know what I mean, Myles. Do you like her as more than a friend?"

His gaze was unblinking as he stared at me. Then, finally, he nodded. "Yeah... I do. But that doesn't matter."

Now I was confused. "That seems like the only thing that matters."

He shook his head, his face melancholy. "She doesn't want to be with me. That's why she's avoiding this. She doesn't want to risk our friendship on something...that could go either way. So really, how I feel...doesn't mean shit. And you know it, don't you?"

Looking at him, seeing his pain…it was too much. My eyes watered, betraying my knowledge. Myles smirked, then nodded. "Yeah… I thought so."

"I'm so sorry, Myles. I truly am."

Standing, he nodded at me. "I know. But hey, it could be worse. She could want to date that hot new mechanic you hired." He raised an eyebrow at me, his voice dripping sarcasm. "Thanks for that, by the way. Just what I needed right now…competition."

Digging my hands into my palms, I closed my eyes. I hadn't thought Myles had really noticed Dex, but apparently, even in his state of extreme concentration, he'd spotted the exotic man who was going to be hanging around the garage every day. Myles could probably strengthen his bond with Hayden by bitching about it to him.

"It wasn't intentional, Myles, and technically, *I'm* not the one who hired him. John did." I opened my eyes to punctuate my point, but it didn't matter. Myles was gone. With a groan of defeat, I let my head drop with a thud to my desk. So much for the new year being less stressful.

CHAPTER 10

Dex coming onto the team was both a blessing and a curse. It was great, because we needed him. Nikki could deny her situation as much as she wanted, but every day she was getting bigger and bigger—like it or not, the baby was coming. It was bad because having Dex around seemed to *add* to my workload, not ease it, like I'd originally thought it would.

It wasn't that Dex was bad at his job—far from it. He was already showing himself to be both capable and talented. No, the problem was coming from my staff, who was either opposed to someone new on the team, or resentful of Dex taking Nikki's place. None of them seemed to believe it was temporary. And of course, Dex's good looks had all of them puffing up their chest, trying to prove they were top dog around here. Especially Hayden and Myles. Those two in particular, were driving me absolutely nuts.

"What are you doing?" I snapped, grabbing a can of shaving cream from Myles's hand.

He gave me a smile that oozed innocence. "What does it look like? I'm shaving. Wouldn't want Cox Racing to look like it was being represented by someone who didn't care about their appearance." His smile slipped. "Because appearance matters, as you know."

He was still annoyed that I'd hired a man who looked like a model to closely work with Nikki for the next few months. And it didn't help anything that Nikki seemed to be the only one on the team who had adjusted to Dex. She constantly told me that looking at his ass made the fact that she was leaving a lot more bearable. I reprimanded her for it every time she said it, but deep down I had to admit, she was right, he did have a nice backside. Not as nice as Hayden's of course, but still…

My lips quirked into a small smile, but there was no humor in my eyes. "As I've told you a thousand times by now, I didn't hire him, John did, so you can stop accusing me of hiring him for his looks. It's incorrect, and disrespectful of my relationship with Hayden—my *boyfriend*."

Myles cringed, and genuinely looked chagrined. Dex had been on the team for a couple of months now, and I'd heard that remark from Myles damn-near daily. It was time for it to stop. Time for a lot of things to stop.

Lifting the can of shaving cream, I sternly told him, "As for your 'story'…one, you're in the locker room, not the bathroom. Two, this is Dex's locker, not yours. And three, you have the nozzle facing the wrong way, and you've gotten it all over the locker while completely missing you." I indicated the inside of Dex's locker, which was now coated in mint-scented foam. "How is that shaving?"

Myles sniffed, then shrugged. "I'm clumsy? I apologize."

Letting out a frustrated groan, I tossed him a towel. "Just clean it up before Dex gets here." I did *not* have time to babysit my employees. Daytona was just around the corner.

Myles rolled his eyes as he caught the towel. "And just when *is* he getting here? He's been late almost every single day."

Chewing on my lip, I glanced at the clock on the wall. "Yeah, I know. Guess he's Nikki's replacement in more ways than one." Up until Nikki had started living with Hayden, she had been perpetually tardy. It used to drive my dad crazy, and now I understood why. There were better things I could be doing than watching a clock.

From behind me, I heard Myles grumble, "Dude should be fired, if you ask me. He's still on a probationary status, right? Three months to see if he's a good fit with the team, right?"

Part of me agreed with him, part of me disagreed with him. I scrubbed my eyes and wished I could go back to bed. Lack of sleep from night racing with Hayden was starting to catch up with me. "Maybe, but Daytona is in two weeks, we don't have time to—"

Just then, Dex walked into the locker room. "I'm sorry, I'm sorry," he said, immediately holding up his hands when he saw me.

A weary smile on my face, I told him, "It's starting to become a habit. A bad one. Fix it, please?"

He crossed an X over his heart. "I'll do my best." The apologetic expression on his face shifted into a frown when he realized what Myles had done to his locker. "What happened?"

Myles shrugged. "Weirdest thing...the can just exploded as I was walking by."

Dex crossed his arms over his chest. "Really? The can exploded for no reason, and the shaving cream managed to *only* get inside my locker? Why was my locker even open?"

Face completely serious, Myles said, "I told you it was weird, and as for your locker, well, you're the one who's supposed to shut it tight. You must have forgotten."

Dex gave him a humorless smile. "Yeah...must have."

Myles let out a sigh, then shook his head and handed Dex the towel. "I did what I could, but I gotta get to work now."

He immediately started walking away, but not before I saw a smile stretch over his lips. "Myles," I warned.

He turned his head but didn't stop walking. "Sorry, Kenzie. I gotta get out on the track. Work on my times and stuff." He had the nerve to laugh after he said it. *Kelley, you're gonna pay for this later.*

Grabbing another towel, I turned to face Dex. "I'm sorry about that. I'll help you clean it up."

Dex gave me a warm smile. "Thanks. I appreciate it, and I promise, I *will* try to be more or less on time. Maybe then, stuff like this won't happen. And my tools won't be hidden around the shop, my lunch won't be replaced with garbage, and my notes won't be covered in penis doodles."

My eyes widened at hearing all of the offenses my employees had caused him. "Oh my God, I'm so sorry. It will stop, I promise."

Dex blew off my concern with a wave of his hand. "Don't worry about it, Kenzie. You can't come onto a fully staffed team and not expect a little hazing. They're just testing me, seeing if I'll break. I won't," he said with a wink.

"Maybe so, but you shouldn't have to endure it. I'll talk to Myles." Again.

Dex shook his head. "Getting the guys in trouble with Mom won't help my case any. I'll be fine. Don't you worry about me."

I started to tell him that I wasn't worried, but I shut my mouth. Maybe I was. Just a little. But that was because we *needed* him. It had taken John months to find this guy—we couldn't afford for him to get fed up and walk away.

Forcing a smile to my face, I said, "Okay, fine. *Mom* won't interfere." Saying that made me laugh. I'd considered myself a lot of things over the years, but Mom was never one of them.

Dex tilted his head as he stared at me, and those pale eyes of his seemed to bore all the way into my soul. "You have a wonderful laugh, you should use it more."

While it was true that I did seem to have trouble finding the humor in things lately, the way he'd put it, the look on his face…he shouldn't talk to me like that. Like he could sense what I was about to say by reading my expression, he held up his hands again. "Not flirting, just an observation. You seem…overly tense for a person your age."

A long sigh escaped me. "Most people my age aren't trying to get an extremely expensive business up and running. Most people my age aren't trying to swim against the current, with rapids, rocks, and whirlpools trying to suck them under at every opportunity."

His brows furrowed at hearing my overly-dramatic comment. I waved off his concern with my towel. "My problems can wait. First, let's take care of yours."

"Everything is fine," he insisted.

I ran my towel down the gooey slime coating his locker. "No, it's not. But I think there's a way it could be okay. A way that won't get anyone in trouble." Smiling, I told him, "I think it would help everyone adjust if we all went all out together. Did something fun, something… unthreatening. Are you free tonight?"

The smile on his face was oddly affectionate. "Yes, I'm free…"

I felt like there was an innuendo there, but I'd told him I was a no-go, so it must be something else. It had to be, I didn't need him fawning over me. Hopefully, he was just touched that I was truly going to put a stop to the hazing. A plan firmed in my mind as I nodded. "Great. I'll let everyone know we're having a mandatory meeting at Oysters, six o'clock. Don't be late," I said, smiling.

Hayden walked into the locker room then. His eyes were stony as they darted between Dex and me. I shifted my smile to him, showing him that he had nothing to worry about. Still looking between us, he asked, "Everything …okay?" His voice was cautious, wary.

My warm smile turned into a frown. "I was just helping Dex clean up his locker, since Myles decided to give it a shaving cream bath."

Hayden's lips twitched into a ghost of a smile. "Did he? What a shame."

The amusement in his eyes was all too evident. He was impressed with Myles, which meant I was going to have to have a talk with both of them. Again. No matter what Dex said, I couldn't just sit back and allow it to continue. This was a business, not a frat house.

Dex frowned at Hayden's comment. Turning to him, I said, "Nikki is probably looking for you, Dex. Why don't you go check in with her, and I'll finish cleaning up this mess. Oh, and can you tell Nikki about the meeting tonight for me?"

His face transformed as he switched his gaze to me. "Sure thing, boss." He flicked a glance at Hayden, then turned back to me and gave me an obvious, flirty wink. I could almost feel Hayden's tension triple.

He rounded on me the minute Dex was gone. "What the hell was that?"

I sighed as I studied his face. "That was Dex trying to get under your skin...and succeeding." Narrowing my eyes, I said, "You wouldn't happen to know anything about Dex's tools being hidden, or his lunch being taken...would you?"

Hayden cringed, giving me all the confirmation I needed. "Damn it, Hayden, you know how hard it is to come onto an established team. I figured, out of everyone, you'd be the *most* welcoming. Not the least."

Hayden sighed and looked away. When he looked back at me, his face was somber. "I know, and I'm sorry, I just... I still don't like him around you. And I know that makes me look like a Neanderthal, but, well, maybe that's what I am." He frowned. "This is harder for me than I thought it would be."

With a sigh, I stepped close to him and laced my arms around his neck. "I understand jealousy. I *really* do. But if we're going to work, then you need to let it go. Or...*try* to let it go. And trust me, I understand how hard it is to do that."

He gave me a sheepish smile. "And I know how hard you try. Agreeing to hang out with Rodney and Felicia... It blows me away how hard you try." Closing his eyes, he shook his head. "And here I am, allowing myself to be a jackass to someone with absolutely no ties to you, just because I'm…" He opened his eyes, and they were soft with emotion. "Just because I'm scared. I'm sorry, Kenzie. I'll do better."

Smiling, I gave him a soft kiss. "Thank you. I'm your girl, Hayden, and that's not going to change." Pulling back, I smiled even wider. "I could be at the Playgirl mansion with three dozen men like Dex and nothing would change. *You* have my heart…and my body."

Hayden laughed then smirked. "I don't think there is a Playgirl mansion."

"Well, there should be," I said with smirk of my own.

Hayden shook his head at me, then squeezed me tight. "So…what's this about a meeting tonight?"

Remembering my plan, I nodded. "Yeah, tonight at Oysters. Six o'clock. It's mandatory…so I should probably go tell everyone about it."

"What's it for?" he asked.

"It's a *Quit being a dick to Dex* meeting." Hayden laughed, and I smiled. "It's just a chance for us to get to know each other. We need to gel before Daytona. We're running out of time." And I still had so much to do…

Hayden looked thoughtful for a moment, then nodded. "Yeah, okay, I'll go help you spread the word."

"Thank you," I said, giving him a parting kiss.

* * *

After work—and after making sure everyone got the message about the meeting—I headed over to Oysters. Hayden and I walked in together, hand in hand. Eli, Ralph, and

Kevin came in next, followed by Nikki and Myles. I'd given John and my father a pass for the evening—they'd just roll their eyes and make ridiculing remarks about our immaturity. And they'd have a good point. A part of me resented the fact that I had to leave so much crap on my desk to come down here and make everyone play nice...another part of me was grateful for the excuse to set it all aside and have fun with my friends.

The group of us found a table while we waited for the last member of Cox Racing to arrive: Dex. Nikki was fidgeting in her seat while we waited. "He's late all the time, just like you," I told her.

She smiled, then cringed, then smiled again. "You all right?" I asked.

She flicked a glance at Myles, who was ordering drinks from Glenn. She opened her mouth, looked over at me, then pursed her lips. "It's fine... I'm fine."

Wondering if anything more had happened between her and Myles—like she'd changed her mind about risking their friendship for love—I squeezed her hand and whispered, "Tell me later?"

She sighed as she nodded, her eyes locked on Myles the entire time he returned to the table. He sat next to her, giving her a brief smile, but even I could feel the ocean between them. It broke *my* heart, so I could only imagine the turmoil they were going through.

Dex walked in a few moments later. I waved him over and he joined us, taking the open seat to my right. Hayden glanced at him, inhaled a deep breath...and smiled. Grateful that he was genuinely trying, I stood up to get everyone's attention.

The individual conversations died, and everyone looked my way. I was about to speak, when Kevin timidly raised his hand. "Hey, Kenz...you didn't call us all here to fire anybody...did you? 'Cause I really like working for you."

Smiling at him, I shook my head. "No...we're here to drink."

Myles immediately slammed his hands on the table. "Yes!" Standing up, he yelled, "Glenn! Make everything a double!"

The guys all laughed. Nikki cracked a smile and looked at Myles with total adoration. Rolling my eyes at Myles, I looked down at the newbie in our group. "We're here to properly welcome Dex as a Cox Racing member... as *family*. Because as much as you guys hate change, the painful truth is...change is coming, and we need to accept it. Embrace it even."

Everyone shifted to look at Nikki. She flushed, and Myles patted her shoulder, his eyes soft with sympathy... and more.

I raised my hand to get their attention again. "That being said...if the pranks on Dex don't stop, I *will* start benching people." Very deliberately, I pointed at Myles... then Hayden. They shared a look of *Is she serious?* and I immediately let them know I was dead serious.

Leaning toward Myles, I said in my most menacing voice, "Don't test me, Kelley. Defending champion or not, I *will* bench you."

Myles shook his head, then looked over at Kevin. "Still like working for her?"

Kevin laughed, then slapped his hand over his mouth.

With a sigh, I looked around the table. "If the childishness is over...we can drink."

The guys all looked around at each other, then looked at Myles—since he was clearly the ringleader. Rolling his eyes, he muttered, "Fine...we'll stop."

"Good," I said, right as the waitress dropped off a tray of assorted cocktails.

As more drinks flowed, conversations loosened. Myles never approached Dex, but the others did. Even Hayden made an effort to get to know him. By the end of the night, everyone was talking and laughing. Everyone but Myles. Standing off to the side, he watched Nikki and Dex so intently, it was like he was trying to read their lips.

"Hey, Myles. How's it going?"

Frowning, he looked over at me. "Would you really bench me for practical jokes?"

My lips compressed into a thin line. Here was where being a friend *and* a boss was difficult. "I'd hate it, but yeah...if you still did it after I warned you, I'd have no choice. So please don't make me do that, because I really don't want to bench you. You're my best rider." Looking around, I whispered, "Don't tell Hayden I said that."

Myles let out a small laugh, then he sighed and took a sip of his drink. "I won't prank him anymore, I swear." His gaze still locked on Nikki and Dex, he frowned and shook his head. "What are they laughing about? They're always laughing. You should make a rule about *that*," he said, glancing at me.

"She's not into him, Myles. If you'd been paying attention, you would have seen that her eyes have been on you all night."

He turned to me, his expression full of disbelief and pain. "And what am I supposed to do with that, Kenzie? She's still...she's hiding behind a wall."

With a sigh, I nodded. Then I reconsidered. She'd shown me...something...earlier. A crack. "Maybe not, Myles. Don't give up on her. Sometimes all you really need is patience, and time will take care of the rest." My eyes naturally drifted to Hayden. Patience had certainly been our glue. Patience, understanding, and a giant mound of mutual determination.

Myles didn't look as sure as I felt, but he nodded.

He took off not too much later. Nikki watched him go with a conflicted expression, like she wanted to talk to him, but at the same time, she didn't. Eli, Kevin, and Ralph left together, mentioning something about bar hopping. Nikki said her goodbye, and I hurried over to her before she got too far away. "Hey, want to talk now?" I asked.

She looked so vulnerable, I thought for sure I could open her mind to the possibility of saying yes to Myles. But then...she shook her head, and her expression hardened, the crack closing. "I really am fine, Kenzie. No worries. None at all." She smiled, but it did nothing to make her seem happy. Now she just seemed...hollow.

"Nik, come on...let's do a girl's night, just you and me."

She shook her head. "I'm really tired, I just want to go home."

"Movie night?" I asked, not wanting to give up.

Again, she shook her head. "See you Monday, Kenzie."

Unless I was going to force my presence upon her—which would only make her shut down even more—all I could do was watch her walk away. My heart was heavy when I returned to the table with Hayden and Dex.

Hayden frowned as he studied my face. "She okay?"

I shrugged. "She's not talking to anyone, so who knows?"

Hayden studied the table. "Maybe I should stay home tonight, keep an eye on her."

I hated that—I really liked climbing into bed with him—but I was worried about my best friend. "Yeah, that's probably a good idea."

He nodded, then stood up. "I'm gonna get us some more drinks first."

I watched him the entire time he walked to the bar. Dex broke my concentration. "He lives with another woman?"

The smile on my face was both amusement and annoyance. *Why did everyone get hung up on that?* Swinging my gaze to him, I said, "Yes, and it's fine."

Dex shrugged, like he didn't understand, but it was none of his business. His lips pursed in thought as he watched me. "Earlier today you mentioned you were struggling with the business."

I cringed, then shook my head. "If you're worried about your job, don't. I *will* get through this year." Even if I had to take out a loan, I was going to race at least one season as the owner of Cox Racing.

An amused smile lightened his expression. "I'm not worried about losing my job. My concern was for you." My expression turned wary, and he added, "For Cox Racing. I like what I see when I look around the place, I like the…feel of it. And I think the business has real potential. I hate to see things with potential go to waste."

I gave him a disbelieving look. "You like the feel of it? Even with all the hazing?"

He laughed. "Even with all the hazing."

My expression shifted into a frown as I studied him. Was he being serious right now, or was this some strange form of flirting? "Don't take this the wrong way, but what do you know about business? How do you know Cox Racing has potential?"

He bit his lip before answering me. "It's kind of the family business to know these things. I've been watching how businesses work since birth. Watching…and learning."

I blinked in confusion. "Family business? What family business?"

Dex spun his glass. "My father runs a company…no, a corporation. A very successful corporation."

Shock made my eyes widen, then my heart started racing. Could this be the good news I was waiting for? "What kind of corporation? Would they like to see their name plastered over my bikes? Because if you're telling me your dad would sponsor the team, I just might kiss you." Realizing what I just said, I quickly amended, "Figuratively. I just mean I'd be extremely grateful, and relieved, and…and God…that's exactly what Cox Racing needs right now."

Dex cringed. "It's not that kind of corporation, Kenzie, I'm sorry." I felt like he'd just socked me in the gut, then I was mad at myself for leaping to conclusions. I shouldn't have gotten my hopes up like that. Seeing my face, Dex reached out and touched my fingers. "Don't be discouraged. My father might not be the right fit as a sponsor, but the companies he works with...they *are*."

The hope began resurfacing. I subtly moved my hand away from him, not wanting to offend him, but not wanting to encourage him either. "I'm listening..." I told him.

Hayden came back to the table as Dex began explaining the situation. We listened—enraptured, intrigued, and a little confused. When Dex was finished, my mind was spinning with information. Dex's family had money—a lot of money. His father was a big-wig in the corporate world with connections—a lot of connections. Dex didn't even need to work for Cox Racing. He could spend all day on a beach somewhere, sipping overpriced drinks while getting a massage. That kind of carefree freedom was mind-boggling to me. Why was he spending so much of his time working for me, making practically nothing?

Seeing we were stunned, Dex smiled as he looked between us. "I gave you a lot to think about, I can see that. I'll get going, let you...mull it over." We nodded as he stood up. "If you want me to set up a meeting with my father, Kenzie, just let me know."

"Thank you, Dex," I said, my voice quiet.

Dex nodded, then leaned forward, his face earnest. "Um...if the two of you could not say anything to the rest of the team about me...about me coming from money, being a trust fund baby...all that... I'd deeply appreciate it. I do what I do because I love it. I don't want them treating me differently because I don't need the job."

I nodded in response, still overwhelmed by everything he'd told me. "Yeah...no, I completely understand. We won't say anything, I promise."

He smiled at me, a little too fondly. "Have a good night…" Like he suddenly remembered I wasn't alone, he added, "both of you."

Hayden didn't say anything until Dex left the bar. Then he turned to face me. I thought he would comment on the smile, but what he said was, "You realize what his father does, right?"

Biting my lip, I nodded. "He finds struggling businesses and makes them better."

With a sigh, Hayden puts his hand over mine. "No, Kenzie. He finds struggling business and buys them out."

Shaking my head, I said, "That wasn't what Dex was offering though. His father is on the board of every business he's purchased. He could authorize sponsorships from every single one of those businesses. Every. Single. One."

Hayden nodded as he stroked my fingers. "He could. And if he did, Cox Racing would be set, no more worries, ever. Or…he could decide he wants your business, and Cox Racing could become another one of his…acquisitions. A meaningless notch on his bedpost. And you, your team…me…our fate would be entirely in *his* hands." His mouth twitched into a sad smile. "And personally, I'd rather have my life in your hands, than some muckety-muck's."

I inhaled a deep breath as I stared at him in silence. While I agreed with everything he'd just said, all I could think about was how hard it had been to keep everything afloat lately, to keep everything running smoothly, or at all. My hands just didn't feel big enough anymore, and I was filled with fear and doubt. *If I can't do this…your career is over.* At least if it came down to it, and I ended up selling the business to Dex's dad, Hayden would still have a job. *Hopefully.*

CHAPTER 11

A couple of weeks later, every member of the Cox Racing team was on a plane to the first event of the season: Daytona. Every member of the team except Nikki, that was. At the last minute, she'd decided that she was too pregnant to fly. It had truly shocked me that she'd come to that decision on her own, without any interference from anyone. But then I started to worry that maybe she'd decided not to go so she could get a break from Myles. God, I hoped that wasn't the reason.

Myles was on the other side of the plane from me, a few rows back. Every time I turned to look at him, he seemed glum, almost depressed. It was strange to see him so down. He hadn't been this dour since he'd broken his collarbone and had been forced to sit out for a season. And just like back then, I had no idea how to help him.

Dex was in a seat directly across the aisle from me. He was chewing on his nails, looking nervous, and I had to smile at him. "Don't like to fly?" I asked.

He immediately pulled his fingers away from his mouth. "Bad habit, sorry." Looking around the airplane, he shook his head. "Flying doesn't bother me, I'm just... freaking out about the race. I wish Nikki had decided to come. But, of course, her not being there is the entire reason I have a job in the first place."

I gave him a comforting smile. "You'll do fine. Don't stress about it."

His piercing eyes turned inquisitive as he stared at me. "How about you? How is your stress level?"

I knew exactly what he was really asking. Was the business too much? Did he want me to contact his father? I still wasn't sure. Did I want that kind of help? But a meeting never hurt anyone, right? "I was thinking...maybe I *should* meet your father."

Dex smiled. "Well, it's a good thing he's coming to Daytona then."

My eyes widened at hearing that. "Did you invite him knowing I'd say yes?"

His expression grew amused. "While I love the fact that you think I know you that well already...no, I invited him for me. So he could see what I do, and maybe see why I love it."

He frowned, and I tilted my head at him. "He doesn't approve of what you do for a living?"

Dex picked at a napkin on his tray. "It's not that he doesn't approve, he just wants me to do what he does. Help *him*, instead of...myself. But the suit life...that's not me, never has been."

He gave me a charming smile, and I found myself returning it. Then I felt someone poking me in the ribs. I looked over to see that Hayden had removed his headphones and was staring at me. "Everything all right?" he asked, indicating Dex.

I nodded, then told him, "Dex's dad is going to be at Daytona. We're going to meet him."

Hayden frowned at Dex, then leaned in close. "Are you sure, Kenzie? If we do well at Daytona, someone will approach us, wanting to sponsor us. Money speaks louder than politics."

I'd considered that, I truly had, but what if it didn't happen? How long could we go on without a major player backing us? "It's just a meeting," I told him. "I haven't agreed to anything yet."

With a sigh, he nodded. "I can't believe I'm about to say this, but maybe we should talk to Jordan? See how he feels about this idea?"

Chewing on my lip, I pondered that. But while I occasionally went to Dad with questions or concerns, I typically avoided it. I wanted to do this on my own, *succeed* on my own, without Jordan Cox being able to take any amount of credit for it. I might still have a chip on my shoulder when it came to my dad. He'd hurt me so badly…it was a wound that was proving to be slow to heal. And besides, I was pretty sure I knew what he would say—don't do it. Dad could be a little old-school when it came to sponsors.

Not knowing how to explain any of that without sounding petty, I told Hayden, "Maybe."

* * *

Saturday morning, I woke up feeling more alive than I'd felt in a long time. It was race day! God, I loved Daytona. I couldn't believe I was here. It was almost like it was my first race again, like somehow, I was a rookie again—a virgin. Every breath I took was full of eagerness and anticipation. My entire body vibrated with energy, and suddenly every stress the business part had caused me seemed completely worth it. Today was going to be amazing.

Hayden and I went to the garage early, since I had more to do at an event than I ever had before. I was ready though. As was typical, my father beat me there. The first thing he said to me was, "I hope you didn't go out last night. I've seen your times…when you've actually made it onto the track. You were much stronger before you took over the business. You need to be as well-rested as possible, and hopefully that will make enough of a difference."

My smile was tight as I stared at him. Nope. Definitely not asking his opinion about doing business with Dex's father. "You'll be happy to know Hayden and I were in bed by nine o'clock." I knew Dad wouldn't be happy to hear about Hayden and I sharing a mattress…which was exactly why I'd said it.

His lips twisted into a brief, awkward smile, then he excused himself to talk to John. Hayden lifted an eyebrow at me, and I laughed in response. Making my dad uncomfortable seemed to be my new favorite pastime.

The rest of the guys filtered in much earlier than usual. Everyone was pumped about today. Even Myles was somewhat smiling. I almost asked him how he was doing, but if he'd found some semblance of peace, I didn't want to disrupt that right before the race. I'd talk to him afterward.

Dex was the last team member to arrive. He looked really green, like he might throw up…or he already had. "How are you doing?" I asked, rubbing his arm.

His color seemed to come back as he glanced at my hand. I immediately dropped it to my side. Soft smile on his face, he nodded at me. "I'm fine, I'll be fine. It's fine, everything's fine."

I couldn't stop the smirk. "Usually when someone says 'fine' that many times, they're anything but fine."

"Got me." He inhaled a deep breath. "I'm sort of terrified."

Shrugging, I told him, "If you mess up today, all that means is that we didn't train you well enough. Whatever happens today is a reflection on us, not you."

His entire posture relaxed as he absorbed my words. "Thank you. That actually makes me feel better."

"You're welcome. So…when is your dad dropping by?"

"Anytime actually. He said he wanted to wish me luck." He laughed after he said it, then stared at me with adoring eyes.

Feeling uncomfortable, I backed up a step. "Well, come find me when he gets here, okay?"

Dex nodded, and I could feel his eyes on me the entire time I walked away.

When I got back to Hayden, he was grinning ear to ear. "It's almost time," he said. His joy was infectious, and I felt lighter just being near him. The qualifying round had just begun, and once everyone who made the cut was stacked into positions, the race would be on. I couldn't wait.

Not too much longer after that, John let me know that it was time for me to race my qualifying round. Since everything depended on these initial laps, nerves bubbled up inside my stomach. *Breathe. In…out.* Yes, I had to do well on these laps to be included in the race, but there would be no one else out there—no obstacles. Just me and the road. I'd done it before, and I could do it again.

After grabbing my helmet and gloves, I walked up to Dex to get my Ducati. "Is she ready?" I asked.

Dex looked uncertain. "Yeah, I think she's…" Inhaling a deep breath, he calmed his features. "Yes, she's ready."

Grabbing the bike from him, I briefly looked it over. She appeared ready to me, too. "See you in a few," I told him. He gave me a thumbs-up, the smile on his face still overly affectionate. Maybe I shouldn't have lifted his spirits quite so well.

As I walked my bike to the grid boxes, my concern about Dex shifted into thoughts about Nikki. It was so weird not having her there, not seeing her confidence, her certainty in her skills, and in mine. Nikki always thought I'd be number one, every time I raced, and it was only now, when she wasn't here, that I realized how important that unwavering support was. And knowing that she was hurting right now, missing us, missing this world, it made a trace of melancholy seep into my joy. *Hope you're doing all right, Nik. I miss you.*

But being here, living out my dream, quickly evaporated the feeling. Being out on the track filled me with so much radiant energy, I was sure the people watching could see the air shimmering above me. And for a moment, as I watched the lights, I forgot everything that had caused me worry today—the stress and rigors of both owning and racing for a team, Keith Benneti's obvious sneers whenever he saw one of my riders, and the fact that this race would be the first time Felicia and I competed at the same time. All of that slipped away, and all that was left when the light turned green was the thrill of racing. That do-or-die, I-can't-live-without-this feeling, that made everything worth it.

I bolted off the line, not too quick, not too slow. My form was flawless, my lifts and lowers timed to perfection. Everything on the asphalt was going my way, and my grin was a mile wide when I finished the final lap.

As soon as I was able, I glanced up at the scoreboard showing the standings. It gave me an unparalleled amount of joy to see my name listed above Felicia's. *This is how it should have been last year.* But no need to dwell on that misery anymore, because my future was bright. Gleaming, shining, I-need-sunglasses bright. Assuming I could keep Cox Racing going, of course.

Pushing that unwanted thought aside, I scanned the screen, looking for Hayden's name. He'd had a remarkable finish too—third, if he could hold it. Eli and Ralph had done well, too, both making the cut so far. And Myles…he was sitting right at the top. Good. He deserved to be there.

Dex was beaming when I returned my bike to the Cox Racing garage—beaming at the bike. "That was amazing!" he exclaimed. He was standing next to an older man with slicked-back, black hair, wearing a gray suit that looked completely out of place. His father.

Ignoring the sudden flurry of nerves in my stomach, I told Dex, "Thank you. It ran like a dream."

Dex grinned, then indicated his father. "Dad, this is my boss, Mackenzie Cox. Kenzie, this is my father, Richard Covington."

Taking off my glove, I extended a hand to him. "It's very nice to meet you, Richard. Your son is extremely talented."

Dex beamed at me now, and I knew I probably shouldn't have said that right in front of him. He seemed to take praise as encouragement. Richard shook my hand right as Hayden joined us. "It's nice to meet you, Mackenzie. Dex has told me nothing but good things about you."

Hayden's jaw tightened at that, but it relaxed quickly. I indicated him to Richard. "My boyfriend, and fellow Cox racer, Hayden Hayes."

The two men exchanged pleasantries and shook hands, then Richard turned to me. "I'll admit, I don't know much about racing. My son's interest with it has always mystified me. But I'm excited to learn more about your… business."

A strange chill went up my spine, but I released it with a small shoulder roll. "Well, if you have any questions, don't be afraid to ask."

He lifted a dark eyebrow. His eyes were the same shocking shade of blue as Dex's. "My son mentioned that you're looking for investors?"

"We call them sponsors, but…yes. We are…very interested in creating some mutually beneficial partnerships." I had to stop myself from crossing my fingers.

Richard gave me a smile that was both calculated and charming. "I'll keep that in mind. Good luck out there, Miss Cox."

"Thank you," I answered, a mixture of positivity and uncertainty swimming in my gut. Was that a good meeting, that was going to lead to something amazing…or the exact opposite? Only time would tell.

* * *

Waiting for the race to begin was difficult. Now that I was here, now that I'd had a taste in the qualifying round, I just wanted to ride. That was the basis for *everything* I did in my life—the pinnacle. When it was time, we transferred vital equipment and personnel to the pits. John and my father helped get everything and everyone in place. Dex bounced up and down, like he had springs in the bottom of his shoes. His blue and white Cox Racing jumpsuit was streaked with grease, just like Nikki's always used to be. "This is crazy," he told me. "So intense...like a dream. A great dream."

Laughing at his eagerness, I told him, "Listen to John and my dad. They'll help you be where you need to be, do what you need to do." He nodded and smacked his hands together.

The call went up for all the riders to be in their starting positions. Hayden gave me a *Let's do it* grin as he grabbed his bike. I returned his eager expression as I grabbed my motorcycle. *It's time. Finally.*

It was a beautiful day—bright, sunny, clear—a perfect day for racing. As I moved into my appointed spot—in freaking fifth position—I looked around at my competitors. Hayden was above me in third, Eli and Ralph were closer to the back, and Myles was in the lead, his entire body rigid, focused on the goal in front of him. Two spaces behind me, in seventh, was Felicia. As I stared at her perched on her bike, visor down and locked in place, her roving head stopped on me. Even though I couldn't see her eyes, I knew our gazes were connected.

While I'd had an antagonistic relationship with Felicia last season, I didn't feel the same way about her now. I only saw her as a worthy competitor, one I was eager to compete against.

I nodded my head at her in acknowledgement, and she matched the gesture. Then her gaze swung back to someone behind her. Rodney. Sitting up on her bike, Felicia smacked her ass. Rodney flipped her off, and I had to laugh—they reminded me so much of Hayden and me, back in the beginning. Twisting back around to the front, I saw that Hayden was staring my way. His visor was up, and I could see the excitement and love in his eyes—eyes that were only for me. He was ready, too.

Like he knew time was about to run out, Hayden slapped down his visor and faced the front. Almost as soon as he did, the light turned green and we were off. Adrenaline rushed through me as quickly as my motorcycle leapt forward. I accelerated, faster and faster. The euphoria of racing instantly alleviated all of my stresses, all of my troubles. There was freedom in the speed, peace in the danger. God, I loved this.

I kept Hayden's backside in my sights. Like before, he was my sole focus, even now that we were a team, unified. Chasing him made me smile, made me feel like giggling, and passing other riders, I kept pressing closer and closer to him. The outside world shut off, and all that was left was the two of us. Until I felt someone pull up beside me.

Flicking a glance to my left, I spotted Felicia trying to squeeze past me. My attention instantly shifted from Hayden to her, and a renewed sense of purpose rushed through me. *Oh no, you're not beating me.* Not today.

I pressed my bike harder, pushing its capabilities. *Come on, Dex, show me what you gave this baby.* Every turn, I stayed ahead of Felicia, keeping her at bay, and holding my lead. Extending it even. It felt like mere seconds had passed, but before I knew it, they were waving the white flag—one more lap.

Felicia was still behind me, and my heart started thudding in my chest. This was it. I had her, all I had to do was stay the course, keep doing what I was doing, and I would beat her. And, even though this was just one race, beating her today would be the highlight of the season for me. A precedence for every race to follow. And I was *so* close.

Control, maintain focus. Relax, live, breathe. I gathered every scrap of advice, every second of training, and wrapped it around myself, made it my armor. My victory. And somehow, some way, I found it in me, in the bike, to go even faster.

I pulled ahead of her like she was standing still and crossed the finish line seconds before she did. Holy shit... I did it. I got her. And actually... I got *everyone*. I scanned the track ahead of me for another rider, but there wasn't one. Peeking back, I saw Hayden slamming his fist into the air with one finger raised—then he pointed it at me. Number one... I was number...one. Holy, fucking shit.

With my intent wrapped up in Felicia, I'd totally missed passing the last few people...including Hayden... and Myles. Oh my God...oh my God! I'd done it! I was stunned, shocked, and roiling with emotion. Tears coursed down my cheeks, as sobs wracked my body. I'd done it...with no interference, no unknown third party paving the way for me. I'd done it with my skill, my training, my bike, and my team. *We'd* done it.

The racers were slowed, then the top three were ushered to the side for their interviews, and their moment in the spotlight. As soon as we hopped off the bikes and removed our helmets, Hayden grabbed my hand. "Enjoy this moment, Kenzie. You earned it."

His green eyes were full of pride and happiness, and I inhaled a deep breath, savoring every second. Felicia walked slightly behind us, a small smile on her face. She'd come in third, just behind Hayden. Stopping, I waited for her to catch up to us. Around me, photographers and cameras were catching every moment of this, and that somehow felt right.

Felicia stepped up to me, uncertainty in her eyes. We weren't exactly friends. My smile grew as I stared at her. Then I extended a hand, in shared victory, and camaraderie. "Great race, Felicia."

Her smile growing more confident, she grabbed my hand. "You too, Kenzie." She didn't even once look at Hayden, and not because she was purposely ignoring him...he just wasn't her focus anymore.

Two female riders finishing in the top three had the media in a frenzy, and they swarmed us before we even had a chance to get to the designated areas. Poor Hayden was all but forgotten in the rush of everyone wanting to speak to Felicia and me. "Kenzie! Felicia! Tell us how it feels to be first and third!"

It was hard to see with all the flashing lights, and the bodies crowding around me made me a little claustrophobic. Holding up my hand, I drew all the attention to myself. "I think I can safely speak for both of us when I say...it feels freaking amazing!" The reporters laughed, and Felicia nodded as she beamed.

One of the reporters turned to me, shoving a microphone in my face. "Kenzie Cox, you seemed more focused than ever out there. What was going through your mind?"

Even with everything that had been swirling around my thoughts today, there was only one thing in my head as I'd crossed the finish line. I knew the reporters would love it, so with a laugh, I told them, "Beat Felicia. That was pretty much it."

They all laughed again, and even Felicia joined in. "Well, congratulations on your first-place win, a record here at Daytona. One that you took from Felicia, with her fourth place win last year," the reporter added with a wink at Felicia. "You must be very proud of your accomplishment, Kenzie."

Yes, yes, I was proud. Proud of myself, proud of my gender, and proud of my sport. And I felt a newfound determination to see my team succeed. We were going to make it. All of us. Whatever it took.

The minute Hayden and I were released from the winner's circle, we headed back to the Cox Racing garage. Everyone was freaking out when we got there. My ears were assaulted with the sounds of boisterous cheers, the reverberation of multiple stomping feet, and the pops of several bottles of champagne being opened. Most stunning of all, though…my father was smiling. Full-mouth, teeth-baring smile. I'd never seen him grin so big.

Dex looked stunned when we approached him. "I did it," he murmured. Then he shook his head. "I mean you did it. Both of you." His smile was a mile-wide, though, and pride in his abilities shone through his expression.

"See," I said. "I told you you'd be fine."

He laughed then scooped me up into a hug that lifted me off my feet. Hayden immediately interceded, pulling me out of his arms. Stiff smile on his face, he said, "I'll let that one go, because you *did* do an awesome job, but in the future...hands off."

I gave Hayden an amused look, and Dex sheepishly backed away from us. Then I spun around looking for Myles. He'd started out the race so well...but he'd ended up in sixth place. Still a great finish, but honestly, I'd been expecting him to win. Something—or someone—had messed with his head. God, I hoped he worked things out with Nikki soon, for the sake of his personal life *and* his professional life.

I didn't see Myles anywhere, but instead spotted someone I hadn't expected to see—Dex's father. Bright smile on his face, Richard walked over to me, arms stretched to his side. "Congratulations, Mackenzie. I have to say, that was pretty spectacular display of skill and stamina. You...and your team...are quite remarkable." His voice oozed charm.

"Um, thank you," I responded, still suffering from disbelief.

Richard firmed his lips, then nodded. "You'll be hearing from me soon, Mackenzie Cox. Very soon."

His lips curled into a smile that oddly reminded me of the Cheshire Cat from *Alice in Wonderland*. But it didn't really matter if he gave me an eerie feeling, or if my gut told me not to trust him. Richard Covington could be Cox Racing's salvation. And I wasn't about to pass up a chance to save my company. To save Hayden.

CHAPTER 12

Winning Daytona…changed me. Every day I found myself wanting to be on the track more and more. I wanted to be racing, riding, keeping my form as perfect as possible, not stuck in an office all day. But I still had a business to run, a business that was really starting to struggle, and I knew, if things didn't change quickly, I wouldn't get to go out on the track anymore. Not as a Cox Racing rider. Dex's dad was my greatest hope…but I hadn't heard from him yet.

I was kind of a wreck waiting for him to contact me, and as the days turned into weeks, I became convinced that he'd changed his mind about supporting the business. Or maybe that wasn't what he'd meant. Maybe he'd just been implying that he'd love to watch another event, and "You'll hear from me soon" had nothing to do with a sponsorship. Maybe I'd gotten my hopes up for nothing. I prayed that wasn't the case, because after using up so much of our resources at Daytona, Cox Racing was hurting.

"Kenzie, this probably isn't my place to say anything, but…we're kind of running low on…everything. Are you gonna…order stuff…soon?"

I looked up from my desk, grateful for the excuse to stop staring at the multiple past due notices in my hands. "Yes," I told Dex. "I'm working on it, I promise."

Concern on his face, Dex walked around the desk and sat on the edge, close to me. "Is everything okay?"

His eyes drifted to the bills in my fingers, and I subtly flipped them over. "Yeah, it's fine. I'm just...running behind on things. But I'll catch up, don't worry."

Dex's worried expression didn't change. "Your cash flow is running low, isn't it?" Low was an understatement. I couldn't tell him that, though, so instead I gave him a tight-lipped smile. He nodded, understanding. "Maybe I can help. I do have a boatload of cash, just sitting in a bank account doing absolutely nothing."

I immediately shook my head. "No, I can't let you do that. And besides, this is only temporary. Cox Racing had three riders in the top ten at Daytona. There's no way someone won't want to work with us. Soon." That hadn't been the case yet, but surely it would be.

Dex didn't look convinced. Halting any further attempts to give me money, I stood up and hastily arranged some of the more haphazard piles on my desk. "I'll work on getting more supplies in, but not right now. Now, I need to get going to Nikki's baby shower."

Nodding, Dex stood from my desk. "Okay, Kenzie," he said, his voice soft. Then he reached down and grabbed my hand. I was so shocked, I didn't pull away, and he clenched my fingers tight. "Just know you can come to me, for anything. Money, advice... Even though I chose not to follow my father's footsteps, I'm actually quite good at this stuff." He nodded toward my desk.

I tried moving my hand away, but he was holding on pretty tightly. "I appreciate that, and I might even take you up on it, because I'll be honest... I'd rather be on the track than up here. But..." I lifted our joined hands, "...this has to stop. I'm with Hayden. It's highly inappropriate."

He immediately dropped my hand, his pale eyes widening. "I'm sorry, I wasn't even really conscious of the fact that I was..." Closing his mouth, he shook his head. "I just... I like you, Kenzie. You're smart, talented, beautiful, determined..." I opened my mouth to object to all of that, and he held a hand up to stop me. "And taken, and my boss. I understand. I'm just letting you know...it's hard for me to not...make a move on you."

His honesty was...refreshing. And problematic. "If it's that hard for you, maybe...maybe working here isn't a good idea." My heart started thudding in my chest at the thought of him leaving. I'd won Daytona partly because of his skills, Nikki could give birth any day, and Road America was right around the corner... I literally couldn't replace him in time.

Dex's posture straightened, and his expression grew determined. "No. I know you need me, and this is where I want to be. And I actually can ignore a pretty face and do my job. It's just the occasional flirting that I have difficulty controlling. Everything else is...fine."

I wanted to believe that, but his expression was a little too soft...too tender. But there was nothing to be done about it now. I needed him. "Just do your best, please."

A warm smile spread over his face, and I sighed. He reminded me of a preteen girl suffering from a severe dose of puppy love. And I had a feeling no matter how many times I told him I wasn't interested, it wouldn't make a difference. Unless I was outright cruel to him, his crush on me would continue. There was no convincing him out of this.

Giving him a brief smile, I grabbed my things and headed for the door. He followed closely behind. I waited for him to leave the room, then locked my door. Dex was still smiling when I turned back around. "Have a good night with Nikki. I'll see you tomorrow."

I nodded, then asked, "Have you heard from your dad? I was kind of expecting a phone call."

Dex frowned, then shook his head. "I haven't, but that's not too surprising. With his fingers in as many pies as they're in, Dad is...really busy. I'm sure he'll call you soon though. I gave him your number."

I nodded and thanked him, and he practically skipped his way back to the garage. I was shaking my head at him when Hayden walked up to me. "What?" he slowly asked, seeing my expression.

"Nothing. Ready to go?" Hayden nodded and grabbed my hand, and I reveled in *his* touch.

Thirty minutes later, Hayden and I pulled up to the apartment he shared with Nikki. It was a little strange to think of the apartment as part his, since he stayed at my place most nights. Truly, his apartment had become more of a glorified closet than anything else. Nikki was even using his room to store all the extra baby stuff she'd been receiving from her massive family. A family that was all here.

There was barely room for Hayden and me to step into the living room, it was so stuffed with the Ramirez family—Nikki's mom, dad, grandma, grandpa, aunts, uncles, cousins, and her six brothers and their wives and children.

Nikki had told them a few times that they didn't *all* need to watch her open presents, but they insisted on being a tight-knit group, so they all came. That kind of family unity was an oddity to me. My family tried, but… I think we failed more often than we succeeded. Hayden seemed mystified too, but then, his family was…gone. His birth family anyway.

Nikki looked flustered and tired when she gave me a hug. "Thank you for coming," she told me. "I know you're super busy at the track." She frowned after saying it. She hadn't been into work much since Daytona, and it wasn't only because her due date was quickly approaching. We had done so well with Dex at the helm, that I think she felt like she didn't belong anymore. But the truth was the complete opposite of that. So long as Cox Racing existed, Nikki would always be a part of it.

"Of course, I'd come," I told her squeezing her tight. "I want to celebrate every moment with you. And it's been lonely at the track without you."

We separated, and she gave me a sad smile. "No one misses me at the track, Kenzie. You don't even need me…" Her eyes filled with tears, and I instantly squeezed her again.

"Of course, we need you. It's not Cox Racing without you." Pushing her back, I stared into her eyes. "Your spot will always be there, waiting for you. No one is taking it. No one."

I made my face firm, so she'd understand and believe me. She sniffed then nodded. Then groaned. "I did congratulate you about winning, didn't I?"

Laughing, I nodded. "Yes, you did. You were crying at the time, but you did."

Wiping away a stray tear, she shook her head and said, "God, I suck. I'm so sorry for being such a self-absorbed prima donna lately. I really *am* proud of you, Kenzie. Even if it does terrify me that you don't need me anymore, I'm bursting with pride. I hope you know that."

"Well, now that it's clear that I *do* need you, you don't need to be scared anymore. I hope *you* know that."

She cringed, then rubbed her back. "I do. Thank you, Kenzie."

"You all right?" I asked.

She nodded. "Yeah, just sore and achy today. Nothing to worry about."

I shrugged then looked around the packed room. There were about twenty conversations going on as people mingled. Hayden was talking to Carlos, Nikki's eldest brother. Nikki's mom, Marie, was waving at me to come over. Her dad, Juan, seemed to be taking a nap. And then, in the far corner of the room, partially hidden by three of Nikki's sisters-in-law, I noticed Myles. My eyes widened when I saw him staring into a cup, looking dejected. I was so shocked to see him here. He'd been a ghost lately.

"Myles is here," I murmured, not meaning to say it out loud.

Nikki sighed "Yeah, he's been moping the entire time he's been here. He'll barely even talk to anyone." She sucked her lip into her mouth, looking worried and conflicted.

"Have you talked to him much recently? Did he tell you...what happened at Daytona?"

Her dark eyes misted up again. "That wasn't my fault. He can't really blame me for that, can he?"

My eyes narrowed as I tried to understand. "He only told me he lost focus. What did he tell you?"

With a sniff, she shook her head. "He told me…he couldn't stop thinking about me, and the race just didn't seem important anymore. He told me…" Closing her eyes, she shook her head. "He told me he loved me."

My jaw dropped open. "Oh my God, Nikki, that's—"

She interrupted my outburst with a glare. "That doesn't change anything. We can't… We're not—The two of us…" She sighed, unable to finish any of her thoughts.

Putting my hand on her arm, I softly said, "Don't make it so hard. Do you love him?"

Twin tears rolled down her cheeks. "I do…as a friend… I do."

A heavy sigh escaped me. I knew she was lying, but she was lying to herself, so there was nothing I could do about it.

Nikki wiped her cheeks, then cringed again. "God, this is really starting to piss me off," she said, rubbing her back again. "It's been off and on all freaking day."

"Do you want me to get you a hot pack?" I asked, stroking her arm.

Nikki shook her head, then her cringe shifted to a look of outright pain. She breathed her way through it, then as the pain apparently faded, Nikki's eyes widened with some hidden insight. "Oh my God, Kenzie, I don't think this is a backache. I think I'm in labor."

My heart started erratically thudding in my chest. "Oh my God, oh my God…okay…um, we need to…" Looking up, I announced to the packed room, "Uh, guys… I think we need to go to the hospital. Nikki thinks she's in labor."

Myles immediately pushed through the room to get to her. Nikki's mom was close behind him. Taking my place, Myles wrapped his arms around Nikki. She clung to him like he was the only thing keeping her grounded. "It's okay, Nik. I've got you."

She looked up at him, love and fear in her eyes. All the earlier conflict and confusion was completely gone. "I'm scared," she whispered.

Smoothing back her hair, Myles started moving her toward the door. "I know, but it's gonna be okay, I promise." Looking back at me, eyes hard with determination, he firmly said, "Her bag is in her room. Grab it and follow us."

I nodded, then darted down the hallway. Behind me, I heard Nikki's mom screech, "Don't you dare leave without me, Myles Kelley!"

When I got back to the living room, people were hustling out the door, swarming to their vehicles. Nikki's dad was still asleep. I quickly woke him up, then hurried over to Hayden. Lifting the bag, my heart thudding with excitement, I said, "Let's go."

I asked Carlos to stay until everyone left, so he could lock the apartment door, then Hayden and I hopped on our bikes and took off for the hospital. I felt a sense of urgency the entire time we rode, but after we got there, and I fulfilled my duty, giving Nikki's bag to her nurse, there was nothing to do but wait. It was excruciatingly boring.

I passed the time by chatting with Nikki's extensive family. Most of them were excited, but her mom…she was pissed that Nikki hadn't let her into the room.

"She said she just wanted Myles in the room with her, can you believe that?" Her small brown eyes narrowed at me. "Myles, a man she insists is only a friend, instead of me, her mother. It's just not right."

Smiling, I told her, "You know they're more than friends, don't you, Marie?"

With a sly smile she told me, "Of course, I know, I'm not an idiot. I'm just waiting for my daughter to figure it out. So stubborn, that one. Always has been."

Laughing, I nodded. "Yeah, definitely." Sighing, I looked over at the hallway that led to the room where Nikki was probably in a ton of pain. "I hope she's doing all right."

Marie touched my knee. "She's fine, honey. Nikki... she's tough. She had to be with six older brothers." I smirked. While I didn't have personal experience growing up with brothers, I had to believe what she'd said was true.

It felt like we all waited there for days, but in truth, it was only a few hours later when Myles walked into the waiting room with a dazed look on his face. "It's a girl," he whispered. Then he started laughing. "Nikki was right, it's a girl."

I saw a few of Nikki's brothers exchange money—they gambled even more than she did—then I couldn't see anything through the tears clouding my vision. Making my way to Myles, I slung my arms around him so hard, he grunted and backed up a step. "Oh my God, Myles! Congratulations!"

He exhaled a shaky breath as he hugged me back. "Thanks, Kenzie. I'm still...in shock, I think."

Pulling back, I grabbed his arms. "How is Nikki?"

His gaze softened, and tears pricked his dark eyes. "She's doing good. Just tired. She was amazing, Kenzie. Just...amazing..." He seemed awed, overwhelmed, and on the verge of an emotional collapse. I rubbed his arm in support, since I didn't know what else to do for him.

Everyone else gave Myles their congratulations. Once the whole crowd had a chance to acknowledge him, Marie asked a question we'd all been dying to ask. "Can we see her? Her and the baby?"

"You mean Maria?" Myles asked, a small smile on his face as he locked eyes with Marie.

Her jaw dropped, and tears pooled in her eyes. "The baby's name is Maria? After me?"

Myles nodded, then shifted his gaze over to me. "Maria Louise Kelley. Nikki gave her my last name." His voice was shaky, like he was about to lose it. I already was.

Tears streaming down my face, I repeated Marie's question. "Can we see her, Myles?"

He nodded, swiping under his eyes. "Yeah, just a couple at a time though. Nik's wiped."

Marie instantly started speed-walking down the hallway, on a mission to see her daughter. None of us stopped or argued with her.

Hayden and I let the rest of the family see Nikki first, and it was late by the time we strolled into her room. We wouldn't have long to visit, but that was okay. Truly, I just wanted Nikki to know I was here.

Nikki looked barely awake when we got there. Myles was sitting at the head of the bed with her, his arms cradling her close. He was lightly stroking her arm with his thumb, and his cheek rested against her head while she rested hers against his chest. The look on both of their faces was perfect peace. Maria was snuggled in a pink blanket, asleep in her mom's arms. Pausing in the doorway, I lifted my phone and snapped a picture of them. If one of them ever tried to argue with me that they didn't belong together, I was going to tape that photo to their forehead. Or staple it. Whatever drove the point home best. They looked like nothing less than an ideal family right now.

They both looked up when Hayden and I approached the bed. Nikki beamed at me, but I could clearly see the exhaustion on her face. Angling her arms, she showed me Maria's adorable, little scrunched face. "It's she beautiful, Kenzie?" she said, her voice as tired as her face.

Feeling like I was going to cry again, I nodded. "Just like her mom." Myles's gaze shifted to Nikki, and I could see he agreed.

Nikki held her hands out to me. "Want to hold her?"

I had to admit, touching that tiny, fragile-looking package intimidated the hell out of me, but I wanted her too much to let that stop me. Nodding, I carefully removed her from Nikki's arms. She was so warm, like a hot water bottle, and so tiny. Her skin was so soft when I touched her too-small-to-be-real fingers, but what really struck me was how good she smelled.

My grin was huge when I looked over at Hayden, standing close beside me. "Now you want one even more, don't you?" he asked, his face just as bright as mine.

Studying his jade eyes, I nodded. God, I couldn't imagine anything more wonderful than having Hayden's babies. But all in due time. I had too much to do right now. "When the time is right," I told him.

He nodded, then reached out to stroke her arm. "I love how soft newborns are," he murmured.

Nikki giggled, and I looked over at her. "You two...if you make it to the altar *before* you're pregnant, Kenzie, I'll be shocked."

Myles had both of his arms draped across her chest, and she was holding them to her, holding *him* to her. I almost told her if she didn't wise up and marry that man beside her, I wouldn't let her back on the team, but that felt a little...drastic. Since I couldn't flip her off, I stuck my tongue out at her. Myles laughed, then kissed Nikki's hair. God...they were killing me with how perfect they were together. I hoped this finally changed things between them.

My gaze drifted back to Maria. Her eyes were tightly shut as she dozed. There was pitch-black hair peeking out of her pink cap, a lot of it from the looks of it. Whenever she yawned, I giggled. I felt like I could hold her forever, but I knew everyone in this room needed rest, including me.

I was just about to hand her back to Nikki when my phone rang. Even though the ringer was on low, it seemed super loud in this sanctuary. I quickly passed Maria off to Hayden since he was closer. He took her a lot less awkwardly than I had. Hayden had a bit more experience with babies.

Apologizing to Nikki, I headed out to the hallway and answered my phone. "Hello?" I said, my voice soft.

"Mackenzie Cox... Richard Covington, is this a bad time?"

My heart started thudding in my chest. "No, not at all. It's nice to hear from you, Mr. Covington." I bit my lip while I waited to hear if he was going to help me or turn me away.

"I'm sorry it took me so long to get back to you. There were a few meetings I needed to have first."

I crossed my fingers. Meetings were good, right? "Not a problem. It's been busy here as well." Busy with stress, worry, and impending financial doom...not that I was going to mention that.

A soft laugh met my ear. "I can only imagine how swamped you must be, riding and racing at the level that you do. But maybe I can help ease your burden."

The fluttering of hope ticked my stomach. "Oh?"

"Yes, I've spoken with every board member of one of my businesses... Burger Barn. Perhaps you've heard of them?"

My throat accidentally closed on me. Um, of course I'd heard of them. They were one of the top five fast food restaurants *in the world*. "Yes, of course."

I could practically hear Richard smile. "Good. Because they'd like to sponsor you."

It was a good thing there was a chair in the hallway, because I couldn't keep standing. "Oh my God...um...yes, that would be amazing. That would be huge for us, I can't even..." Knowing I sounded very unprofessional, I inhaled a quick breath. "Tell them thank you for me, please."

Richard laughed in my ear. "Of course. And I'm going to speak with some of the others that I think might be a good fit. Keep up the good work, Mackenzie, and I'll do the same."

"Thank you, Mr. Covington."

"Please, we're practically family now. Call me Richard."

Again, a weird shiver ran up my spine. And again, I pushed it away. *This will save Cox Racing.* "And call me Kenzie."

"Enjoy the rest of your evening, Kenzie. I'll speak with you soon."

He disconnected the phone before I could say goodbye. I stared at my phone in shock for a moment, then I leaped out of the chair and started dancing and silently screaming. We did it!

CHAPTER 13

There wasn't a lot of time to get the new sponsor plastered on everything before Road America. It took a week to sign papers and get Burger Barn's official logo, then I had to rush-order decals for the uniforms, vinyl for the bikes, swag for signings. Dex was invaluable during the transition, and I was positive I wouldn't have gotten through it without his help. He even managed to set my tire vendor straight—threatening them with a self-imposed discount if they didn't get our order right. Ever since, they'd been perfect.

Relief filled me, both because money was coming in again, and because I had competent, reliable help in the office. Help that didn't come with hidden strings or belittling remarks. Just the occasional flirting. But it was fine, because letting Dex handle bits and pieces of the business was giving me time to ride as often as I wanted—*finally*—and when it was time to pack up and head out for Road America, I felt fully prepared, ready to take on the world.

Myles was once again dour when we left, but this time, it was for a slightly different reason. Showing me a picture of Maria on his phone, her face frozen in the world's cutest smile, he let out a wistful sigh. "It's only been a day, and I already miss her, Kenzie. Like there's-an-ache-in-my-chest miss her."

Smiling up at him, I asked, "Maria? Or Nikki?"

His grin turned goofy, lovestruck. "Both."

I laughed at his expression, then chewed on my lip. "Are you okay being around her? Nikki? Considering she still doesn't want to..." A sad sigh escaped me. I'd truly thought Nikki would have melted into a relationship with Myles after seeing them at the hospital together, but she still insisted they were better off just being friends. Personally, I thought it was just the exhaustion speaking.

Myles's smile slipped as he put his phone away. "I don't... I'm trying not to think about it. Just focus on Maria, you know?" His eyes drifted to the ground. "But yeah...it sucks, and it hurts like hell that she doesn't... want me." He looked up at me, a small smile on his face. "But at least we're still friends. That's something, right?"

Patting his arm, I nodded. "That's everything." Nikki would come around once she'd adjusted. I was sure of it. But even still... I didn't want to mention that to him, just in case.

Giving him one last squeeze, I went to make sure the rest of my team was ready for the race. Eli was pumped, Ralph was throwing up, per usual, and Kevin was triple-checking everything. John and my dad were quietly talking, and Dex was talking to...his dad. What was Richard doing here?

Hayden approached me while I was staring at Dex and his father. Richard was again wearing a tailored suit that looked completely out of place in this environment. I had a feeling he never dressed in anything else. "He's back," Hayden said.

"Yeah... I wonder why."

"Maybe he just wanted to make sure we did a good job representing his sponsor," he said with a shrug.

Leaning into his side, I looked up at him. "If that's the case, he should be satisfied. It looks like Burger Barn threw up on our bikes. And us," I added, glancing over my shoulder, where I knew the logo was covering almost every inch of my back.

Hayden laughed, then smiled down at me. "It's good to see you more carefree."

There was a very subtle pause in his sentence, but I caught it. "But...?"

Hayden sighed, then looked over at Dex. "I just... I think maybe, you're giving Dex too much freedom...with the business."

Pulling back, I looked at him with furrowed brows. "Not really. All he's done is helped with some vendors, helped get the sponsor logos ordered and applied, made some flight arrangements, and...handled some bills for me."

"Right...he barely did anything," he said, his voice dry with sarcasm.

Shaking my head, I assured him everything was fine. "He knows this stuff, Hayden. He knows what to say to people, knows how to work deals. Hell, he got our embroidery guy to give us 20 percent off the order. A *rush* order. He's got skills I just don't have."

Hayden's eyes, still on Dex, narrowed. "He's got an agenda you don't have either."

I followed his gaze and watched as Richard patted Dex's shoulder in clear approval of...something. "What do you mean? If this is about him flirting with me, because I've already—"

Hayden's eyes snapped to mine, fire in them. "If he doesn't stop that, my fist is going to have some serious words with his face." I pursed my lips at him and he sighed. "But no, that's not what I meant." His raptor gaze returned to Dex. "I just meant…his dad trained him to be like him, and his dad is a shark. He smells blood in the water and attacks. I just worry that, while you think Dex is helping you, what's he's actually doing…is making the cut deeper." His eyes returned to mine, soft with concern. "I don't want you to lose everything because you trusted the wrong person."

My heart softened as I took in his worry for me. I knew Hayden made a good point, but my gut told me Dex was different than his father, that I could trust him. But not blindly. "I'm watching him, Hayden, and if he does something underhanded, then he's gone. It's as simple as that."

Hayden smirked. "No, it's not, Kenzie. You need him. And now, you need his father too. And do you really think Richard Covington will continue to sponsor Cox Racing if you fire his son? You're tied to them, *both* of them." His eyes hardened. "And I hate the thought of you being bound to anybody." A small grin lightened his face. "Except me, of course."

I wanted to laugh at his remark, but my heart was suddenly pounding, and my blood felt chilled. He was right. I needed Dex *and* I needed his father, and if either one of them was screwing with me…there was nothing I could do about it.

The dread inside me tripled when I spotted my father making his way over to Dex and Richard. Then my eyes widened. I hadn't told Dad anything about how I'd secured the Burger Barn account. I'd let him think I'd convinced them with my skills and charm. I seriously doubt I'd fooled him.

"Crap," I muttered, then I hurried over to intercept. Too late, though. Dad was shaking Richard's hand when I got there.

"*The* Richard Covington," my dad said, his eyes wide with recognition. Shit. He'd heard of him.

Richard seemed impressed that he had. "The one and only." His eyes shifted to me. "Mackenzie, I'm so glad to catch you before the race. I have excellent news."

He smiled that grin that creeped me out, but before I could respond to him, my dad grabbed my arm. "Excuse me, Richard. I need to speak with my daughter for a moment."

He pulled me away so hard, my arm started to ache where he was gripping me. "Jesus, Dad, let up," I said, yanking my arm away.

Hayden glared at my father, and Dad glanced over at Dex and Richard. Once he was convinced they couldn't hear us, he turned to me, fire in his eyes. "What did you do, Mackenzie?"

I was surprised by the anger in his gaze, but I was mad, too, at this point. I wasn't a child he could just pull around whenever he felt like it. "What I *did*, was save Cox Racing. You said we needed a big sponsor, so I got one." To make my point, I showed him the logo on my back.

Dad jerked his thumb behind him. "By working with Richard Covington? Do you know who he is?"

Gritting my teeth, I nodded. "Yes. But he's not interested in buying the company. He just wants to help with sponsors."

Dad ran a hand down his face. "I can't believe you got into bed with that man. He will devour this company, Mackenzie, and you won't even see it coming." Determination firmed his face as he straightened. "No, I *forbid* this. Go over there and tell him we don't want his tainted money. Tell him we're done."

My eyes widened at his declaration. "You *forbid* me?" I must have had a violent expression on my face, because Hayden put his hand on my shoulder. "You mistake yourself, Dad. This isn't your business anymore, and while you have my ear, you don't have the reins. *I* do. And I can handle Richard Covington."

Dad's expression hardened, then the stone evaporated in a weary sigh. "For your sake, and the sake of your employees... I hope you're right, Mackenzie."

He walked away without another word, and I realized I was shaking. God... I hoped I was right too.

"That went well," Hayden mumbled beside me.

I twisted to face him. "Oh my God, Hayden, what if he's right? What if I just set a match to Cox Racing. What if this blows up in my face? What if I just ruined everything?"

Hayden grabbed my shoulders, making me look at him. "Remember what you said, Kenzie. You have the reins. *You.* Not your dad, not Richard, you. They're all just advisors, and nothing is going to happen without your consent."

I felt myself relaxing, but my underlying concern was still there. "I could still destroy this, Hayden."

He cupped my cheek, nodding. "You could, but you won't."

"How do you know?" I asked him, mystified. "You just said I was messing up by trusting Dex too much."

Hayden cringed, then shrugged. "Yeah, I know, but I also know you'll fight ten times harder for this business than they will." He pointed over at Richard, who was leaving Dex's side and walking over to us. "To him, Cox Racing is an opportunity. But to you...to you, it's your soul. And in the end, that will make the difference."

Smiling at his answer, I grabbed his hand and turned to face Richard. He glanced at where my father had disappeared before speaking. "Everything all right?" he slowly asked.

"Yes," I stated. "My father just had something he needed to take care of. You said you had news for me?"

Richard's face morphed into a smooth smile. "Yes... another one of my businesses has decided to work with you...with a certain, small condition."

"What condition?" I asked, instantly suspicious.

His smile grew wider. "Nothing to worry about now. We'll discuss the finer details once you get back to Oceanside. Have a great race, Mackenzie."

I wished I could, but my stomach had just turned to lead.

* * *

Even though my dad had made me mad, and Richard had unnerved me, once I got on the racetrack all my worries dissolved, and all that was left was my bike, the road, my teammates and my competitors. And for just a moment in time, life was nothing but sheer bliss.

It ended far sooner than I would have liked it to end, and when it did, I found myself sitting in the top three, just having edged past Hayden and Felicia. While I would have loved to score another first-place victory, I was thrilled with who did nab the honors—Myles. He was beaming with pride as he walked over to be interviewed, and the first thing he said was, "I raced that for my new baby girl, Maria. Daddy misses you, sweetheart. You and your mom."

But as happy as he was in that moment, he was even happier on the plane, when he was flying back to his baby and his best friend. As I smiled at Myles's content face, Hayden nudged my shoulder. "Rodney wants to go out tonight when we get back. To celebrate."

Dex, across the aisle from me, heard him and said, "You're going out to celebrate tonight? Care if I tag along? I don't want to go back to my huge, empty house. I'm too...amped."

Hayden sighed when I looked back at him, then rolled his eyes, then nodded. With a shrug, I told him, "Sure. I've got a ton of stuff to do tomorrow, but I can relax tonight." And strangely, the thought of hanging out with Rodney and Felicia wasn't as repulsive as it once was. When we arrived back in Oceanside, I was almost looking forward to it. *Almost.*

We ended up meeting them at Oysters. Rodney and Felicia were already there when we arrived, sipping on drinks. I had to laugh when I saw that Rodney was drinking The Myles. "I thought you said that was a chick drink?"

He took a long slurp before answering me. "It is. And it's damn tasty too." Standing up, he gave me a quick, friendly hug. "Congratulations on your third-place finish, Kenzie." Letting out a low whistle, he grinned and said, "I never thought there would be a day when I was congratulating a Cox. Keith would have an aneurysm if he heard me say that."

Felicia crooked a smile. "He'd probably fire us if he knew we were here with them."

Rodney lifted an eyebrow at her. "He'd fire me in a heartbeat. *You*, he practically worships."

She shrugged, then looked up at me. "Congratulations, Kenzie. Next time, you're mine though."

I couldn't contain my grin as I sat down. "We'll see."

As Hayden was about to sit down, Dex walked into the bar. He spotted us, waved, then hurried our way. Felicia's lips twisted into a half-grin. "Call me crazy, Kenzie, but I think that boy has a crush on you. I've seen the way he practically falls all over himself when he's around you."

Hayden narrowed his eyes, and her grin grew. "Don't kill the messenger," she told him.

"It's not the messenger I'm going to kill," he murmured.

I subtly elbowed him in the ribs as Dex approached our table. Extending his hand, he immediately introduced himself to Rodney and Felicia. "Hi, I've seen you guys around the track, and at events. You ride for Keith Benneti, right?"

Felicia grasped his fingers. "Yes… Felicia Tucker, nice to meet you…?"

Dex gave her a charming grin. "Dex. Dex Covington. I work for Kenzie."

"Yes, I know," Felicia said, her dark eyes amused. "I've also seen you around the track and at events." Her eyes shifted to mine. "Such a handsome face is hard to forget." She winked at me, and biting back a smile, I restrained myself from flipping her off.

Rodney stood and extended his hand, interrupting Dex and Felicia's overly long handshake. "Rodney. Hey." Rodney's face had the same strained look that Hayden usually got around Dex.

"Nice to meet you." Dex briefly shook Rodney's hand, then took a seat. Like they'd planned it, the only available chair around our table was between Hayden and Rodney. Dex didn't seem bothered as he sat, though. He just seemed happy to be included.

We ordered food, and a few more drinks. While we waited, I said to Dex, "So... I noticed you and your dad talking before the race. It seemed like he was...congratulating you?"

Dex tilted his head, thinking, then he nodded. "Oh, yeah... I'd mentioned how I'd been helping you out with the business side of stuff a little, and he said he was proud of me for kind of following in his footsteps." Dex let out a brief laugh as he shook his head. "He's never actually said those words to me before—*I'm proud of you*. I have to admit, it stunned me a little."

Hayden and I shared a look. Then I tentatively asked Dex, "You don't happen to know what condition he was talking about, do you? With the new sponsor he lined up?"

Rodney's eyebrows lifted. "Dex's dad is finding you sponsors? Fuck, don't tell Keith that. He'd schmooze that guy like he's trying to get in his pants."

Felicia smacked his knee, and he looked her way with a confused expression. "What? You know it's true. Keith is a whore for sponsors."

She frowned, then sighed and nodded. "Yeah, that's actually true."

Dex laughed at them, then shifted back to me. "Sorry, Kenzie. I have no idea what he was talking about. He never mentioned any conditions to me. But I'm sure it's nothing major, just some trivial fine print."

I gave him a smile, but in my experience, fine print was generally *not* trivial.

The rest of the night was surprisingly...fun. Hayden and Rodney did their best to include Dex in the conversations, and with them sitting on either side of him, forcing down his natural flirtatiousness, he didn't say or do anything that made them mad. He even made them laugh a time or two.

When Hayden and I were driving home together, I felt oddly...optimistic. If somehow Rodney, Felicia, Dex, Hayden, and I could all hang out together, then certainly everything else in the universe could work itself out in a favorable manner. Who knows, world peace might even be possible.

Since I was in such a positive mood, I attacked Hayden the second we stepped into my living room. Hopping into his arms, I wrapped my legs around his waist and murmured into his ear, "Take me to bed."

Hayden laughed, but did what I asked and took me to the bedroom. Setting me down, he began stripping off my clothes. Just when he was about to undo my bra, my phone started ringing. "Ignore it," he said, his breath fast.

"It could be Nikki. Or Izzy. Or someone equally important."

He sighed but let me go. Fetching my phone from my bag in the entryway, I glanced at the screen, frowned, then answered it. "Richard...hello. This is a surprise."

Also frowning, Hayden mimed disconnecting the call and walking back to the bedroom. Then he made a movement with his hands that made it all too clear what he wanted to do to me after that. With great difficulty, I managed not to laugh.

"Kenzie, I'm sorry for calling so late. I wasn't sure what time you'd be home, relaxing after a weekend like that."

"It's fine. I was just...watching TV."

Hayden raised an eyebrow, then made that motion with his hands again. I had to cover my mouth that time.

"Yes, well, I just wanted to go over the small request the new sponsor had. If now is a good time?"

All the humor left my body. "Now is great. What do they want from me?" Closing my eyes, I counted to ten. *Please don't let this be something unreasonable, something that will make me say no. I need this to go smoothly.*

"This company, well, they feel their dollars would be better spent on something more visible than stickers on a bike."

I cracked an eye open to see Hayden staring at me, inquisitiveness on his face. "What are they thinking?"

"Television. They'd like to do some cross-promotional ads with Cox Racing. More specifically... with you."

"Commercials? They want me to do...commercials? They know I'm not an actress, right? I mean, have they seen my interviews?" While I was getting better at them, I was far from polished.

Richard laughed in my ear. "They have, but still, they think you'd be a perfect representative, and I happen to agree with them."

"All right... I suppose that could be...okay." Furrowing my brow, I said, "You haven't mentioned the company. Who exactly is our new sponsor?"

There was a very long pause from his end, then he said, "Ashley's Intimates."

I felt like he'd just socked me in the gut. "Underwear?" Hayden's eyes were fire-red hot after hearing me say that. It matched the inferno in my belly. "No, nuh-uh, not on your life. I've worked too hard to prove myself as an equal in this sport. I'm not giving all that up to prance around in my skivvies for the camera." Heat flushed my cheeks as I remembered the humiliation of prancing around for Keith. Never again.

Richard merely laughed at my outburst. "It's a tasteful company, and their plan for the commercial is to flaunt your strength, not your body. Trust me, no prancing will be involved. And before you completely reject the offer, I feel I have to remind you...they are one of the most recognizable names on the planet. Right behind those...male underwear people. You know, the ones who only hire A-list actors to promote their stuff?"

I knew what he was doing—using the fact that men sold sex all the time and it didn't demean them in their profession. But still...this was against *everything* I stood for. But God...it was a massive sponsor. I couldn't flat-out turn it down without looking at every angle. Inhaling a deep breath, I told him, "Before I agree to anything, I want to see—*in writing*—the outline of the entire ad. Every single second of it."

"Done," he said. "You'll have it by the end of the week."

I hung up the phone, already regretting my decision.

CHAPTER 14

I dropped my phone into my bag, then turned to face Hayden. His eyes were narrowed, his jaw clenched tight...he did *not* look happy about what he'd just overheard. "He wants you to do an underwear commercial? *Underwear*? Why are you even considering this, Kenzie?"

A long sigh escaped me. "Because it's *Ashley's Intimates*. That's huge, Hayden. And he said it would be tasteful, not a body parade."

Hayden's jaw clenched. "Right. Just like Keith's job for you was tasteful? I didn't like what Keith did to you back then, and I don't like this now."

His comment about Keith made me cringe, but I understood the similarities. I felt them too. "I know you don't."

"You know I don't. But you're gonna do it anyway." His eyes narrowed as he studied me.

Shaking my head, I told him, "I'm not going to make a decision until I can see the complete picture. If it crosses a line, I'll tell them no. If it's empowering and thought-provoking, well...then, I just might tell them yes."

Hayden rolled his eyes. "How can underwear be thought-provoking?"

Holding out my arms, I twisted back and forth, showcasing the underwear that I was currently wearing. Underwear that just happened to be from Ashley's Intimates. "This doesn't inspire any provoking thoughts?" I asked, my voice low.

Hayden's eyes snapped to my body. His expression grew heated, like he just now remembered what Richard's phone call had interrupted. His lip twitched in amusement. "The thoughts they inspire are more...primal than provoking."

"Hmmm," I said, tapping my finger on my lip. "You might need to show me the difference."

Hayden growled deep in his throat, then jumped over the couch to sweep me into his arms. I laughed the entire time he carried me—over his shoulder—to the bedroom.

* * *

The next morning, Hayden still wasn't sold on the idea. He told me not to do it, no matter what the outline said. I left him stewing about it at the house, while I grabbed my board and caught some waves before work. It was so nice to be back on the water, almost as satisfying as being back on my bike. After spending far too long enjoying the smell of the sea and the sound of the surf, I headed home to change for work.

Hayden was still there, fretting. "Kenzie, I really think—"

"Can we put a pin in this argument? At least until we see the outline?"

He frowned but nodded. "Fine. But don't think you can distract me with sex again. From here on out, I'm immune to your charms, Twenty-two."

God, I really wanted to test that proclamation, but unfortunately, I'd spent way too much time giving my stress to the ocean, and I was massively late for work. Hayden too. So, all I did was smile as I speed-walked to the shower.

I could tell Hayden wanted to bring it up again. Every time I saw him, he just had this look on his face—this *I think you should say no* look. Whenever I ran into him at work, whenever he came over to my house, whenever we met up at the track, he'd give me The Look. In response, I'd pointedly raise my eyebrow, silently telling him to wait for the outline, then he'd roll his eyes and let it go. Until the next time. It was our new "thing."

And by the end of the week, other people had picked up on it. "Kenzie…don't get mad at me if I'm overstepping, but…is everything all right between you and Hayden?"

I was in my office, going over paperwork with Dex. With his help, I'd whittled the stack that had been haunting me for months to almost nothing. We were even starting to prep for next year. Life was so much easier when there was money coming in. Kind of. Some things didn't change no matter what your bank account looked like.

"Uh, yeah, we're fine." Dex's face fell at my answer, like he'd been hoping I'd say the exact opposite. "Why do you ask?" *Please don't say because you love me or something equally flowery and heartfelt. Don't make me the bad guy, you know I'm not available.*

Dex chewed on his lip, then shrugged. "Just...it seemed like you were...fighting or something, that's all."

"We're not, not really. He's just...not thrilled about a request the new sponsor made."

"Ashley's Intimates," Dex said, his voice quiet. His cheeks flushed with color, and his pale eyes looked anywhere but directly at me. What he was thinking about *right now*, was exactly why Hayden didn't want me to do this.

With a sigh, I nodded. "They want me to do a commercial for them, but Hayden thinks it's a bad idea."

Dex met my eyes, surprise on his face. "Oh... I didn't know about that. I think... I think you'd do great." His eyes briefly flicked down my body. Yeah, I bet he thought that.

My smile tight, I told him, "I haven't agreed to anything. I'm waiting to see the proposal. I won't be made to look like a...meaningless sex object." I'd worked too hard to be taken seriously. In this case, the money wasn't worth it.

Dex's gaze softened as he stared at me. "I don't think you'd come across that way, Kenzie. I think... I think even more people would look up to you. Admire you..." A soft smile lifted his lips, and his expression grew dreamy.

Frowning, I said, "I don't want to be admired. Not for my body. The only thing I want people commenting on is my skill on the track."

Dex frowned, his brows drawing together. "That's not what I meant. I didn't mean...just your body. A commercial is like a window, and regardless of what you're promoting, it will show people your fire, your passion, your...soul. That's what I meant by people would admire you. They'll admire your spirit."

His eyes had gotten that wholly-absorbed look again, and I felt like I couldn't let this one go. "Dex, that's really sweet, and it actually kind of makes me feel better about saying yes, but...you know that I'm...that Hayden and I are still..."

Turning his face from me, Dex nodded, "Yes, I know. Happy, in love, destined to be together forever... I get the company newsletter." He looked back at me, a sly smile on his face.

A small laugh escaped me, then I sighed. "Okay. I just wanted to make sure, because sometimes..."

"Sometimes what?" he whispered.

"Sometimes it seems like..." *You're hopelessly in love with me.* Shaking my head, I forced a smile to my face. "Nothing, don't worry about it."

Dex looked thoughtful as he nodded, and an awkward tension grew in the room. Thankfully, it was disrupted by a knock on the door. "Yes," I answered.

Myles poked his head in. "Hey, Kenzie... Dex." Walking forward, he dropped a padded envelope on my desk. "Delivery guy just dropped this off."

I stared at the package, knowing what it contained: the dreaded outline. "Thanks, Myles." He started to walk away, and I looked up at him. "Hey, Myles, give that little girl a kiss for me, okay?"

He gave me a dopey, in-love-with-the-world grin. "Yeah, sure thing. I'm going there tonight after work." I figured he was. Nikki said he was there every night. He even stayed sometimes, sleeping on Hayden's bed, since Hayden was rarely there. Myles really should just move in with her...and Hayden should move in with me. Were we ready for that? Yeah... I finally felt like we were.

Depending on what was in this envelope, of course. With a forlorn sigh, I ripped it open and pulled out the stack of papers. Dex hovered over my shoulder, trying to read it. "So? Clothes or no clothes?" he asked.

I frowned at him, then continued looking through the outline. "Well, damn," I said. "Your dad was right. This is really tasteful. Kind of powerful even..." I looked up at Dex, shock and surprise on my face. "I think this could work."

He grinned, then tucked a strand of hair behind my ear. "Of course, it will work," he tenderly said.

I instantly took a step back and raised a finger at him. He sighed, holding his hands in the air. "I'm just being supportive, and you were about to eat your hair."

Grabbing the papers, I smirked and told him, "Next time let me eat it, okay? I'm heading out. Lock up for me?"

He nodded, looking both wistful *and* amused.

Later that night, I showed Hayden the outline. He had a scowl on his face the entire time he read it, even when he set it down on the coffee table. "Oh, come on," I said, "What's wrong with that? I'm not even in underwear. I'm on a bike, Hayden. Fully clothed. It's kind of awesome."

Frown still on his face, he said, "I know."

I straddled him on the couch. "Then why do you look like that?"

With a sigh, he looked up at me. "Because now I have to let you go away to film this. And that sucks for me. If you hadn't noticed... I kind of like having you around."

"And I like having you around, too...all the time." I bit my lip, wondering if now was a good time to talk about officially moving in together.

Hayden studied my face, then his eyes dropped to my lips. As I felt his need growing beneath me, I decided that maybe that conversation could wait until later...

* * *

Two weeks later, I found myself driving to L.A. to begin filming the commercial. I would be gone for an entire week, a fact that filled me with dread. I'd never left the business for that long, and I was a little worried that everything might fall apart while I was away. But then I remembered that I had a great team, and they could hold down the fort while I was away. For a short time.

John had everything dialed down in the garage, and he would make sure my guys were still training. Not that they wouldn't—every rider had their own motivation to improve. It was usually more difficult to get them off the track than to get them on it. Left to their own devices, riders would blow through every tire and drain every tank of gas. Me included.

Dex was taking care of the day to day business stuff for me. Something that had Hayden—and my father—on edge. They both seemed to think he was going to empty my bank account and skip town or something. Well, that was what Hayden thought. My dad thought Dex was going to change the locks and hand the keys over to his father. Okay. Hayden thought that too.

But I'd been watching Dex for weeks now, and all I saw when I looked at him—besides adoration for me—was the desire to help Cox Racing.

Once I checked into the hotel Ashley's Intimates set me up in—a swanky place with expansive marble floors and crystal chandeliers everywhere—I headed to the studio where the commercial was being filmed. It was an intimidating place, with rows of massive warehouses, people ambling about, and an armed guard at the gate. I felt completely out of place once I stepped inside, but I pushed the feeling to the back my mind. All the people here were just doing their job, same as me.

My first day at the shoot was spent meeting people and getting prepped. After being introduced to the entire Ashley's Intimates publicity team, I met the director, the stylist, the coffee guy...everyone. Then I was whisked away to wardrobe, hair, makeup. Everything was a discussion—the outfit, the bike, the makeup, the hair...they wanted it all to be perfect. I appreciated perfection, but the entire time they worked on me, my mind was split between worrying about work, and worrying about being on camera. I hated being filmed.

But we ended up wrapping for the day without filming a single frame, which was sort of a relief, sort of a frustration—the sooner we finished, the sooner I could get back to the track. I trudged back to my hotel room, exhausted for absolutely no good reason. I called Hayden, but he didn't pick up. I called Nikki, but she didn't pick up either. Myles either. Feeling lonely, I debated calling Dex. But then I decided that was an exceptionally bad idea, so I turned out the light and went to sleep.

The next day we started filming, but it was all racing stuff, so it didn't actually feel like I was acting. They had me with a group of guys on a track, and all I had to do was stay ahead of them. Since the guys they hired weren't professional riders, it was easy. Almost pathetically easy. I kind of felt bad for them.

When we called it quits for the night, I again called my boyfriend. This time, he picked up. "Hey, you," he said in my ear. "How's it going?"

"For being half-naked all day, it's going fine." Dead silence answered me, and I laughed. "I'm kidding, Hayden. Fully clothed, remember?"

He laughed, but it sounded hollow. "Not funny. At all."

I giggled again, then asked him, "Where were you last night? I called but you didn't pick up."

"I…uh…Rodney wanted to go out. We went down to Oysters…"

His voice was strange. Strained. "What's wrong?" I asked.

He let out a huff of breath. "I thought I was just going to meet Rodney, but… Felicia came too. I wasn't sure what to do once she showed up, but… I ended up staying. The three of us hung out all night, and now… I feel really weird about it."

An odd, tightening sensation wrapped around my chest, and my heart surged like the light had just turned green at an event. I had no idea what to say to him. I had no idea how I felt. All that was going through my head was the image of the three of them laughing, drinking… snuggling. But no, it wouldn't have gone down like that. It was nothing. "Oh," I finally said.

Hayden sighed in my ear. "Are you okay, Kenzie? We never really talked about this happening. I never really expected it to happen…"

I wanted to be cool with it, wanted to brush it off like it was nothing, but my chest still felt like the life was being squeezed from me. "It's fine," I whispered.

Now Hayden sounded angry. "I can hear it in your voice that it's not fine, Kenzie. If this bothers you, tell me...don't lie to me."

His words made a sudden surge of anger wash through me, easing the constriction around my chest. "Okay, then yes, it does bother me. I hate the fact that you were chumming around with your ex last night. But I know in my head that's not what happened. You were chumming around with *Rodney*, not her. I'm adjusting to this, but it's not...easy."

Hayden was quiet for a moment, then he said, "Thank you. I just wanted a truthful answer, even if you felt bad giving it to me. And I'm sorry, I wish they weren't a packaged deal, but...they're kind of inseparable."

That made me smile, and thoughts of them—Rodney and Felicia, together, as a couple—flooded my mind. "Yeah, they are. It's a little sickening."

Hayden chuckled. "Not as sickening as the two of us."

A quiet laugh escaped me, and Hayden sighed. "What do you want me to do, Kenzie? In the future, when I want to hang out with Rodney and he brings her...what should I do?"

Wasn't that the million-dollar question? Or maybe it wasn't such a big deal. We'd hung out together so often now, it didn't feel like it did before. So long as clear lines were drawn, so long as it was Hayden and me, and Rodney and Felicia. If it ever became Hayden and Felicia, and Rodney and I dropped by the wayside, well, that was when we'd have a real problem.

With a sigh, I told him, "You have fun hanging out with your friend, and you tolerate his girlfriend's presence."

"Are you sure, Kenzie? Is that something you can be okay with? Truly?"

I took a few seconds to consider that before I answered—I wanted to be sure. "Yeah, I understand that it might happen—Rodney is your friend, Felicia is his girlfriend. The two of you are going to see each other. But Hayden...out of respect to me, could you please not make it a habit? Maybe tell Rodney you want to hang out with just him. You know, a guys' night? I'm sure he'd understand if you told him I'm not completely comfortable with you guys double-dating when I'm not there."

I could practically hear Hayden smiling into the phone. "Of course, Kenzie. That's a perfectly reasonable request. The next time we hang out... I'll talk to him."

A long, relieved exhale left me. "Thank you." Biting my lip, I added, "And Hayden...if he doesn't understand, and he invites her anyway... I need you to tell me right away. I don't want to be blindsided by this."

"Of course, Kenzie. I love you."

"I love you too," I said with a smile. "I'll see you soon."

* * *

The next couple of days were very productive. We finished the racing scenes, then focused on my scenes. Those were the most nerve-wracking for me, but after the first few takes, I relaxed and started having more fun. It was pretty easy too. All I had to do was tear off my helmet, start walking away from the camera, stop, then look back over my shoulder and say, "Strength comes from within, support comes from Ashley's."

Surprisingly, everything went so smoothly, we wrapped a little early. I was eager to get home, get back to the track, get back to Hayden and my friends, so I returned to Oceanside that night, instead of waiting for the morning. The entire time I was riding back, I waffled between going to my house, going to Hayden's place, or going to the track.

While I really wanted to check on the track, make sure Dex hadn't burned the place down, I ended up driving to Hayden's instead. Being apart from him had been harder than I'd expected it to be, and I missed him. Anticipation coursed through me as I raced to his apartment, but it turned to ice the second I pulled into the parking lot...and realized his bike wasn't there. He wasn't home. Why wasn't he home?

Dread pounded through my veins as I tried to imagine where he was. He wasn't expecting me until tomorrow, so he could be anywhere, with anyone, secure in the knowledge that I was miles away, and I'd never find out what he was doing. Tears stung my eyes as I stared at Nikki's door. I could ask her if she knew anything. But she had a newborn. Sleep was a sacred thing to her right now, and I didn't want to be the reason she didn't get enough tonight.

Twisting my bike, I headed out of the lot. I'd find Hayden on my own.

But as I drove deeper into the city, guilt stabbed at me. Hayden and I were working on trust, honesty, and respect. Riding around aimlessly, trying to find my boyfriend, wasn't exactly the epitome of those ideals. I had to believe that no matter where he was and what he was doing, it wasn't something nefarious, something that would hurt me. Maybe he was just out with Rodney. And... maybe Felicia was there, because he hadn't had a chance to talk to Rodney about putting limits on their friendship. If that were the case...then it was...fine. I'd told him I would understand if it happened—on occasion—and while it didn't thrill me, I *did* understand. I just hoped he lived up to his word and told me about it himself. As soon as possible.

Knowing there was nothing else for me to do, I went home. I guess I should have stayed in L.A. and gotten a good night's sleep. There was no reason for me to rush home. Pulling up to my dark, little house, I began to fill with melancholy and loneliness. While I'd always enjoyed the peace of living alone, now it seemed...too quiet at my house. It was better when Hayden was there. Somehow, he made it a home, and not just a place to sleep at night.

Hoping I was able to shut off my mind, so I could get some tiny amount of sleep tonight, I opened my garage door and walked my bike inside. And that was when I noticed something, something that made my heart thud inside my chest. Was I hallucinating, or was that really Hayden's bike tucked beside my truck? He was here? Hayden didn't have a key to my house, but that really wasn't a problem for him—breaking and entering was as easy to him as breathing. My smile was a mile wide as I closed my garage door. He really was here.

Wanting to surprise him, I quietly entered the house. Everything was dark, silent, still. If I hadn't seen his motorcycle, I never would have guessed that anyone was home. I tiptoed down the hallway to my bedroom, then toed open the door. My heart leapt into my throat when I saw the shape of him, under the covers, inside my bed. God…coming home to him waiting for me, was better than anything I could have imagined. He wasn't out doing something mischievous. He was sleeping in my bed, missing me. It stirred something deep inside me, and my heart surged with love.

Careful and quiet, so I didn't wake him, I removed my boots, then my jacket. Eyes locked on his sleeping form, I removed every piece of clothing I was wearing, then gently climbed into bed beside him. He stirred when I kissed his shoulder, his head turning my way in the dark. "Kenzie?" he asked, his voice groggy with sleep.

"Hey," I said, giving him a kiss. "You're here? In my bed?"

He turned to face me. "I hope you don't mind that I broke in. I missed you."

"I'll forgive you, this once."

I leaned forward to kiss him, and I felt his arms slide up my body. He pulled away from my mouth to say, "You're naked."

A low laugh left me, as I found his lips. "I know. You should probably do something about that…"

His chest rumbled with an erotic, amused noise, then he twisted me to my back, and his mouth began trailing down my body. Yes, this was definitely how I wanted to come home every day. I made a mental note to give him one of my spare keys in the morning.

CHAPTER 15

The commercial started playing just a few days before we left for Barber. Nikki was the first one of us to see it, since she was staying pretty close to home with Maria right now. I was a little worried how she was doing financially, but Myles told me he had everything under control. I wasn't sure how that was possible, since Myles was renting a freaking palace with Eli and Kevin and didn't have much to spare. And that was when I overheard Ralph talking to Eli about moving into Myles's room.

"You took his place? Where is Myles living?" God, had he officially moved in with Nikki, and neither one of them had mentioned it?

Eli immediately scuttled off, clearly not wanting to be a part of this. Ralph looked uncomfortable under my gaze, so I tried to relax my expression. Finally, he said, "He's still living there...he's using the couch."

"The couch? He's sleeping on the..." Closing my eyes, I shook my head and went in search of my self-sacrificing rider. I found him in the gym, looking exhausted for more than one reason. Climbing on an elliptical next to him, I said, "Hey, Myles. How's it going?"

He gave me an odd look. "Fine..." Changing his expression, he said, "Have you seen your commercial yet?

Nikki recorded it if you haven't. It's good, Kenzie. You did a great job."

I felt my cheeks heat as I accepted his praise. Hayden had made me watch it last night, and while I had to agree, it had turned out great, I wasn't a big fan of watching myself on screen. "Thanks..." Feeling uncomfortable now, I blurted out what I knew. "You're living on a couch now? Really?"

Myles stumbled a bit on his machine. "Who told you? Kevin?" His eyes narrowed. "They weren't supposed to say anything."

With a sigh, I shook my head. "What are you doing, Myles?"

His gaze focused straight ahead. "I'm helping Nikki and Maria. She can't work right now. Well, she doesn't want to work right now. She wants to be with Maria for a little while longer, and I support that." He looked over at me, a warm smile on his face. "I want to be with her too, but...you know, one of us needs to make money."

His expression turned sad, remorseful. "Why the couch, though?" I asked. "Why don't you just move in with Nikki? It sounds like Ralph took your spot on the lease. It sounds like you're free?"

He cringed, then shook his head. "Nikki's not...that's Hayden's room. I don't want to step on his toes."

"It doesn't have to be Hayden's room," I flatly told him. I'd given him a key, and we were ready for that next, final step—he spent most nights with me anyway and moving his few possessions out of his room would be easy.

Myles snapped his gaze to mine. "Don't, Kenzie. Things are fine the way they are. Don't interfere, please?"

I ground my teeth together but nodded. I could butt out. For now.

Hopping off the machine, I headed to my office. Dex was there, smiling as he looked over the papers on my desk. "Hey, Kenzie. Good morning."

"Morning," I murmured, Myles and Nikki still on my mind.

Dex stopped what he was doing and walked over to me. "Are you okay? Are you worried about the commercial? Because I just saw it, and you…" He exhaled a slow breath. "You looked amazing."

The look on his face combined with how close he was standing to me made me feel guilty. I wished I could turn off his attraction. I had a feeling that commercial had only made it worse. Giving him a half-smile, I sidestepped away from him. "Thank you. No, I was thinking about something else."

He followed me. "Oh? What?"

Safely putting my desk between us, I gave him as patient a look as I could. "It's personal."

Putting his hand on my desk, as close to me as he could get away with, he said, "You can tell me personal things. It's okay."

With a sigh, I collapsed into my seat. "Dex, remember that line we're always talking about? You're starting to cross it."

He immediately pulled his hand back. "Sorry…it's not intentional."

Closing my eyes, I nodded. "How about you help John start packing everything up? We're leaving for Barber in the morning."

I opened my eyes to see him nodding. "Yeah, okay, Kenzie."

He left my office, and I laid my head back on the chair. Much to my relief, he'd done a good job holding down the fort while I'd been away. His help was so nice, but his unending adoration was...grating. I rested there for a minute, letting the stress dissolve.

I was just about to get moving when my cell phone rang. Grabbing it from my bag, I glanced at the screen, then answered it. "Hello, Richard. How are you?"

"I'm excellent, Kenzie. I'm just calling to tell you that Ashley's Intimates couldn't be happier with the commercial. You've made them very happy, so happy in fact, that they'd like to do more with you."

There was something in his voice that instantly put me on edge. "More? Like what?"

"Like another commercial. Something a little more... enticing."

Closing my eyes, I felt the weight of my decisions bearing down on me. Somehow, I'd known that opening the door, giving them an inch, would lead to them wanting something I couldn't give. "Enticing kind of sounds like what I didn't want to do. I'm not pimping my body for them, or anyone."

"Rumor around the league has it that you didn't always feel that way. Didn't you model for your rival, Benneti Motorsports, last year?

My eyes shot open. "How do you know about that? Did you talk to Keith?"

"I talk to a lot of people, Kenzie. It's a vital part of my job. So is research. I've seen photos from your Benneti days, and his outfit for you was anything but tasteful.

What's being offered now is quite a step up, and if I were you, I wouldn't be so quick to dismiss it." There was something in his tone that was almost…threatening. It raised the hairs on the back of my neck.

"Well, you're not me, and I'm not going to do it. I was desperate when I agreed to work for Keith. I'm not anymore, so I'm saying no. Please tell Ashley's that I'm flattered, but that's not the kind of partnership I'm looking for."

The pause on his end was so long, my heart started thundering in my chest. "I'll let them know, Mackenzie, but I feel I need to tell you…they want this to happen, and it's either going to happen with you, or with someone else."

Surprise made my blood go cold. "Are you telling me they'll leave if I don't say yes? Because we have a contract."

"A one season contract. They're free to go their way at the end of the year, as are you, if you feel it's not working out."

My head dropped back to my chair. Was I going to have to do this all over again next year? And again? And again? I really didn't think I could do it over and over. It was too hard, too stressful. "Tell them… I'll think about it."

"Excellent. They'll be thrilled to hear that."

He disconnected the line while I began to speak, and he never heard the words, "I'm only thinking about it. I haven't agreed to…anything."

* * *

As the team headed out to Barber, I found it impossible to tell Hayden about what I'd partially agreed to do for Ashley's. The words just wouldn't form when I was around him, and not being able to talk to him about it filled me with guilt. We'd sworn to be honest, brutally, painfully honest. I *should* tell him. But I wasn't even sure if I was actually going to do it. I might back out, let the sponsor go and try my best to replace them next year. I mean, I still had Burger Barn. Would it really be all that bad if I lost Ashley's?

Yes. It would hurt to lose them. We'd adapted to the higher cash flow, and we relied on them now. I didn't want to say goodbye, but I didn't want the image of me in their underwear plastered everywhere. That was for Hayden's eyes only. Eyes that I suddenly realized had been staring at me for several minutes.

Refocusing my gaze, I locked eyes with him. "There's my girl," he said with a smile. "Where were you? Visualizing the track?"

I loved the fact that he knew my routine and hated the fact that I wasn't doing that. "No, I…" Knowing I had to tell him now, I inhaled a deep breath, taking in the exhaust and excitement from one of my favorite venues. A venue I wasn't even currently enjoying. God, how I wished I could let go of this worry and just *race*. That was my passion, not…management.

"We might lose Ashley's Intimates at the end of the year," I told him, my breath and my heart heavy.

Green eyes widening in surprise, he said, "What? After how great that commercial turned out? How they could possibly be upset with everything you've done for them?"

"That's just it, the commercial was good...too good. Now they want more, and I...don't really want to give it to them."

His brows bunched in confusion. "More? Like...what more?"

I sighed when his eyes flicked down my body, then I nodded. "Yeah, more skin, more sex appeal, more...everything I didn't want to do in the first place. And because I won't do it, they're going to go find someone who will. And we're...screwed."

Grabbing my face, Hayden shook his head. "No, we're not. We have other sponsors, we don't need them." Another weary sigh escaped me. Raising his eyebrows, he repeated, "We don't need them, Kenzie."

Gently removing his fingers from my cheek, I said, "I told them I'd think about it."

His expression instantly turned stony. "No, you're not going to think about it. You don't want to do it, you said so yourself." I opened my mouth and he instantly steamrolled over my objection. "No. You're not doing something you don't want to do. Not again. I'd rather go back to street-racing than watch that happen again."

I pursed my lips, silently telling him that he'd be street-racing over my dead body, then I nodded. "Okay. I'll tell them no. Then they'll leave...and we'll make do."

Tossing an arm over my shoulder, he smiled wide. "Just like we always do. And we'll be fine. I promise."

I wanted to tell him he couldn't promise me something like that, but there was no need. He understood, the same as I did, that the future was fluid, and it was quite possible that we could lose everything. But I knew what he really meant by his promise—that even if we did hit rock bottom, even if we had to live out of my truck…the two of us, we would be okay. And knowing that gave me strength, made me feel like I could call Richard right now, and tell him there was no way in hell I was going to do a racy underwear ad. And then, once I hung up with him, I wouldn't spend one second worrying about what that meant for Cox Racing.

Yes, that was exactly what I was going to do…right after the race.

Putting that stress from my mind, I waited with the rest of my crew until it was time for the main event. When we were told to line up, I grabbed my bike from its resting place and headed for the grid boxes.

Adrenaline and excitement surged through me while I waited under the heat of the afternoon sun for the light to turn green. Hayden had qualified under me, and when I looked back at him, he was shamelessly enjoying the view. Even though he was firmly on the *Don't Do It* side of the Ashley's Intimates issue, I had a feeling he'd been picturing me in a sensual underwear ad all day. He was going to be crawling all over me when we got back to the hotel. I couldn't wait.

Myles had had a great qualifier, ending up in the number one spot again. His head was down, though, while he waited, like he was asleep. I wished I had something to chuck at him, to wake him up, but just as I was thinking that, he shifted his gaze to the sky. Not sleeping then. But still…his head wasn't in the game, that much was clear.

I wished I could check on him, but instead, I stayed glued in my spot, waiting. He'd snap out of it once the light changed. Hopefully.

As we got closer to start time, everyone around me tensed in preparation. My heart seemed loud in my ears, louder than the bikes and the cheering fans. Eyes glued in front of me, I waited for that magical moment. Green suddenly filled my vision, and I released the pent-up need inside of me, surging forward with the pack.

All my day-to-day worries vanished as I pressed my bike harder and faster, and all that existed was the road, my bike, and me. The three of us began a conversation, an intimate, perfect discussion that had me sweeping past the other riders like they were standing still. Time froze, and yet, at the same time, it inexplicably sped up, and before I knew it, the last lap flag was being waved.

I'd been so intent on just enjoying the feel of racing—of letting go—that I had no idea what position I was in. There were three people ahead of me...none of them Myles. Was I in fourth? Had Myles slipped out of the top three? I quickly glanced behind me, hoping to spot him. Instead I saw Hayden, practically eating my rear tire. Grinning, I faced forward. *If you want this, Hayes, you're gonna have to work for it.*

Pressing for speed, hoping to get away from Hayden, I started in on the number three position. The finish line was zooming toward me—my last chance to get around this guy. Feeling like laughing, I gave it everything I had...and passed him mere seconds before our tires crossed the line.

Euphoria burst through me as I pumped my fist into the air. It wasn't first place, but it was top three, and I'd take it. Glancing back, I saw Hayden sitting in the fifth position, just behind the guy I'd passed. I could make out Felicia and Rodney a few spots behind Hayden...but I couldn't see Myles. It wasn't until I stopped and looked at the board that I figured it out. Tenth. He hadn't finished that low…in a long time.

Concern for my teammate, and to a lesser extent, my business, was at the forefront of my mind as I did my mandatory interviews. When my moment in the sun was over, I headed back to the Cox garages, hoping to get some answers. Dex was beaming when I spotted him. "Kenzie! That was amazing! Watching you ride… God, I could do that all day."

"Thanks, Dex," I said.

As I looked around for Myles, Dex added, "Don't take this the wrong way, but you're different when you're out there. Like this weight is off you."

With a sigh, I stopped searching and met his eye. "Racing is all I've ever wanted to do, since I was young. All this…stuff that comes with it…it's not my passion. I can't… I can't stand it," I said, feeling the truth of honesty lightening my shoulders.

Dex looked thoughtful as he nodded. "I can understand that."

He looked like he wanted to say more, but I finally spotted Myles and excused myself. Calling his name, I jogged over to where he was standing, staring at nothing. "Hey, Myles…everything okay? What happened out there?"

He let out a long, weary sigh, then discreetly looked around. "Can we talk, Kenzie?"

Dread filled my stomach. "Yeah…what's going on?"

He ran his hands through his hair, repeatedly. "I just… I'm having a really hard time…here…at events."

With sad eyes, he shook his head. "I'm miserable, Kenzie. I just want to go home."

My eyes widened in shock. "But you won the last race? And you qualified in first again? I thought... I thought racing in Maria's name was making it easier?"

Cringing, he nodded. "Yes...and no. Sometimes the racing is enough to...make up for everything else. Sometimes it's not. The travel, being away...missing Nikki and Maria." His expression morphed into a disappointed frown, and a humorless laugh escaped him. "I knew Nikki would have a hard time being away once the baby was born, but I never expected that I would too. It's been *so* hard on me, so I was thinking..."

"You were thinking what?" I asked, lead forming in my belly.

"Don't kill me, but...what if that was my last race? What if I retired?"

I felt like he'd socked me in the gut, my eyes even stung from the blow. "You can't...you can't retire. You said so yourself...one of you needs to make money."

He fell onto a nearby stool. "I know. And deep down I know I can't *really* quit. I can't do that to you, I can't do that to Nik, and I actually don't think I could stop... I'd miss racing. I just... I can't stand being away from them. From *her*...from Nik."

Sinking down in front of him, I put a hand on his knee. "It's temporary, Myles. Nikki wants to come back, and she will...next season." God, I hoped that was true. She was awfully content being at home with Maria. Shit. What if I lost Nikki...and Myles?

Shaking that horrid thought from my head, I desperately tried to come up with something to sway him. "Why don't...why don't we invite Nikki out to the next race. It's Monterey...it's close. Her mom can watch Maria overnight, and we can all go out...have fun, like we used to." *Please don't leave yet.*

Myles peeked up at me, warmth on his face. "That does sound...nice."

"Good," I said, standing. *Thank God.* "Then it's settled. You aren't quitting."

A dry laugh escaped him. "Yeah... I'm not quitting..."

That should have been reassuring, but there was an odd tone to his voice, a sorrowful sound. And I didn't know if it was because he felt bad for himself, for the fact that Nikki wasn't here...or if he felt bad for me, because he knew that his heart was leaning toward a more permanent solution.

"I'm gonna head back to the hotel, pack up...see if I can't get an earlier flight back." I nodded at him, and he gave me a half-smile. "See you later, Kenzie. And I'm sorry I sucked today..."

I had to swallow the lump in my throat as I watched him shuffle away. I never thought I'd see the day when racing wasn't Myles's entire world. As an owner, it terrified me. But as a friend...it broke my heart.

CHAPTER 16

"I broke him, didn't I? Myles?"

I paused in rocking Maria to look over at Nikki. She was chewing on her fingernails as she watched me. There were bags under her eyes, but the exhaustion was laced with joy. She was exactly where she wanted to be—home with her little girl.

Glancing back down at the little being in my arms, her head fully covered in a shocking amount of black hair, I shrugged and told her, "No…he's fine. He'll be fine."

Nikki snorted. "I watched the race, Kenzie. He qualified first, then wound up tenth. It wasn't his bike, wasn't a crash, wasn't anything but his head. This never would have happened before…" She paused, then sighed. "I broke him. I ruined Cox Racing."

Looking up at her again, I pursed my lips. "Now you're being dramatic. Nothing is ruined. And besides, if it does go down, it won't be because of you…"

She tenderly put a hand on my arm. "I'm sorry you lost Ashley's Intimates. And I totally erased your commercial from my DVR. Those bastards don't deserve you."

"Thanks," I said with a smile. I'd called Richard as soon as I'd returned home from Barber, and a week later, he'd called me back with the bad news. Ashley's was going with someone else next season. I'd lost them. While I was still reeling from the blow, I wasn't surprised. They'd wanted more than I could give them. We just weren't a good fit.

As I sat there, processing that, I cringed internally. I was sitting on news Nikki needed to know. The problem was, I had no idea if she'd be bothered by what I had to tell her. She could be indifferent, not really caring one way or the other, or she could be happy for me. I'd be fine with those last two reactions. It was not knowing if she'd be upset that was making me hesitant to talk to her.

She must have sensed my turmoil, because she cracked open the door for me. "You look like you just ate something sour. What is it?"

With a long exhale, I put my finger in Maria's tiny palm. "As you know, Hayden and I are going away for a long weekend, a little R&R before Monterey. And…when we get back…we're gonna move his stuff into my place." She opened her mouth to speak, and feeling nervous, I quickly blurted out, "He's going to give you two months' rent, and he's going to leave all the furniture…in case you want to get a new roommate. Maybe Myles? Since he's here…so much…anyway."

A small, tight small formed on Nikki's lips. "Was this your idea or Myles's?"

"Mine. But I do think it's absolutely ridiculous that he's sleeping on a couch when you have…" I let that thought linger with a sigh. "Hayden and I are ready. We want to live together, and since Myles is helping you with rent, and you don't really need Hayden's help anymore, we figured…now was a good time."

Her smile relaxed. "It's fine, Kenzie. I saw this coming. The only thing shocking here is that he stayed as long as he did. And I know that was because of me, and I love you both for it, but he should go, so the two of you can... be happy."

She suddenly looked worn to the bone, the joy from being a mom suddenly tucked into a corner, just out of reach. "You could be happy too, Nik. You and Myles both."

Closing her eyes, she shook her head. "We *are* happy. When he forgets that he's...in love with me, we're fine. We're great. It's just when he gets all serious and melancholy...when he starts racing like shit because he's *distracted*." Her dark eyes turned fiery. "I'm seriously going to kick his ass if he does that again. If he wants me, then he should show me by kicking ass out there and winning. I'm not going to be with a Debbie Downer."

I couldn't stop the grin that erupted on my face. "You're going to be with him?"

"If you weren't holding my daughter right now, I'd smack you in the face with a pillow. No, I'm not. I'm just saying...if he wanted to change my mind, *losing* isn't the way to do it."

A small laugh escaped me. "You want him to change your mind?"

"Oh my God, give me my daughter so I can smack you."

I clutched Maria tighter, using her as a shield. Nikki laughed and shook her head. When her expression leveled, I told her, "I'm really glad you're coming to Monterey. It...just hasn't been the same without you."

Nikki frowned. "Yeah... I know." She flipped her lips into a smile. "I'm glad I'm going, too. I've missed you guys."

Because I couldn't resist, I said, "Some of us more than others?"

Nikki groaned and tossed a burp rag at my face. "You can leave now...bitch."

Laughing, I gently handed Maria to Nikki. "Here, take your daughter...bitch."

She laughed, then her face completely transformed as she took the warm, soft, sweet bundle from me. Smiling down at the content mother and daughter, I felt a pull inside me that went all the way to the center of my soul. Someday that would be me. And Hayden. Later, when I was ready to take a couple of years off racing. That would be weird. But as I said goodbye to Nikki, I reconsidered. She'd been so worried to leave, and now the only thing stressing her out was Myles—not the baby, not work. I would adapt, the same as she had.

After leaving Nikki's apartment, I headed to the track. I was meeting Hayden there, then we were taking our bikes up the coast to a quaint bed and breakfast that Hayden had found. The photos of it looked like peace personified, and with how crazy and hectic this year had been, it sounded like heaven.

It was a Wednesday afternoon, so the track was swarming with activity when I got there, both on the Cox side and the Benneti side. As I glanced over to Keith's garages, I saw him out front, talking to Felicia and a person that seemed familiar...somehow. It took a few seconds to register, and when it did, my hands tightened on the handlebars so hard, I thought my fingers might be bruised.

They were talking to an Ashley's Intimates rep; I'd met her when I'd filmed the commercial.

With the way everyone was smiling, I wondered if Felicia was going to be Ashley's new spokesperson. Probably. I had a feeling she would do *everything* I'd been reluctant to do. I wanted to be angry about that, but truly…this wasn't about Felicia and me. It wasn't like she had swooped in and stolen Ashley's from me. I'd said no and turned them away. If she was the one who'd knocked on their door and said yes, then I couldn't blame her for seizing an opportunity. So long as it was *her* idea. If Keith was forcing her to do this, well that, I had an issue with.

I put it from my mind as I rode to the Cox garages. This weekend was about peace, not stress or regret.

Hayden was in the garage when I walked in, talking and laughing with Eli and Ralph. I paused for a moment to watch him. He fit in here now, no awkwardness, no tension, no lingering doubt. He was one of us, wholly and completely, and it made a warm, fuzzy feeling dance across my stomach. My eyes even hazed with happy tears.

"Mackenzie? Are you…all right?"

I turned to see my father staring at me with concern in his eyes. "Yes, Dad, I'm fine," I said, blinking away the stinging sensation.

Dad's lips pressed into a firm line. "I think we should talk about this trip. Now really isn't the time to—"

"To have a life?" I countered, cutting him off. "Now is exactly the time, Dad."

I started heading upstairs, to check on my to-do list before I left town. Dad followed me. "The next race is right around the corner, Mackenzie," he said, walking up to my desk with me.

I started flicking through papers. Most of them had notes from Dex attached to them. He was already handling things. Glancing up, I told Dad, "John and Dex have everything under control. It's just a few days. It will be fine."

Dad shook his head, pursing his lips. He still didn't trust Dex, but he was biting his tongue on that subject. "I didn't mean that, I meant…you should be training. Now isn't the time to slack off."

The words were so familiar, I smiled. "Yeah, I probably should be, but I'm not. Instead, I'm going to spend some quality time with my boyfriend, resting, drinking, and possibly eating pasta."

Dad's frown deepened. "Is this because you lost Ashley's? Because, I really think if we just—"

I held up my hand to stop him. "It's not because of that. It's because… I don't want to sacrifice my happiness, my *life*, for a business…even *this* business. I want balance."

The look on Dad's face turned sympathetic. "You might not believe me," he quietly said. "But I understand that."

I waited for him to say, "But…" but surprising me, he didn't. He simply smiled and said, "Enjoy your weekend, Mackenzie." Then he turned and left my office. I was so stunned, I was still staring at the door when Hayden walked through it.

"There's my girl, ready to go?" Since I was still looking at the door, he turned and glanced over his shoulder. "Something going on?" he asked.

His eyes returned to me, and I locked gazes with him. "I think hell just froze over…but other than that…everything's fine."

Hayden laughed, his expression confused. Smiling, I walked over and laced my arms around his neck. "Yes, I'm ready. Let's go for a ride."

I double and triple checked a few things before we left my office, but there was no need. Dex had already checked them and made notes for me. Amazed and relieved, I left my office with Hayden. Dex was in the garage when I got there, going over Myles's bike with Kevin, like they were both sure what had happened at Barber was mechanical, not mental.

"Hey, Dex, great job upstairs. I was going to take care of some last-minute things before I left, but I see you already did."

Dex turned away from Myles's bike, and his eyes locked onto my hand laced in Hayden's before lifting to my face. "Right...yeah, you're leaving..." With a shake of his head, he said, "After what you said at Barber, I just wanted..." He paused to sigh. "I want coming here to be fun for you, not stressful."

I gave him a sweet, but professional smile. "Well, I appreciate it, thank you."

Dex glanced at our fingers again, and I felt Hayden's hand grip mine tighter. Knowing he was a few seconds away from smacking the longing look off Dex's face, I said, "See you Monday. Call if there's any problems."

That was when Hayden finally did interject. "What she meant was, *don't* call if there are any problems. Fix them yourselves."

"Hayden," I said, glancing up at him.

He shrugged and smiled, and I rolled my eyes. "*Call me* if there are any problems," I repeated, while Hayden subtly shook his head, telling them no again. I let it go so we could walk away and get out of there.

Twenty minutes later, Hayden and I were following the coastline north. The ride along the water was beautiful and relaxing, even with Hayden and I playfully jockeying for position, passing each other over and over again until we finally reached our destination. The B&B Hayden had found was tucked away in an adorable, picture-perfect coastal town. Our room overlooked a marina, filled to the brim with sailboats and small yachts. The tranquil water was the same peaceful shade of blue as the sky, and I felt all my tension melt away as I stared out over the softly rippling waves.

"What do you think?" Hayden asked. Coming up behind me, he wrapped his arms around my waist.

"I think...it's absolutely perfect." I twisted in his arms to face him. "Just what we needed."

He grinned, then nodded over to a corner of the room. "Did you notice the jacuzzi?"

My grin matched his as I nodded. "Yeah. That's the sole reason you booked this room, isn't it?"

A playful smile on his face, he shrugged. "Maybe." Stepping away from me, he said, "I'm going to fill it up. You start stripping."

Feeling like I was going to be spending most of this weekend naked, I laughed as I moved over to the bed. Sitting down, I started undoing my boots while Hayden messed with the water. "Should we get some wine?" I asked. That would be the perfect way to start my mini-vacation.

"Taken care of." Hayden pointed over to the nightstand, where a bottle was resting in a bucket of ice.

"Perfect." Kicking off my boots, I slipped off my jacket.

Leaving the water running, Hayden walked over to me and extended a hand. I took it, and he helped me to my feet. Pulling me in for a hug, he gave me a soft kiss. "I love you. So much."

"I love you too," I murmured under his lips.

He helped me undress, then I helped him. Once we were bare, he grabbed the bottle of wine, I grabbed a couple of glasses, and we made our way to the tub. I carefully stepped inside, then sank into the water with a relieved groan. Hayden raised an eyebrow as he did the same. "I should be the one making that noise come out of you," he said, a smirk on his face.

"You booked the room, so in a way…you did," I answered, a satisfied grin on my face.

Shaking his head, he said, "Later on, you'll be making that noise because of me, and *only* me."

Even while I let out a soft laugh, my body tingled with awareness. I was already looking forward to it. But for right now, I was just going to enjoy doing nothing except relaxing and drinking. Taking a sip of wine, I told Hayden, "Thank you for this. My dad thinks it's a horrible time to get away, but… I think I needed it."

"I know you needed it. And you're welcome," he answered with a smile.

Hayden turned on the tub's jets. I giggled as the soft air exploded against my back, then relaxed into the massage. Hayden watched me for a moment, his expression thoughtful. "What?" I finally asked him.

He looked down before responding. "After the race at Barber, I overheard what Dex said to you…and what you said back to him." I scrunched my brows, trying to remember the conversation, but I couldn't. Hayden continued, "Dex commented that you're different when you race, lighter, less stressed. And he's right...you glow when you ride. Everything about you changes...you're free."

I sighed, then looked down at the water bubbling around us. "Yeah... I wish that was all I had to worry about. I wish the business stuff was..." I sighed, not able to finish my wish.

Hayden grabbed my hand under the water, concern on his face. "What if it could be?"

"What do you mean?" I asked.

He pressed his lips together, like he was trying to think of just the right way to tell me his idea. "Just...your dad ran the company for years. Why don't you let him... handle all the stuff you don't want to touch?"

Wishing I could, I shook my head. "Because he's a control freak, and he can't run the business without running me as well. Besides, he ran it into the ground, remember?"

Hayden nodded, but he still had a strange look on his face, like he thought I should reconsider my thought on the matter. It was a pretty remarkable change of heart, considering how Hayden felt about my father. But that was how strongly he wanted me to love my job again—love *every* part of it again.

I forced it from my mind for the rest of the weekend, and just enjoyed the free time with Hayden. It was bliss. Pure, perfect bliss. I never wanted it to end, but of course, it had to, and eventually it was Sunday morning, and we were packing up to head home. I didn't feel sad about it though. We were getting Hayden's stuff today, officially moving in together. It made leaving our love nest a little easier, knowing we were taking a huge step forward in the process.

"I'm going to miss this place," Hayden said, zipping up his bag. His eyes flashed to the tub and the bed, the two places where we'd spent the most time.

"Me too," I told him. "We'll just have to make sure we come back."

"Maybe for our honeymoon?" he suggested, eyes fixed on his bag.

My heart thudded in my chest as I stared at him. He was asking me to marry him...well, he was probing the marriage waters anyway, seeing how I felt about it. Sucking my lip into my mouth, I bit down, hard. I wanted to say yes, toss my arms around his neck, and ask him to take me to the courthouse today. But, honestly, we weren't there yet. But we would be one day.

Smiling, I told him, "No."

His eyes snapped to mine. Smile widening, I explained. "We're going somewhere tropical for our honeymoon."

His expression relaxed as he realized I wasn't saying no to marrying him. I was most definitely saying yes. "I can do tropical."

"Well, first things first. Let's get you moved in to my place."

I'd never seen such joy in his eyes as he nodded. Grabbing his bag, he slung it over his shoulder, then held out his hand for me. I was just about to grab it when my cell phone started ringing. Hayden pursed his lips, silently telling me to ignore it. "It could be important," I told him.

"They've managed all weekend without you. I hate to admit when I'm wrong, but Dex is actually pretty good help." Telling me that made him look sick to his stomach.

With a laugh, I dug my phone from my bag. "See, I told you he..." My voice trailed off as I saw who it was—Richard. I wanted to ignore it, I really did, but instead, I connected the call. "Hello, Richard."

"Mackenzie, hello. I hope I'm not bothering you."

My eyes flashed to the rumpled sheets. If only he'd called earlier, then I would have legitimately been able to avoid the call. "No, not at all. How can I help you?"

"Yes, well... Burger Barn has come to me with a... request for the next race."

My chest instantly filled with ice. "What kind of a request?"

"Well, first off, they're very impressed with you, and love their partnership with Cox Racing. But...what they'd really love to see, is *you* being Cox Racing's top rider. Apparently, whenever you place in the top three, sales are through the roof. After doing the ad for Ashley's, you're very...recognizable."

I furrowed my brows, confused. "Okay...well, tell them that's my goal at every race. First is always where I want to land, but it's a very competitive sport with some extremely talented racers. I can't guarantee them a win." Hayden looked at me with a questioning expression. I wanted to tell him something, but I wasn't sure what was going on yet.

"Ah, yes," Richard said. "They understand that. But they also understand that Cox Racing is a team, and maybe your team could...help make that happen."

My heart surged and my body tensed, like a coiled spring. "Help make that happen? What is that supposed to mean?"

"It means," he slowly said, "that as a team, your employees should know and understand that sometimes the best way they can help is…by *not* being the best. Their main focus should be on helping you succeed."

My jaw dropped, and heat flamed my cheeks. "I hope I'm misunderstanding you, because it sounds to me like you're asking my riders to purposely let me pass them." Hayden mouthed the word *'what?'* but I lifted a finger, asking him to wait.

"Is that such a horrible request?" Richard said. "You *are* the owner. Shouldn't they automatically let you beat them?"

I could hardly believe what I was hearing. "Absolutely not. That's not how this works, and you can tell Burger Barn to go—" My mouth clamped shut, cutting off my vulgar response. "You can politely tell them that I will never ask my riders to concede their position to me. The race plays out as it plays out, and I hope they can understand and accept that."

"I see. Well, I have to warn you, they'll be very disappointed to hear you say that."

"I don't care. I'm not playing that game."

"Understood. Enjoy the rest of your day, Mackenzie. I'm sorry to have wasted your time."

The phone disconnected before I had a chance to respond, and my heart was racing when I looked up at Hayden's confused face. "What happened, Kenzie?"

Shaking my head, I told him, "I'm not sure…but I think I just lost us our biggest sponsor. I fell onto the bed, feeling utterly defeated. So much for my stress-relieving mini-vacation.

CHAPTER 17

With heavy hearts, we set up at Monterey. We'd received word from Burger Barn a few days ago—they were out at the end of the year. The rejection was a surprisingly emotional blow. My head told me it was just business; my heart screamed in pain. But what they'd wanted me to do…it wasn't the way I operated. Me, or my team. We were better when we pushed each other to succeed when we competed. And we were all itching for a win now.

"We're going out tonight, right? Because everyone on this team looks like they could use a good time. Even John and your dad."

Smiling over at Nikki, I nodded. "Definitely." And then, just because I was so relieved to have her here, I hugged her.

She laughed as she hugged me back. "I leave Cox Racing for a couple of events, and everybody emotionally falls apart. I know you guys love me, but sheesh…get a grip on yourselves."

Laughing, I swiped under my eyes. Damn. She might have a point. I looked around the garage, seeing if we were ready to head out. Everything seemed to be in its place, and everyone seemed…dour. Yes, we were ready for a good time. "Myles," I called out. "Did you find a place for us to go?"

He raised his hands, giving me a *Come on, it's me* look. "Yep, just one question…how do you feel about bugs?"

I instantly crinkled my nose. "If they're on the menu, absolutely not."

Myles grinned. "They're not." He wouldn't elaborate beyond that, though, which wasn't a good sign. But I was too happy to see him excited and relaxed to really care. He was like his old self again.

Dad and John decided to go to the hotel, but the rest of us headed out with Myles. When we got to the bar, and I saw what he meant about bugs, I started belly-laughing. "Cockroach racing, Myles? Seriously?"

Nikki clapped her hands as she jumped up and down. "Oh my God, you can bet on them!" Huge smile on her face, she grabbed Myles's hand and started pulling him to that corner of the bar. "Let's go bet on the green one." Myles grinned ear-to-ear as he followed her.

Hayden smiled down at me. "Want to place a bet?"

"On bugs? No, I think I'd rather drink…maybe dance."

I wriggled my eyebrows at him, and he grinned in response. "That sounds like a great plan."

Eli and Ralph joined Nikki and Myles, while Kevin and Dex joined Hayden and me. As our group laughed and sipped on drinks, I could see the tension in my team dissolving. Everyone seemed to be having a good time, not worrying about things they shouldn't be worrying about anyway. It was my job to worry, not theirs.

Eventually, the gamblers of the group returned to us, and our expanded group made our way to the dancefloor. As Hayden and I danced close together, I saw Dex, laughing with Kevin. Dex's eyes instantly flicked to me, like he could feel me watching him. Not wanting to give him the wrong idea, I quickly shifted my gaze to Nikki and Myles.

They were slow dancing to the fast beat, just like Hayden and me, and Nikki seemed lost in the moment as she threaded her fingers through Myles's hair. I knew, just by looking at them, that they were going to wind up in bed again. And if Nikki stuck to her usual pattern, she'd go back to ignoring Myles in the morning...and he'd be a wreck on the track tomorrow. I needed to get them to stop this cycle, or both of them were going to implode from the strain.

Leaning up, I said in Hayden's ear, "I'll be right back."

I started to pull away from him, but he kept his arms around me. Glancing at Nikki and Myles, he said, "What are you going to do?"

"Something I should have done a while ago."

He grinned, then took my hand, and we walked over to them together. Nikki saw us coming, and instantly took a step back from Myles. *Too late, Nik. I already saw. And it's time you did too.*

Myles looked confused and disappointed by Nikki's retreat. Then he spotted Hayden and me. "Hey guys...are you leaving or something?"

Shaking my head, I crossed my arms over my chest. "No, I'm not leaving until you two stop this."

Nikki's lips pressed into a firm line. She was mad. Myles just seemed even more confused. "Stop what?

We're not...doing anything." I could hear the sadness in his voice, perfectly evident even through the noise and music.

My eyes turned to meet Nikki's. "Yes, you were. You were falling in love and torturing yourselves by not acting on it."

Myles said nothing. Nikki did. "Stop it, Kenzie. That's not what's going on here, and you know it. We're just friends." Her words were laced with anger, but her eyes...they were brimming with terror.

I put a hand on Nikki's arm, trying to quell her temper and fear. "Nik, I saw the look in your eyes...that wasn't friendship. You were five seconds from hopping into his bed again...because you love him."

"You're ridiculous," she said, shaking her head. She started to leave, but Myles grabbed her hand. Hayden shifted his weight, like he now felt really weird about being here. I sympathized, but Nikki needed a firm hand right now. No more walking away.

"Nik? Is that true? Were you gonna sleep with me again? And ditch me again?" Myles asked, his expression turning angry.

"Of course not, Myles. I wasn't going to sleep with you. We're friends, we don't do that." Her eyes were shimmering now, confusion clear on her face.

Something flashed in Myles's eyes. Determination and resolve. He was done with this. "Right," he murmured, then he grabbed her neck, and yanked her mouth to his. She resisted him for all of three seconds, then she melted. Then it was like someone had poured pheromones over the two of them, and as they voraciously made out, I started to worry that they were going to have sex—*right here*.

Hayden quietly laughed as he watched them cave into their long pent-up passion. My cheeks felt on fire as I took in the searching hands and probing tongues. I tried shoving them apart, but it was like trying to tear apart giant magnets—they just didn't want to separate. When they finally did, they were both panting, fire in their eyes.

Holding them apart, my gaze shifted from one to the other. "Myles, are you in love with Nikki?"

His response was instant. "Yes. She's everything to me."

I turned to Nikki, her eyes met mine, and they instantly turned pleading. *Sorry, Nik. You're not getting out of this.* "Nikki…are you in love with Myles?"

She clamped her lips shut, and they started quivering as her eyes watered. "No lies, Nik," I said with a sigh. "No half-truths. No avoiding it. Just tell him what's in your heart. Because…in case you're unaware of this…it's written all over your face."

Her gaze shifted to Hayden, and he nodded at her, a half-smile on his face. "Sometimes it's easier if you close your eyes," he said with a wink.

Nikki rolled her eyes, but then she did what he suggested. Closing her lids, she faced Myles. "Yes," she whispered. "I'm in love with Myles."

My heart surged in my chest, but it was nothing compared to the look on Myles's face. He leaned in to kiss her again, but I held him back with a hand to his chest. To Nikki, I said, "As more than a friend, right? You love him as more than a friend?" She'd escaped that way once… I wasn't letting her do it again.

She peeked an eye open to glare at me, then tightly closed it again. "Yes, I love him as more than a friend. A lot more…" Her eyes slowly opened as she faced him. "I love you so much…and that terrifies me."

Myles's smile grew as he stared at her with wet eyes. "It terrifies me too. But not as much as you telling me we can only be friends. I don't want to be just your friend anymore. I want to love you, I want to raise our daughter with you, I want to grow old with you. And I really want to make love to you…like all the time."

Nikki laughed, then wiped some stray tears off her cheeks. "But what if it doesn't work out? What if we don't work out?"

Surging forward, Myles cupped her cheeks. "What if we do?" he said, searching her eyes.

Nikki searched his face, too, and I held my breath. Finally, she exhaled and said, "I love you, and I want to be with you."

Myles grinned in response. "I want to be with you, too." Then he crashed his lips back to hers.

They didn't stop making out, and I had a feeling I wouldn't be able to pry them apart again. Instead of trying, I patted their shoulders, and said, "See you guys at the track tomorrow. Don't be late. Oh, and don't break him, Nikki. He's got a race to win." She paused long enough to laugh, then sought his lips again.

Shaking my head, I started pulling Hayden toward the doors. My job here was done.

* * *

The next day was bright and beautiful, my favorite kind of race day. The entire team was energized after our night out, especially Myles. He was so radiant when he walked into the garage—holding hands with Nikki—that I had to shield my eyes.

He tossed a rag at me when he noticed what I was doing. "Funny," he said. Then he smiled over at Nikki; she looked just as at peace as he did.

"So," I asked them, "are you guys ready for today?"

Myles met my eyes with a nod. "Absolutely. Let's do this!"

Nikki laughed at him, then tilted her head at me. "What do you mean you *guys*...plural? What is there for me to do?"

With a sly smile, I pointed a finger at my bike. "I was hoping you'd give it a onceover before the qualifiers."

I didn't have to tell her twice. Mammoth grin on her face, she dropped Myles's hand and raced over to my Ducati, practically shoving Dex out of the way. I laughed at her eagerness, then looked over at Myles. "Things good?" I asked him.

His face morphed into sappiness. "So good. She came back to my room, and—"

My hand instantly covered his mouth. "I'm thrilled you two are finally together, but I don't need a play-by-play. Watching you make out was bad enough."

I could feel him grinning under my fingers, so I slowly pulled my hand away. His grin didn't fade when he left to go check on his bike. God, it was so good to see him happy again. Dex came up to me as I was shaking my head at my two stubborn friends. "Hey," he said. "Nikki kicked me off your bike, so I don't really have anything to do..." He frowned as he looked back at her. "Is she coming back already?" He twisted back to me. "I thought I'd have more time…here." His pale blue eyes studied my face like he was seeing it for the last time.

With a sigh, I shook my head. "No, you're not off the hook yet, but as you know…this *was* a temporary position."

He looked overjoyed for the first part of my sentence, then full of melancholy. "Yeah… I know, Kenzie. And it's fine, it's just… I'm really gonna miss it here. I finally feel like I fit in." A small laugh escaped him. "No one's stolen my lunch in at least a week."

I grinned, and a soft sigh escaped him. "I'm gonna miss that smile, too." My expression changed, and he held up a hand. "I know, inappropriate. I'm gonna…go help Kevin." He turned and left, still looking defeated. So much for the entire team being in a great mood today.

"He sure loves it here. It's a shame he'll be leaving next season. I've never seen him so happy."

Recognizing the voice behind me, I spun around, heart in my throat. "Richard, I didn't know you were coming out to the race. I figured…you wouldn't have much to say to me, since all the sponsors you brought my way have decided to not continue sponsoring me."

He gave me a small, sad smile. "This might sound strange to you, but I'm genuinely sorry that those partnerships didn't work out. I tried to line up some more…but seeing two of our biggest companies reject you…well, that spoke volumes, and in the end, they *all* said no."

So that was it. No more opportunities coming from Richard Covington. Deep down, I'd known that was coming, but still…the finality of it stung. "You could have called me to tell me that. You didn't need to come all the way down here."

Nodding, he flattened the lapel of his pristine suit. "True...but I wanted to run something by you, and I felt a face-to-face discussion was best."

There was something about his tone, his face, that tickled the hairs on the back of my neck in warning. "What?"

His lips cracked into a small smile. "Well, I know you're struggling. And I also know you don't really enjoy the business aspect of your sport. You want to be on a bike, not behind a desk." His eyes flashed to his son before returning to mine. Had Dex told him all that? What else had he told him?

"Yeah, I suppose that's true. But...someone has to run the company," I said with a shrug.

"Very true, but that someone doesn't necessarily need to be you."

A rock began to form in my stomach. "Who else would it be?"

"Me," he said, simply and directly.

I was so stunned, all I could do was say, "You..."

He shrugged, like what he'd said wasn't at all crazy. "You've seen some of the companies I'm partnered with. Do you know what they all have in common?"

"No...what?"

"They were all struggling, barely holding on...then *I* stepped in, and made them better. I saved them, and now they're thriving. I could do the same for Cox Racing. I could *save* you, Kenzie. And free you. Wouldn't you like your only worry to be out there...?" He pointed in the direction of the track.

My chest tightened with grief. *God...yes.* I was so tired of the grind, of the stress, of never knowing how we were going to hold on, day to day, minute to minute. But still…my gut told me Cox Racing would never be the same if I gave it to Richard Covington. He'd slice it, dice it…turn it into something I didn't even recognize.

"I…"

He cut me off with a wave of his hand. "Don't give me an answer just yet. Think on it a few days. Have a great race, Mackenzie. And while you're out there, imagine how it would feel if being out there was all you ever had to think about. When you're racing, see how good it feels…to let go."

* * *

I tried to forget what Richard had said, tried to push it from my mind, but it was with me for the rest of the day. After my qualifying lap, when I finished fourth, I wondered what it would feel like if all I had to do was revel in that victory. When I sat in my grid box, waiting to begin the race, I imagined a world where waiting to explode with speed was the only thing on my mind. As the light turned green, and my blood spiked with excitement, I pictured this high being the only feeling I routinely experienced. And as I finished the race in second place, right below Myles, I felt tears of desire coursing down my cheeks.

I wanted that kind of freedom. I wanted all the shit that I didn't care about to be over with, so all I had to focus on was racing. I wanted to stop stressing, stop worrying, stop pulling my hair out in frustration. I wanted the salvation Richard was offering. And wanting that made me feel like I was betraying everything I believed in.

When we got back to Oceanside, I was restless. Hayden, however, was perfectly content as he sat on the couch, like he was ready to pop in a movie and relax all night. I knew I couldn't do that, so I told him, "I'm gonna grab my board and hit the water."

He immediately stood from the couch. "I'll come with you."

His devotion was sweet, but it was clear he didn't actually want to go surfing right now. "No, you just got comfortable. You can stay."

A soft smile on his face, he shook his head. "Kenzie, I know something's going on up there." He pointed to my brain. "Let me come with you, and maybe I can help you figure it out. And if not, then at the very least, I can be your friend and support you, 'cause you look like you need that right now."

Remembering I wasn't alone in this made a weight lift off my chest. "Thank you." God, he was amazing.

Hayden and I got into our swim clothes, then headed out to my truck. It made me smile to see all his things in the garage, and around the house. And sure, he was a little messy, and I had to stop myself from cleaning up after him every twenty minutes…but that was a stress I welcomed. It was just part of sharing a life with him. And I was becoming a little less anal about it. I hoped.

Not too much later we were walking down the partly hidden trail to my favorite secret beach. It was late afternoon, just approaching evening, and we had the beach to ourselves. The sound of the waves crashing against the shore, the tang of salt in the air…my head was already beginning to clear.

We slid our boards into the water, then paddled out beyond the breakers. We sat in silence for a moment on the fluctuating water, waiting for the perfect wave to ride. I spotted one, and Hayden gave me a nod, telling me to go for it. I paddled as hard as I could, gathering speed. When I felt that moment—that second between calm and chaos—I hopped up into a low crouch. Every muscle in my body contracted as I held that fine line of balance. The wave was perfect—swift and surging—and I rode it all the way to the shallows. My heart pounded with the rush of it as I slipped into the gentler water. Much like racing…and Hayden…surfing was a joy I couldn't get enough of. Grabbing my board, I paddled out, to do it all over again.

Hayden and I took turns mastering the waves, until finally, we were too tired to go out again. Sitting at the edge of the shoreline, the crashing waves tickling our feet, we sat in silence, just enjoying the tranquility. Hayden was the first one to break the moment with words. "So…want to talk about what's bothering you?"

I smiled over at him. "Nothing's bothering me now. This is…perfect."

He grinned and nodded. With a shrug, he changed his question. "Want to talk about what was bothering you earlier? You should have been high on life after that spectacular finish at Monterey, but you seemed…off."

With a sigh, I looked out over the darkening water. "I feel like you're not going to like it."

"Which is exactly why you're going to tell me," he said, placing his hand over mine on the sand.

Twisting my wrist, I clenched his fingers. "Yeah, okay…" I turned to look at him. "Richard offered to buy Cox Racing."

Hayden's jaw flexed as he closed his eyes. "I knew it…you told him no, right?"

He opened his eyes to look at me, and I shook my head. "I didn't tell him anything."

"But you're *going* to tell him no, right?" he asked, brows furrowed.

"Honestly? I don't know." I felt tears stinging my eyes as indecision washed through me. "Richard told me to race Monterey imagining that I had nothing to worry about but racing, and I did…and I *loved* it." A tear dropped to my cheek as I stared at him. "I love having Cox Racing back, I really do, and I am *so* grateful for what you and my father did…but I hate being an owner. I hate having to deal with the construction people, the tire people, endlessly buying parts, keeping inventory, having machines break down left and right, making sure there's always enough fuel, and all the freaking paperwork… I just hate it. I want to be on the road, not stressing about money and sponsors and…crap I don't care about."

Hayden was silent a moment as he studied my face. "So, you're going to tell him yes?"

More tears fell from my eyes as I shook my head. "I feel like if I do… I'll lose Cox Racing just like I did before. Sure, he'll make it better, just like he did with his other businesses, but…it will never be the same. And I'm pretty certain he'll fire almost everyone—Kevin, Eli, and Ralph for sure. Maybe even John. Maybe you…" I let out a frustrated sigh. "But maybe I can protect everyone… include them in the deal or something. I don't know. I just don't know." I dropped my head into my hand as stress exploded in my brain in a throb of pain.

Hayden released my hand to rub my back. "Hey, it's okay, Kenzie. It's okay to not know what to do. And it's okay if we just sit out here some more and think about it, without making any decisions. We have time, right?"

Wiping my cheeks dry, I nodded. "Yeah... I've got my sponsors 'til the end of the season, so...we've got until then, I guess."

Smiling, Hayden cupped my cheek. "We'll figure it out before then...but not tonight. Tonight, all we're going to do is enjoy how beautiful it is out here. How beautiful *you* are out here."

He leaned forward to kiss me, and like his lips were magic, my headache—and my worries—instantly disappeared.

CHAPTER 18

I found myself going surfing nearly every morning to clear my head, but I was still a mass of confused, conflicted feelings, and no clear decision was showing itself to me. Sell, don't sell. Stay in control, honoring Hayden's sacrifice and my father's legacy, or take the carrot dangling in front of me, and release the extra burdens so I only had to worry about the one job that truly mattered to me—racing.

The inability to make a decision—*any* decision—was starting to give me ulcers. I couldn't stand not knowing what to do. Hayden tried to help, offering comfort and support, but in the end, the decision was mine, and so was the stress.

Hayden approached me one afternoon, with an unsure half-smile on his face. "This is probably the last thing you need right now, but..."

He moved aside and two people I hadn't expected to see swarmed into my office—Izzy and Antonia. A mile-wide smile on my face, I leapt up from my desk to clasp my arms around Antonia. "Oh my gosh, no...you guys are a welcome distraction. What are you doing here?" I asked, looking over at Izzy.

She grinned as she stood beside Hayden. "Antonia just got the results back from her last checkup. All clean, still. We're going out to get ice cream to celebrate. Come with us?"

I felt the weight of the world on my shoulders, but there was no way I could say no to that request. "Yeah, of course. Absolutely, yes, let's celebrate."

Once I grabbed my bag, we all funneled out of my office. While Antonia and Izzy walked along in front of us, Antonia entranced with everything she was seeing, Hayden leaned in close to me. "I know you're swamped, I'm sorry to spring this on you. They just showed up, and Antonia wanted you to come so badly, I couldn't say no."

I brushed off his concern with a kiss to his cheek. "Don't be sorry. I'm glad they dropped by. Antonia's good health is something we should definitely be celebrating." Every second of every day.

Hayden gave me a warm smile, clearly sharing my silent declaration. When we got to the garage, Antonia had to stop to see Maria—Nikki had come by with her. She'd been doing that more and more frequently, like she was itching to get back to work. "Oh my God, she's so cute!" Antonia squealed.

Myles and Nikki both looked down at their daughter with matching content expressions. Myles had officially moved in with Nikki almost the second we got back from Monterey. And aside from his hours here at the track, he was rarely apart from them. Nikki had told me a couple of times that she was glad her lack of sleep was due to something far more interesting than a baby crying. And Myles, well, he just wouldn't stop grinning. It was sickeningly adorable, but I was thrilled for them.

Before we left, I quickly introduced Antonia and Izzy to the rest of the crew—Eli, Ralph, Kevin, and Dex. Izzy was all smiles as she shook Dex's hand, but he seemed... preoccupied. As we said our goodbyes, he stepped close to me. "Hey, Kenzie, when you get back from lunch, can we talk about...the last tire order?"

My brows furrowed as I wondered what he was talking about—there hadn't been anything wrong with the last order. "Uh, sure, no problem. We won't be gone long."

Dex smiled, then waved goodbye before heading over to my bike. When we were outside, Izzy giggled and said, "He's cute."

A long sigh escaped Hayden's lips. "Don't even, Iz."

She frowned as she looked up at him. "What? I can't think a boy is cute?"

Expression completely serious, he told her, "Not around me, no."

Antonia and I shared a laugh, right as we passed the entrance to the track. Rodney and Felicia were on their bikes, having just finished their training. They popped open their visors when they spotted us, and we all gave them a wave in response.

They rode our way, pulling to a stop before Izzy and Antonia. "Hey Felicia, Rodney," Izzy said. "We were just getting some ice cream to celebrate Antonia's clean bill of health. Want to come with us?"

Felicia smiled brightly at Antonia. "Absolutely. Just let us put our stuff away." She looked over at Rodney, and he nodded. Seconds later, they were maneuvering their bikes back to the Benneti garages.

Izzy's cheeks instantly turned pale. She twisted to meet my eyes. "Crap. Was that okay of me to invite them, Kenzie? I didn't even think about it..."

"It's fine, Izzy," I said with a laugh. "Felicia and I... we've made a lot of progress this year. And there actually *is* something I want to talk to her about."

Hayden lifted an eyebrow at me, but I only smiled at him.

A half hour later, we were all back in Oceanside, walking along the pier, eating ice cream. It was quite possibly the best lunch break I'd ever had. As Hayden carried on a conversation with Rodney, Izzy walked close to my side. "So, Kenzie, how are things going? How are they *really* going? I saw on TV that you lost both of your major sponsors."

I gave her my most convincing, untroubled smile. "It's nothing...this kind of thing happens all the time with sponsors. We'll find someone else soon."

She studied my face for a moment, then smiled, relief in her dark eyes. "Good, I was worried."

"Don't be," I told her. "Everything's going to be fine." I had no idea how it would be fine, or what I should do...but it was all I could tell her.

Felicia left Rodney's side to walk next to Antonia. "I'm so glad to hear you're doing so well," she said, putting an arm around Antonia's shoulders.

Antonia smiled brightly up at her. "Thank you. Uncle Hayden says if my next test comes back clean, he's going to buy my puppy Sundae a playmate."

Izzy's face instantly shifted expressions. Stopping in her tracks, she looked back at Hayden and Rodney. "Hayden, you are not buying my daughter another dog."

Hayden raised his hands. "Every kid needs a dog, Iz."

"Yes, one dog. *One*."

"Mom," Antonia sighed, as she walked back to her. "Sundae needs a friend."

"Sundae has you, Antonia."

Felicia and I continued walking forward as Izzy, Antonia, and Hayden discussed adding another puppy to the family. Well, Antonia and Hayden were discussing it. Izzy was just repeatedly saying no while Rodney laughed. Felicia shook her head as she looked back at them. "Hayden's always had a thing for dogs."

"Yeah," I laughed. "He keeps trying to talk me into one, but I don't know. We're gone so much..." Felicia nodded in understanding. "So..." I slowly began. "Rumor has it you're the new face of Ashley's Intimates."

With a groan, Felicia stopped and face me. "Are you angry?"

"Well, that depends...rumor also says you agreed to do some ads that are a lot...sexier than mine. Is that true?"

Felicia cringed. "Yeah...that was part of the deal. Now are you mad?"

I stared at her a second, then shook my head. "I'm only mad if Keith forced you into it. If this was your idea, great, I hope it works out well for you. If this was his idea, and he's bullying you into it, well, then I'll probably stop by his office after lunch."

Felicia laughed. "Really? You'd pester Keith for me?"

Smiling, I shook my head. "I'd do it for any of the women in this sport, if they were being coerced into something like that. Especially when they're one of the best racers I've ever seen."

Felicia looked genuinely moved by my response. Then she sighed. "While I'd give just about anything to see you go off on Keith...no, he didn't coerce me or bully me. They approached me with the idea and I thought it sounded great. Rodney is ridiculously excited about it," she added with a laugh.

"Good, I'm glad to hear it."

She tilted her head at me, confusion on her face. "You're really not mad that I'm working with them?"

Shaking my head, I told her, "I turned them down... I didn't want to do it. I can't hold anything against you for saying yes when I said no."

She brightened. "Good. Because... I think it would bother me if you were mad at me."

I had to raise my eyebrows at that. She laughed again. "Yes, I know how that sounds, but it's true. You've proven yourself to be pretty amazing, on and off the track. I'm glad we're friends. Or...getting to be." She shrugged and cringed, like she knew I hadn't instantly forgotten last year or anything.

I gave her a soft smile, then nodded. "I'm glad we're...almost friends too."

Rodney ran up to her then, wrapping his arms around her waist and lifting her into the air. The expression on her face was utter joy, and a flash of jealousy raced up my spine. Not because of Ashley's Intimates, not because she was a damn good rider, and not because she was heads over heels for Rodney—I was actually thrilled about that. No, the momentary jealousy was because her life seemed so...simple. All she had to do was ride. All she had to worry about was whether she could work off the extra calories from the ice cream she just ate. Those problems felt so surmountable, while mine often felt too large to tackle.

But I knew that was an illusion. Everyone had more problems than they let on. And Felicia had certainly had struggles in her life. Her lonely childhood, her fear of loving someone too much, walking away from Hayden out of that fear, and then everything she'd gone through last year, when she'd wanted Hayden back but hadn't been able to steal him away from me. None of that had been easy for her.

Every last trace of jealousy vanished as I watched Rodney and Felicia bond. Sure, I'd been having a rough couple of years, but it was nothing compared to what she'd been through. And if she could come out of her darkness with that much hope and optimism, then I had every confidence I'd come out of mine feeling equally positive. All I had to do…was make a decision and stick to it, come hell or high water.

* * *

Once the dog decision was firmly decided—with a resounding no from Izzy—Izzy and Antonia made their way home, and the rest of us returned to work. Hayden was grinning the entire way back to the track—Antonia's news had lifted his spirits. It had lifted mine too, but still, as I walked down the hallway to my office, the indecision over what to do about Richard was like a boulder on my back, hunching me over with its weight.

Like he could somehow feel the heaviness of my burden, Richard called me almost the moment I got inside my office. I considered letting my phone go to voicemail, but I knew no good would come from that, so I picked it up, almost angrily swiping right to connect. "Hello... Richard, how are you?"

"I'm doing very well, Kenzie. It's been a couple of weeks, I was just wondering if you'd made a decision about my offer."

Wearily, I ran a hand down my face; I felt heavier with every breath I took. "Um...actually... I haven't reached a decision yet. I was hoping I could decide sometime after the last race...so I could just focus on riding for the rest of the year."

"You could just focus on nothing but riding every year, Kenzie, all you have to do is say yes."

"I know," I said with a sigh. "But this is a hard decision for me... I hope you understand I need more time."

He was quiet for long seconds. Then he finally said, "All right. I can give you more time, Kenzie, but not an endless amount. At the final race of the year, I want an answer. Deal?"

My eyes were so heavy, they closed on their own accord. "Deal." The line disconnected, and I felt a weight around my heart as I set my phone down. That was it. About a month, and I'd have to tell him if we were moving forward together as a team, or if I was moving on alone. Either answer felt devastatingly solitary.

I heard a small knock on my door while I still had my eyes closed. "Kenzie?" I opened them to see Dex standing there, peering around my open door. "Is this a bad time?" he asked.

Waving him inside, I shook my head. "No, it's fine. What did you want to talk about, Dex? I know it's not the tire order."

Dex frowned as he looked me over. "Kenzie... I..." Pausing, he shut my office door. My brows drew together in confusion and concern as he approached me. "I think something bad has happened, and I think it's all my fault."

Tilting my head, I tried to guess what he might be talking about. "You told your dad I didn't enjoy running a business? That's s okay, Dex. It's not a great secret. Every single one of my guys could have told him the same thing."

Dex shook his head. "No...that's not it."

Anxiety and fear began to tickle my belly. Had he somehow betrayed me? "What did you...? What are you talking about, Dex?"

He swallowed what must have been an enormous lump in his throat. "I introduced you to my father, told you he could help you... I trusted him to not go after you, and I shouldn't have."

My veins filled with ice and lead. "Why shouldn't you have trusted him? What has he done?"

Dex's eyes floated to the ground. The piercing blue was duller today, shadowed by guilt and regret. "The things your sponsors wanted from you...that wasn't typical. And... I overheard Hayden telling the guys about... about Burger Barn's request, about why they dropped us. I don't have any proof, but I'm fairly certain they never asked for that. I'm almost positive my dad lied to you."

Heat flared through my veins, burning away the icy dread. "What? He...lied? Burger Barn never asked my guys to cheat?"

Dex cringed, then shook his head. "I really don't think they did. That's not their style, and... I was talking to a friend of mine who is on the board. They were completely satisfied with Cox Racing, with you, until my father ended things on your behalf." I was so stunned, all I could do was gape at Dex. He cleared his throat and added, "And even Ashley's... I'm 99 percent certain Dad told them you'd do racier ads, got them excited about it, then later told them you were out. I'm willing to bet everything I have that they were as shocked as you."

My mind spun, barely working. "I don't... That doesn't... Why would your dad make sure both sponsors left me? Make it seem like I was leaving them? Burn bridges?"

Dex's cringe grew. "To make you desperate enough to sell. That's where you are right now, isn't it? My dad is your only hope to save the business?" I weakly nodded, and Dex sighed. "Yeah...he gave you a taste of the good life, then snatched it away, because this right here is what he wanted. You...needing him to bail you out."

My stomach tightened in a ball of righteous anger. "So...he planned this?"

Dex sighed, then nodded. "I'm afraid so. He wants Cox Racing, so he tried to crush your spirit, so you'd sell. I've seen him do similar things, with other businesses." His expression hardened. "It's one of the many things Dad and I disagree on."

Some of my anger fizzled as I stared at him. "By telling me about this, you're kind of destroying your dad's plans. Why would you do that?

Dex's eyes avoided mine. "I...he was supposed to stay away from you. Help you with sponsors, legitimately, no funny business. He promised me." Grudgingly, his eyes lifted to mine. "He knew...how I felt about you," he quietly said.

Unease danced in my stomach. "Dex…"

Half-smiling, he shook his head. "I know, Kenzie. I know your heart is with someone else. And I… I like Hayden. I like how happy he makes you." He paused to inhale a deep breath. "I…respect what you guys have, and there's no way I'd interfere with that. But I'd love it…if you and I could be…friends. Do you think that's possible?"

I gave him a genuine smile. "Of course, Dex. I'd love that."

A look of relief crossed his expression. "Good, because what matters to me now is keeping Cox Racing alive. I don't want to see my father hurt anyone here. Everyone has become really important to me. You guys… you're my family now."

"Thank you," Dex," I said, awed by his commitment to the team. "Knowing everything you just told me, well, that makes my decision a hell of a lot easier."

He smiled, his pale eyes glowing with happiness. Then his expression grew serious as he locked eyes with me. "Say no to my father, Kenzie. There's another way, he's not the answer."

I inhaled a big breath, then nodded. No, he definitely wasn't the answer. Not if he was intentionally undermining me. I would fight to the death to keep Cox Racing from him now. But even as I felt that decision sliding into place, I knew… I'd never been going to sell Cox Racing to him. Cox Racing was mine, and it always would be. Struggle or no struggle.

CHAPTER 19

Now that my decision was made, time surged forward, and before I knew it, we were in New Jersey, getting ready for the last race of the year. It was overcast, and the ominous clouds above us were heavy with moisture. They looked like they were going to open up on us at any time, delaying the race or postponing it all together. I hoped the bad weather held off. I was ready for speed, ready to finish this.

Nikki was here, going over my bike while Dex looked over Hayden's. I hadn't been too surprised when Nikki had given Maria to her mom for the weekend, so she could be with us for the final event. As much as she loved her daughter, Nikki's heart and soul yearned to be at the racetrack, same as mine.

Even though no one had any idea what was going to happen next season, everyone was in bright spirits. The shock of losing Burger Barn and Ashley's Intimates had worn off, and they all had faith that I'd be able to make something happen soon. I hoped that too.

But in order to do that, I knew I would need all the help I could get. It was time to truly forgive and forget. "Dad…can I talk to you a moment?"

Dad had been surveying the garage, looking for something to do. And it was only just now that I realized he'd been doing that all year—searching for a way to be helpful, but without stepping on anyone's toes. I'd kept him at arms' length, and for the most part, he'd let me. "Of course, Mackenzie," he said, walking over to me. "What is it?"

"You and I...we've had our ups and downs."

Dad let out a dry laugh. "Yes, you could say that." With a sigh, he shook his head. "I fear most of that was my fault. I tried controlling you, instead of understanding you."

Now it was my turn to agree. "Yes, yes you did. But in the end, you came around, you did the right thing. But instead of moving forward, I held on to my bitterness. I've tried so hard to keep everything going, and I had a huge resource in you, but I refused to use it. My pride got in the way, and I'm sorry for that."

"What are you saying, Mackenzie?" he asked, hope on his face as he scanned my eyes.

"I'm saying... I need your help. No... I *want* your help, with the business end of things. I just want to focus on racing."

His lips cracked into a smile. "It would be an honor to help you. It's all I ever..." Shutting his mouth, he gave me a sheepish smile. "Yes, I would love to do that for you."

A weight lifted from my shoulders as I nodded at him. "Good, there's just one tiny detail I should probably mention."

Dad lifted an eyebrow in question. "And what is that?"

Smiling, I looked over at Dex. "I'm going to hire Dex to manage the business. All your expertise will go to him. He'll be your...well, he'll kind of be your boss. Think you can be okay with that?"

Dad frowned as he looked over at our temporary mechanic. "Are you sure that's wise? Are you sure you can trust him?"

My nod was firm, precise. "I'm absolutely sure...he's proven his loyalty to me. Plus, he's good at this stuff, and he likes doing it. But I'd still appreciate your help, your input. This was your baby for years, and... I want you to be part of it."

Dad gave me a smile that was full of warmth. It was an expression that I still wasn't used to seeing on his imposing face. It didn't last long, and a split second later, he was frowning. "What about Richard Covington? There are rumors around the garage that he has offered to purchase Cox Racing. I've been wanting to ask you...if that was true or not." The disapproval on his face was clear. He didn't like that thought any more than me.

A flash of guilt washed through me as I nodded. I should have talked to Dad about the offer, but I knew what he'd say—don't do it, you'll regret it, Richard's a snake—nothing I didn't already know, nothing Dex hadn't unequivocally revealed to me. "Yes...he made an offer on the business."

Dad's lips firmed, but he was calm when he responded. "And have you decided what you're going to tell him?"

A slow smile spread over my lips as I nodded. "I have...and he's not going to like it."

Dad's pleased smile matched my own.

* * *

Richard showed up just after qualifiers. Not too surprising, since he wanted an answer before the race began. Dressed in an all-black suit, he strolled into the garage like he already owned Cox Racing. His pale eyes swept over the everything he believed was *his* asset, before falling on me. "Kenzie, congratulations on your excellent placement for the race. I have no doubt you'll do well today."

I forced myself to smile at him. "Thank you, Richard."

He gave me that creepy smile he was so good at, the one that made my skin crawl. "So…have you come to a decision?"

Hayden came up beside me. Richard didn't even bother to look at him. He'd dismissed him as important, both personally, and for the business. Heat raced up my spine. "I have…and the answer is no."

I felt people behind me and glanced over my shoulder to see my dad standing there, along with John, Dex, Nikki, Myles…everyone. My entire team was backing me up. Richard's eyes flashed to Dex before returning to me. "No? You're turning down my offer to pick you up, dust you off, and get you back on your feet?"

My fingers fisted. "You're the reason we fell. You're the reason the sponsors left in the first place. You manipulated them, and you manipulated me."

His lips pressed into a fine line, and his eyes again flicked to his son. "I have no idea what you're talking about."

I saw Dex stiffen under his father's steel gaze, then he stood a little taller. "I told her everything, Dad, so don't bother trying to deny it."

Richard's eyes narrowed dangerously at his son. "You told her what? What exactly do you think you know...*son*?" The inflection on the word was laced with contempt. Siding with me on this just might cost Dex everything.

I answered Richard before Dex could say anything. "He told me what I already knew. That going into business with you would be a mistake, that selling Cox Racing to you—to *anyone*—would be a mistake. One that I would regret for the rest of my life. I have enough regrets... I don't need another one, so I'm saying no, and ending this partnership."

Richard's fiery gaze turned to me. "Fine. I'll just wait for Cox Racing's inevitable failure. Then I'll swoop in and pick up the pieces. Regardless, in the end, Cox Racing will be mine." He spun to leave, then stopped and looked back at Dex. "I hope you understand just what you've done today, son. Just what you've...sacrificed."

Dex swallowed, then nodded. "I do, and I'd do it again. You gave me your word, Dad." His voice was just as contemptuous as Richard's had been earlier.

Richard shook his head as he continued on to the exit. Once he was gone, I turned to Dex. "What did he mean by that? What did you sacrifice?"

He gave me a sad smile. "I'm fairly certain when I wake up in the morning, my trust fund will be gone." My eyes—and the eyes of everyone around me—widened in surprise. Dex looked at all of us, then held up a hand. "It's okay, I didn't need it or want it. I'm doing what I want to do. I'm happy here." He frowned as he looked at me. "Assuming I still have a job next season."

Nodding, I told him, "For as long as Cox Racing exists, you have a job here."

My father smiled at him. "You're going to be my boss. You're going to run the company with me."

Dex's eyes grew as wide as saucers. Locking on me, he asked, "Is that true? Is that what you want me to do?"

I glanced at Hayden, then nodded. "If you'll take it, yes. I would love for you to do all the crap I don't want to do. And when you're not busy with that, I'd like you to help Nikki and Kevin, because your skill with a bike can't be denied."

Dex's eyes watered as he looked around the garage. "I'd be honored to be a permanent part of the team."

Eli, Ralph, and the others congratulated him. Over all their praise, I told the group, "Don't get too excited, guys. This could very well be Cox Racing's last event."

A sad sigh left me as my chest filled with defeat. Myles grinned at me. He shared a look of optimism with Nikki, then said, "No, it's not the end, Kenzie. This is just the beginning. Trust me."

I kept Myles's words with me, deep inside my heart, as I lined up for the race. I was in third again, Myles just above me, Hayden just below. Myles looked over at me while we waited, then gave me a thumbs-up. Grinning under my helmet, I nodded a thanks to him, then looked back at Hayden. He was staring my way, and I could almost see the satisfied smile on his face. He was in his happy place, same as me.

Letting all thoughts about my team and my teammates fall to the very back of my brain, I focused all my attention on the light, willing it to change color. When it did, I surged forward. My heart pounded with excitement, adrenaline, and joy. And the fact that, one way or another, I'd never have to deal with the minutia of day-to-day business crap made that joy ten times as potent. I was truly free.

I zipped in and out of turns with that thought forefront on my mind. No matter what happened after this, I would never again be shackled to a desk. Hopefully I'd still be racing. Hopefully I'd still be racing for Cox. But I couldn't worry about that now—not while the finish line was calling for me. A call I had every intention of answering.

Myles, Hayden, and I fought tooth and nail for that top spot. It was so familiar racing with them, that it felt like we were back at home, on our track, not at an event, in front of thousands of screaming fans. Lap after lap, the three of us held together as we passed the few other riders in front of us. And then we were in the final lap, whipping around the last corner, the finish line looming just ahead of us. Myles was too far ahead of me to catch, but that was okay, I'd be more than satisfied with a second-place finish. Hayden, though, apparently wasn't satisfied with being third. I saw him in my periphery, trying to inch past me. *Oh, I don't think so, Hayes.*

My competitive spirit kicked into overdrive, as I pressed my bike for every ounce of speed it would give me. Hayden's tire caught up to my seat. If we were street racing—and I wasn't worried about his safety—I could have reached out and kicked him. My grin a mile-wide, I leaned low on my bike, focusing on my form. My smaller size and weight worked to my advantage sometimes, and I managed to hold him off—just barely.

When we crossed the finish line, our positions relaxing as we eased off the gas, Hayden pointed at me. *Next time*, he was telling me. God, I hoped there was a next time. *Don't let this be the end.*

Glancing at the leaderboard, I saw that Myles had nabbed first by a longshot. Hayden and I were milliseconds apart. Rodney and Felicia did well, ending up in the top ten, and Eli and Ralph wound up somewhere in the middle. The clouds had held their rain, and the track had remained dry all day. And now, as we finished, bits of sunlight were streaming through breaks in the sky, covering the riders with shafts of light, like spotlights. All in all, it was a great day, and a great race.

The press was all over us the second Hayden, Myles, and I set our bikes and gear aside—the top three riders being on the same team was a feast for them. They did our interviews together, showcasing the fact that we all raced for the same team—*my team*. "So, Kenzie, how has it been this year, balancing being an owner and a rider?"

I let out the weary sigh that rushed to my lungs whenever I thought about all of my responsibilities. The reporter laughed. "That good, huh?"

I laughed with her. "I'll be honest, it's been really tough juggling both, but I think it's made me appreciate being a rider all the more. That's my passion, my reason for getting up in the morning, and I'm just so grateful… that I get to do this." My throat closed as emotion choked me.

"Are you all right?" the reporter asked, true concern in her eyes.

I nodded, gripping Hayden's hand tighter. "Yeah, it's just been a tough year. My team…we've been racing great, but even still, through no fault of our own, we lost our two biggest backers. If we don't...if we don't get some support soon, I just don't know if there *will* be a Cox Racing next year, and that crushes me."

The reporter looked genuinely sad to hear that. "Well, let me just put it out there then." She turned from me to look directly at the camera. "If any sponsor out there would like to instantly be on everyone's lips, you might want to contact Cox Racing *today*, because these three right here are about to rule the world."

I could have kissed her.

Once our interview wrapped up, all the teams gathered together to hear the conclusion to the championship. Since this was the final race of the year, we weren't just celebrating one victory—we were celebrating two. The final scores had already been calculated, and the champion was about to be declared.

The crowd waiting for the results was huge. Grabbing Hayden's hand, I gave it a squeeze. He smiled at me, a playful twist to his lips. I gave him a quick kiss, then looked over at Myles. He'd had a couple of rough races, but I had no doubt he was about to nab the championship again. Unfortunately, I'd been so caught up in Richard's crap, and administrative crap, that I hadn't paid close enough attention to the points race. I had no idea where everyone was sitting.

One of the officials walked up to the stage, microphone in hand. The riders, crew, owners and sponsors in the crowd hooted and hollered so hard that he had to raise a hand to quiet them. "Ladies and gentlemen, it's with the greatest honor that I get to announce this year's winner of the ARRC." He paused in dramatic fashion, then quietly said into the microphone, "Congratulations, Mackenzie Cox."

I blinked in confusion while my mind fumbled to make sense of what he'd just said. Because it sure sounded like he'd just said *my* name…but that was impossible. Utterly impossible.

When I didn't move, Hayden pushed my back, urging me to go onstage. But why? I couldn't seriously have won…

Finally, I relented to his prodding, and trudged up to the stage. There were tears on my cheeks, but I wasn't conscious of the fact that I was crying. Why was I up here? The official handed me a gargantuan trophy, and the crowd around me flashed with lights as people took pictures. I started sobbing as it sank in. I'd…won. Somehow, I'd won.

A microphone was thrust in my face, but I was too emotional for words. I shook my head, and the official pulled it away, patting me on the back instead. After another few minutes of standing in the spotlight, soaking in the praise, I finally made my way back to my friends. They each congratulated me with bear hugs, even Felicia and Rodney. When they were all done, and I could finally breathe, I shook my head and protested my victory. "This can't be right. I only won one event."

Hayden's smile was huge. "But you were consistent, Kenzie, and consistency is what you need in a points race. You landed in the top three at every event. The rest of us, we were all over the fucking place." He laughed. "Well, except for me. I was consistently behind you. Not that I minded…it's a great view. And in case you're wondering, I knew you could get third and still win the whole damn thing...that's why I went for it. Failed, but went for it." He ended his statement with a playful, unapologetic wink.

I could only gape at them all as I processed what he'd just said. It made sense, but still, I was so stunned, it was really hard to believe. Hayden handed my trophy to Nikki, then wrapped his arms around me. "You really had no idea, did you?"

"No idea?" I asked, feeling half-drunk.

He grinned wider. "You had no idea you were leading the points race. You truly were oblivious."

I shook my head, amazed, then I glanced around at all my friends and colleagues. "Why didn't you guys tell me?"

Myles shrugged. "We didn't want to jinx you...give you the yips. We all agreed to not mention it until you did. And you never did, so..."

"Unbelievable," I told him. Then my smile grew uncontainable. "Un-fucking-believable. I can't believe I won..." My dad came up to me then, his smile full of pride. "You knew?" I asked him. "You knew I was in the lead?"

He raised an eyebrow in a droll expression. "Of course I knew, Mackenzie. But Myles insisted I shouldn't say anything...so I didn't. Congratulations... I'm so proud of you." His gray eyes grew watery, and I could feel my tears resurfacing.

Dad lifted a finger. "Before you start sobbing again... I have a couple of people here who would really like to meet you." He stepped aside, allowing a man and a woman to join our group. "Mackenzie, this is Pat Davis, head of Riser Athletics, and Samantha Dupont, head of Generation

Tires. They're both interested in partnering with the first female ARRC champion." His voice oozed pride.

My eyes nearly bugged from my head as I shook hands with both people. Riser Athletics and Generation Tires…it didn't get much bigger than those two companies. "I'm honored to meet you," I said, hoping my voice didn't sound as overwhelmed as I felt.

Samantha smiled. "Not as honored as we are. We've been following you for a while now, and while you started the year with a certain…cloud over your head, you've ended it outstandingly. We'd very much like a sit-down meeting with you when you return to Oceanside."

"Yes, absolutely…thank you." And for the first time in a long time, I felt nothing but joy and hope.

CHAPTER 20

Three months later, my life was everything I'd always hoped it would be. I felt completely at peace. Home, friends, family…work…every worry was lessened, every stress alleviated. After winning the entire championship—a fact that I still had trouble grasping—the floodgates had opened, and sponsors had poured through. The media—the national media, not just the sports channels—was having a field day with the first female champion, and everybody wanted to attach themselves to me. My father and Dex were sorting through the offers, finding the best fit for Cox Racing, and I was so grateful for their help and expertise. Whether they realized it, they were saving my sanity.

It was exhilarating and strange to have everything going my way for once, especially with all the crazy twists and turns my life had taken over the past couple of years. I was making sure to enjoy every single second of my newfound bliss.

Stretching out, I tangled my legs with Hayden's. He made a deep, delighted noise, and I smiled. I loved having him here all the time. "Did I just wake up next to the sexiest woman in the world?" he rumbled, low in his chest.

My smile grew as he wrapped his arms and legs around me, pulling me tight. "I don't know if I'd say sexiest. Luckiest, definitely."

Hayden laughed, then kissed my neck. "Trust me, it's sexiest too."

His hand on my stomach stroked circles into the skin. We'd fallen asleep naked, and I could feel that he was ready to show me just how sexy he found me. My body started responding, opening under his touch.

A soft moan escaped me, and Hayden let out his own erotic noise as he heard it. His lips found my mouth, and my body surged with energy as his passion seeped into me. The hand on my stomach shifted to my breast—feeling, swirling, circling. Then his lips floated down my neck, traveling to meet his fingers.

I gasped as his mouth closed over my nipple, tasting me, savoring me. His hand traveled down now, and my breath grew faster. His finger slid between my legs, and a loud moan left my lips. *God, yes.*

Hayden shifted his body over mine. His breath was just as fast, just as needy. I pulled on his hips after he settled over me, wanting him inside me. He entered without hesitation, and a low groan left his lips.

A sound of satisfaction filled the air as our hips met. Then he pulled back, and my body exploded with sensation, a sensation that amplified when he pushed forward again. A frantic need began filling my body as every stroke he made coaxed me closer to the edge. Grabbing his body, I pulled him into me harder, faster. I needed more.

The buildup started reaching its apex, and my body tensed in anticipation. The explosion hit me, and a long cry left my lips. Hayden's breath was fast, his body slightly damp from the exertion. He pumped into me a few more times, then let out his own groan of release.

Hayden slumped against me, resting his head in the crook of my neck. "I love waking up with you," he muttered, his words partially muffled by my skin.

I let out a soft, tranquil laugh. "I love waking up with you, too. But we should probably get going. We're late for work."

Hayden immediately shifted his gaze to the clock on our nightstand. Even though I was right, and we were late, Hayden's smile was huge and happy. "Yeah, you're probably right." He shot up off the bed and stood in front of me, in all his beautiful, naked glory. "I'm gonna hop in the shower. Care to join me?"

While I was enjoying the peep show, I shook my head. We had to get going, and if I stepped in there with him, we'd spend a good half-hour exploring each other. Sometimes bliss was really distracting.

My phone rang while Hayden was in the shower, and when I glanced at the screen, I wasn't too surprised by who it was. Richard. I'd been ignoring his calls for months. I considered ignoring this one too, but I had a feeling the phone calls wouldn't stop until I'd given him a firm final rejection. Inhaling a deep breath, I answered the phone. "Hello, Richard."

His voice was saccharin sweet in my ear. "Kenzie, I've been trying to get a hold of you ever since New Jersey. I never got a chance to congratulate you. I knew you'd do well but winning everything…that was quite remarkable."

I could hear the intrigue in his voice. This wasn't simply a call to congratulate me. "Thank you…but I have a feeling that's not the real reason you're calling me. I'm not sure what you're trying to sell me, Richard, but my answer is no. A firm no."

"Ah, Kenzie. I'm not trying to sell you anything. I just wanted to pass along some good news. Burger Barn and Ashley's Intimates have decided to stay with Cox Racing next year."

A weary sigh escaped me. "Led by you, of course."

"Naturally. And just so you know, my offer to buy still stands. If you'd still like to free yourself from the burden of ownership… I can help you with that."

Hayden came out of the bathroom then. Scrubbing his hair with a towel, he gave me an inquisitive expression. Since my hand was clenched in a fist, I probably looked angry. "Again, my answer is no. I have talented people around me who are handling the things I don't want to deal with. And as for Burger Barn and Ashley's Intimates, well…we already have a slew of new sponsors lined up, almost more than we can handle, so you can tell them we're very sorry…but we're going another way."

The sweetness in his voice was instantly gone. "Don't be foolish, Mackenzie. One win doesn't guarantee anything. You *need* me."

"No, actually… I don't. I have your son, and he's by far a better person than you are."

Richard was silent a second, then said, "Dex doesn't have what it takes to survive in this business. He's too busy following his heart."

His tone was so condescending, I couldn't help but stand up for Dex. "Personally, I don't think following your heart is a bad thing." My eyes locked with Hayden's, my smile warm and soft.

Richard scoffed in my ear. "Says the woman who almost lost everything."

"Almost doesn't count, and I didn't lose anything... except the desire to ever speak to you again."

"This is my last offer, Mackenzie. If you turn me down now...my help won't be there when you inevitably fail."

"Goodbye, Richard." I disconnected the line before he could respond, then tossed my phone into my bag.

"You okay?" Hayden asked.

Grinning, I told him, "I'm fantastic." And I truly was. I felt better than ever.

Soon after that, Hayden and I made our way to the track. I was excited to get there—the place was always constantly buzzing with energy now—an excited, palpable energy that danced across my skin, igniting me. The upcoming season flashed through my mind as I rode through the inner gates, heading for the garage. In three more months, we'd back in the race circuit. Hayden and I had been riding really well, and so was Myles. Between the three of us, Cox Racing was sitting pretty for another championship. We were a household name now, our fame stretching outside the sport in an unprecedented way. Even the officials loved us, since we were bringing in new fans left and right. It was everything I'd always wanted for the family team, and I was so proud to be a part of it. And grateful that Hayden and my dad had found a way to keep the dream alive.

Since Hayden and I were a little late getting out of bed this morning, the entire team was already at the garage when we arrived. And so were my sisters and their husbands...and Izzy, Antonia, and Hookup.

My heart started beating harder as I looked around. Why was everyone here? "Daphne, Theresa… Izzy, Tony …what are you guys all doing here?"

Daphne clapped her hands, like she was so excited she could hardly contain herself. She was finally pregnant, with an adorable baby bump signaling the eminent arrival of the newest member of the family. Jeff was standing beside her. He winked at me, then gave Hayden an encouraging nod. The two had grown close over the last several months, while Hayden had been teaching Jeff to ride. Daphne would only allow it to happen in a parking lot, but Jeff seemed content with just that little bit of adventure.

Daphne didn't answer my question, so I shifted to Theresa. She was holding hands with her husband, Nick, but she gave me a thumbs-up. I moved over to Izzy, but she only grinned. Antonia had a hand slapped over her mouth, and she was giggling. Hookup pursed his lips and gave me a nod, but like everyone else, he had nothing to say, no explanation to give.

As I stared at everyone in bewilderment, two more people walked into the garage—Rodney and Felicia. They were the most shocking to see—Benneti riders *never* came over here during the day. Keith was going to have their heads if he found out they were on "enemy" territory.

"What are you guys…?" Stopping my question, I looked up at Hayden. He was beaming at me. "What's going on?" I asked him.

In answer, he sank to one knee. I stopped breathing as he reached into his pocket and grabbed a sparkling diamond ring. Holding the ring up to me, he softly said, "Mackenzie Cox, being with you has made me so incredibly happy. I can only think of one thing that would make me even happier. If you would be my wife. Will you marry me?"

My eyes watered, and as I stared at him, everything—every*one*—vanished. He was all that existed. "Yes," I whispered. Clearing my throat, I nodded. "Yes, absolutely…yes."

A chorus of cheers went around the room as Hayden rose to his feet and slipped the ring on my finger. Tears were streaming down my face as Hayden leaned forward and gently kissed me. Over the sound of cheers and clapping, I heard the sound of champagne bottles being uncorked. Then I felt cool droplets landing on me, as we were sprayed with the bottle's buildup. Laughing, I pulled away from Hayden to see Eli and Ralph holding foaming bottles. "It's okay," Eli said, "We've got more."

Daphne pulled a discreetly placed cover off a workbench, displaying cake, snacks, and several bottles of champagne. I could only gape at how quickly a normal day of work had turned into a celebration. "You all knew about this?" I asked the group, stunned.

Everyone nodded, grinning devious smiles. My gaze shifted back to my boyfriend. No…my fiancé. "You arranged this?"

Hayden grinned, then nodded his head toward my father, of all people. "I had help."

My jaw dropped as I looked at my dad. He shrugged. "All I did was call Daphne. She took care of everything else." Even still, I was shocked that Hayden had even considered asking for my dad's help. Or Dad's blessing, because clearly, he had. The smile on my father's face was warm and untroubled.

After that, I was bombarded by people giving me their well wishes. Rodney looped an arm around each of us, pulling us close. "Kenzie, Hayden, congratulations, guys."

I laughed as I hugged him back. "Thanks, Rodney."

When he let go, Felicia took his place. She extended a hand to me, and as I took it, I searched her face for any sign of stress or sadness. All I saw was joy though. "Congratulations, Kenzie. I'm happy for you. *Truly*," she emphasized.

"Thank you," I told her, grateful to fate that she genuinely seemed to mean that.

Releasing my hand, she turned to Hayden. "Congratulations, Hayden. It makes me happy to see you happy."

"Thank you, Felicia," he told her. Then his eyes drifted to Rodney, busy talking to Myles. Grin on his face, Hayden leaned forward and told her, "Don't freak out, but rumor has it that guy wants to marry you."

She grinned as she glanced over at Rodney. "I know. And I'm not freaked out. I'm not *ever* running away again. I learned my lesson."

Hayden gave her a warm, brotherly smile. "Good. I'm happy to hear that…he's a good guy."

She winked at me. "Yeah, he's all right." As I laughed at her comment, she said, "Rodney and I need to get back before Keith kills us, but we're taking you out this weekend to celebrate."

"Sound good," I said. "Call me."

As she nodded, I marveled at the fact that somehow we'd all become friends. Just like Rodney had predicted.

Nikki flung her arms around me the second she got a chance. "Oh my God, Kenzie! I'm so happy for you guys!" When she pulled back, there were tears in her eyes. Seeing them made my eyes tear up again.

"Thank you, I'm happy for you guys too." I indicated the ring that Myles had put on her finger last week. They were getting married next year at Monterey—the birthplace of their relationship.

"Thanks," she giggled. "Maybe we can have a double wedding?"

"Oh no, after everything it took to get you guys together, you're not sharing your day."

She sighed happily as she looked back at Myles, then she returned her eyes to me with a frown on her face. "Your journey wasn't easy either, Kenzie."

Hayden kissed my head. "Well worth the pain," he murmured, and I sighed in agreement.

Myles congratulated us next, then my sisters, their husbands, and John and my father. Hookup came up to us with Antonia. She squeezed me tight as Hookup said to Hayden, "I always knew you'd end up with Felicia Two."

Hayden smacked his shoulders. "Stop calling her that."

Hookup laughed, then nodded. "Yeah, all right." Antonia let me go to give Hayden a bear hug, and Hookup turned his attention to me. "Congratulations, Kenzinator. I knew you'd make an honest man out of this chump."

I smirked at him, then shook my head and flung my arms around him. He seemed surprised that I was hugging him, but he squeezed back. When I let go, I told him, "Now if we could only find someone to make you an honest man."

He made a dismissive noise as he put a hand on Antonia's shoulder. "Already done. Right, munchkin?"

Antonia looked up at him and nodded. "Yep."

I smiled at the two of them, then looked around for Izzy. "Antonia, where did your mom go?"

Antonia pursed her lips, then jerked her thumb over her shoulder. "She's sharing some cake with that cute guy." She giggled after she said it.

Hayden and Hookup both got the same overprotective look on their faces as they searched for Izzy. I spotted her first, standing in the far corner of the room, and just like Antonia had said, she was indeed sharing a piece of cake with Dex. He laughed as she told him something, and the grin on her face was a mile wide. They were…adorable.

Hayden spotted the pair a split-second later. "What the hell are they—"

Not finishing that thought, he started taking a step toward Dex and Izzy. I grabbed his arm, holding him back, and his jade eyes flashed to mine. Holding his gaze, I said, "Don't even think about it, Hayes. Izzy's an adult and can flirt with whoever she wants." I flicked my eyes between Hayden and Hookup, since Hookup seemed ready to interfere too.

Hayden pursed his lips like he didn't agree. I raised my eyebrows. "Dex is a good guy, even you can't deny that. And doesn't Izzy deserve someone decent after everything she's been through?"

Hookup looked at Hayden for confirmation, since he didn't know Dex. Hayden sighed and rolled his eyes. "I guess, yeah…he's all right. But…it's weird."

I lightly tapped his stomach with the back of my hand. "It's not weird. It's sweet."

Dex and Izzy stayed locked in conversation for the rest of the afternoon, and I made sure Hayden and

Hookup, and even Antonia, left them alone to bond. There was a lot of laughter coming from their corner—it made me exceedingly happy to hear it.

My father came up to me while I was enjoying a piece of my sister's cake. I pointed a fork at him. "If you're about to tell me I shouldn't eat this because it's my third piece, well, you just might find this fork in your arm."

His lips stretched into a relaxed smile. "You're the defending champion, Mackenzie. And you're celebrating a pretty momentous occasion. You can have all the cake you want."

My eyes widened. "What have you done with Jordan Cox?" I asked.

With a small laugh, his gaze dropped to the floor. "I've been hard on you. These past couple of years have shown me that…very clearly." Lifting his eyes to me, his expression turned sad. "It was never my intention to push you away. Just…to push you. But you never needed me to do that for you. You were always a champion, Mackenzie. And you never needed me."

With a sigh, I set down my cake. "That's not true. I did need you. I *do* need you. But not as a coach, or a trainer, or a business partner, or even a friend. I need you…as a father. That's all I've ever needed from you."

Dad's jaw tightened, and his eyes turned glossy. With a stiff nod, he reached out and pulled me to him. Hugging me fiercely, he whispered, "Then that's what I'll be, and that's all I'll be. I'm so proud of you, Kenzie."

His words, his use of my shortened name, made a jolt of joy go through me, and I felt the void of his rejection being forever patched and sealed. Dad left not too much later, inviting John to go out with him for a beer, to celebrate the 'good old days,' he said. Dad seemed lighter, happier. Maybe he'd finally left his ghosts behind.

My sisters left next, dragging their reluctant-to-leave husbands with them. Then Nikki and Myles left to take Maria home. When the afternoon shifted into evening, Eli, Kevin, and Ralph gathered up the remaining bottles of champagne and headed back to their gargantuan house on the coast. Then Hookup left with Antonia. I was just wondering why Hookup had Antonia when Izzy and Dex approached me.

Dex looked a little unsure as he stepped up to me. "Hey, uh, Izzy and I were gonna take off…get some dinner…unless you needed me to do something before I left?"

Smiling at him, I shook my head. "No, there's nothing that needs to be done right now. You guys go have fun."

Dex gave Izzy a shy smile, his bright blue eyes glowing. When he returned his face to me, he looked completely at peace, and I was happy to see the calm. Things had been tense between Dex and his father ever since New Jersey. Richard, proving he truly was a douche, had indeed tried to take away Dex's trust fund. Fortunately for Dex, though, his grandmother adored him, and since she had the real power in the family, she'd put a stop to Richard's retribution. Richard hadn't been able to touch a dime of Dex's money.

"Congratulations on your engagement, Kenzie," Dex said, extending his hand.

"Thank you, Dex," I said, briefly shaking his hand. "I hope you two have a great night." I pointed a finger at him. "But don't be out too late, because we've got a ton of work to do tomorrow."

His expression was even brighter as he nodded. "I know, and I can't wait."

He turned to Izzy, then nodded his head toward the door. "Shall we?" he asked, offering his elbow.

Izzy bit her lip before taking it. "Absolutely."

As they walked away, Izzy looked back at me with an *Oh my God* face. I laughed, then wished them well. When I turned back around, Hayden was watching them leave, too, a small frown on his face. Then he sighed, shook his head, and smiled at me. "So, Future Mrs. Hayes…what would you like to do now?"

My stomach swarmed with butterflies at hearing the words *Mrs. Hayes*…God, I loved the way that sounded. Grinning, I looked around the empty garage, then my eyes settled on my bike. "Well, Mr. Hayes… I was thinking…how about a spin around the track?"

He pursed his lips as he studied me. "Loser has sex with the winner?"

I laughed, then nodded, and a glorious smile spread over his face. "Then I only have one thing to say." Fast as lightning, he grabbed my waist and pulled me into him. "Race me or chase me, Twenty-two."

Lacing my arms around his neck, I examined the way the lights danced across my ring. "Too late… I already caught you."

"True," he murmured. "Very true. But to be fair, I let you catch me. Because your arms…they're the only place I want to be."

My heart swelled with love, adoration, and absolute certainty. "I know." And I'd never doubt that again. I had

Hayden's heart just as surely as he had mine. And together, there wasn't anything we couldn't do.

* * * The End * * *

ABOUT THE AUTHOR

S.C. Stephens is a #1 *New York Times* bestselling author who spends her every free moment creating stories that are packed with emotion and heavy on romance. In addition to writing, she enjoys spending lazy afternoons in the sun reading, listening to music, watching movies, and spending time with her friends and family. She and her two children reside in the Pacific Northwest.

You can learn more at:

AuthorSCStephens.com
Twitter @SC_Stephens_
Facebook.com/SCStephensAuthor

Printed in Great Britain
by Amazon